FALSE PATRIOTS

FALSE PATRIOTS

Charles O'Brien

This first world edition published 2010
in Great Britain and in the USA by
SEVERN HOUSE PUBLISHERS LTD of
9–15 High Street, Sutton, Surrey, England, SM1 1DF.
Trade paperback edition published
in Great Britain and the USA 2010 by
SEVERN HOUSE PUBLISHERS LTD

British Library Cataloguing in Publication Data

O'Brien, Charles, 1927-
  False Patriots. – (French Revolution)
  1. Cartier, Anne (Fictitious character) – Fiction. 2. Women
  teachers – France – Fiction. 3. France – History – Louis
  XVI, 1774-1793 – Fiction. 4. Detective and mystery stories.
  I. Title II. Series
  813.6-dc22

ISBN-13: 978-0-7278-6898-5   (cased)
ISBN-13: 978-1-84751-240-6   (trade paper)

All Severn House titles are printed on acid-free paper.

Severn House Publishers support The Forest Stewardship Council [FSC],
the leading international forest certification organisation. All our titles that
are printed on Greenpeace-approved FSC-certified paper carry the FSC logo.

Mixed Sources
Product group from well-managed
forests and other controlled sources
www.fsc.org Cert no. SA-COC-1565
© 1996 Forest Stewardship Council

Typeset by Palimpsest Book Production Ltd.,
Grangemouth, Stirlingshire, Scotland.
Printed and bound in Great Britain by
MPG Books Ltd., Bodmin, Cornwall.

ACKNOWLEDGEMENTS

I wish to thank Andy Sheldon for helpful computer services. I am grateful also to Gudveig Baarli for assisting with the maps, to Jennifer Nelson of Gallaudet University for useful advice on matters pertaining to deafness, and to the professionals at Severn House who produced this book. My agent Evan Marshall and Fronia Simpson read drafts of the novel and contributed much to its improvement. Finally, my wife Elvy, art historian, deserves special mention for her keen editorial eye and her unflagging support.

LIST OF MAIN CHARACTERS
IN ORDER OF FIRST APPEARANCE

Anne Cartier: *former music hall entertainer, tutor of deaf children, and wife of Colonel Paul de Saint-Martin*

Denis O'Fallon: *elderly aristocratic Oratorian priest, born in Ireland, entered French military service*

Patrick O'Fallon: *deaf servant and son of Denis O'Fallon*

Marthe Boyer: *butcher's daughter from Rouen, deaf wife of Jacques Boyer*

Micheline [Michou] du Saint-Esprit: *deaf artist with studio on Rue Traversine, Anne Cartier's friend*

Jacques Boyer: *patriotic agitator, radical pamphleteer*

Colonel Paul de Saint-Martin: *former Provost of the Royal Highway Patrol, now commander of the Gendarmerie Nationale for the area surrounding Paris; husband of Anne Cartier*

Georges Charpentier: *Saint-Martin's adjutant, experienced investigator*

Jérôme Pétion (1756–1794): *radical author and politician, second mayor of Paris, 1791–1792*

Magdalena Diluna: *young Italian slack rope dancer*

Antonio Diluna: *Magdalena's older brother and an entertainer*

Armand Flamme: *artisan, radical republican*

Jean Guiscard: *wealthy businessman and speculator in nationalized church property*

Madame Marie de Beaumont: *Paul de Saint-Martin's aunt, Michou's patron, and Anne's friend. Formerly a countess, she resides at Chateau Beaumont, an estate south of Paris, and at a Paris town house on Rue Traversine near the Palais-Royal*

Monsieur Augustin Savarin: *Royal archivist and genealogist at Versailles until 1789; thereafter, cryptologist for the Office of Foreign Affairs, husband of Marie de Beaumont, formerly a count*

Jean-Sylvain Bailly (1736–1793): *distinguished astronomer, mayor of Paris, 1789–1791*

Count Axel von Fersen (1755–1810): *Swedish officer in French service and the royal family's friend*

Jeanne Degere: *Fersen's faithful maid*

Pierre Roland: *enlightened young magistrate at the Louvre district police bureau*

Renée Gros: *Armand Flamme's mistress; mental patient*

Aristide Blanc: *barman at The Red Rooster, Jacques Boyer's maternal uncle*

Luc Thierry: *Jean Guiscard's porter*

Benoit Degere: *Jeanne Degere's lame, older brother, army veteran, Fersen's servant*

Lafayette, Marie-Joseph etc., Marquis de (1757–1834): *popular, ambitious commander of the National Guard, hero of the American Revolution*

HISTORICAL NOTE

In the late spring of 1791 the French nation could look back with guarded satisfaction at the two years of its revolution. True, the country's financial crisis continued unabated, and the majority of the population lived in deep misery. But prospects for a better life lay ahead. Their elected representatives in the National Assembly had nearly finished work on a new framework of government, partly inspired by British parliamentary tradition and the recent American constitution.

Guided as well by enlightened principles of freedom, equality and fraternity, the National Assembly had systematically reorganized the country's courts, police, civil administration, and church. It had abolished class distinctions and privileges and had provided for a new, single-chamber Legislative Assembly with the sole authority to make laws for the entire country. The power of the formerly absolute, divine right monarch was severely limited. Louis XVI remained the chief executive but he was allowed merely a suspensive veto over acts of the Assembly. He was also supposed to answer for his actions to the people rather than to God.

Whether these reforms would succeed depended on the harmonious cooperation of the king and the assembly. Unfortunately, they were unhappy, distrustful partners. A messy divorce lay ahead. In July 1789, Louis XVI had merely outwardly accepted the new regime and his much-weakened role within it. He had little choice. In October, a large mob had dragged the royal family from the great palace at Versailles to Paris. There they lived like prisoners in the Tuileries palace in the centre of the city. A devout man, Louis XVI profoundly disliked the new regime's drastic reform of the French Catholic Church. Its property was nationalized, its religious orders abolished, and its clergy elected by the people, be they Catholics, Protestants, Jews, or atheists. Finally, the church's ties to the pope in Rome were cut.

The king's discontent peaked in the spring of 1791 when the National Assembly required the clergy to take an oath of loyalty to the new regime, including specifically the ecclesiastical reforms. More than half the clergy – known as the 'nonjuring' in contrast to the 'constitutional' clergy – refused the oath. They were followed by a majority of practising Catholics, causing a major schism throughout the country. Urged on by his wife, Queen Marie Antoinette, the king attempted to flee from Paris with his family to the eastern frontier. There he hoped to raise an army and to re-establish the old regime by force.

The scheme failed. The royal family nearly reached the frontier but were caught at Varennes and forced to return to Paris in disgrace. Public opinion now shifted dramatically against the king and the new constitution. Moderate reformers, such as General Lafayette and Mayor Bailly, lost credit among the people. Demands for a democratic republic grew much louder and the spectre of civil unrest at home and war with France's neighbours drew closer. With a prophet's eyes the Reign of Terror could be seen on the horizon.

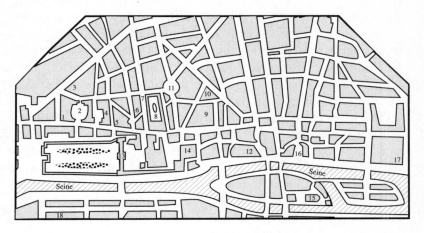

CENTRAL PARIS 1791
1. Residence/office of Paul de Saint-Martin & Anne Cartier, Rue Saint-Honoré
2. Place Vendôme
3. Hôtel de Police, Rue des Capuchines
4. Jacobins Club
5. Church of Saint-Roch, Rue Saint-Honoré
6. Comtesse Marie de Beaumont's townhouse, Rue Traversine
7. Rue de Richelieu
8. Palais-Royal
9. Central Markets (Les Halles)
10. Church of Saint-Eustache
11. Place des Victoires
12. Châtelet
13. Palace and garden of the Tuileries
14. Louvre
15. Notre Dame Cathedral
16. Place de Grève
17. Institute for the deaf
18. Hôtel de Monaco

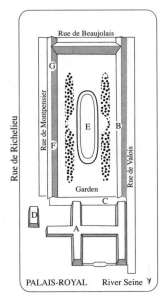

PALAIS-ROYAL 1791
A. The duke's palace
B. Valois Arcade
C. Camp of the Tatars
D. Comédie Française
E. Circus
F. Café Odéon
G. Café de Foy

ONE
A Woman in Distress

Paris, 31 May–1 June 1791

'**M**adame Cartier, there's a priest to see you.' The servant's voice registered a note of surprise. Clerical visitors rarely came to call on Anne Cartier, never in the morning and unannounced. For a moment she was taken aback. Her mind was occupied with household duties. Neither she nor her husband moved in ecclesiastical circles, nor were they 'devout'. So why would a priest appear at her door?

'Did he give his name?' Anne asked.

'O'Fallon,' the servant replied. 'Father Denis O'Fallon from the Oratory at the Louvre on Rue Saint-Honoré. His servant Patrick is with him.'

'Show them into the parlour. I'll meet them in a few minutes.'

Anne knew Denis O'Fallon, and his servant. Nonetheless, she was apprehensive. The priest was a reserved man and this was the first time he had ever called on her. What could be the matter?

While dressing, she called him to mind. A friend and patron of the late Abbé de l'Épée, founder of the institute for the deaf, O'Fallon also supported his successor, the Abbé Sicard. Anne had made O'Fallon's acquaintance at the institute, where she tutored young deaf children how to sign. Initially, he kept her at a distance, probably mindful of her previous career as a London music hall entertainer. Then, one day he came to a public programme where Anne and a young deaf girl demonstrated Épée's method of instruction in signing. Afterwards he had complimented her.

Then, receiving a favourable report from Épée, he began to treat her with respect, greeted her with a smile when they met, and questioned her on problems that deaf students faced. Finally, he had asked her to tutor his deaf servant Patrick at the institute. The priest had legally adopted the young man and given him the O'Fallon name. For the past two years she had taught him to sign. The priest seemed genuinely pleased with his progress.

As she entered the parlour, he was standing with Patrick in front of a map of the British Isles, aiming his cane at London. Anne had hung the map on the wall as a reminder of where she came from and a starting point of conversation with visitors.

Anne nodded towards the map. 'It reminds me of home in Hampstead near London. You may know that my family is Huguenot. They fled from Normandy, the French king's dragoons snapping at their heels.'

The priest smiled wryly. 'Yes, the Abbé de l'Épée told me your story. He was sympathetic, having experienced persecution himself.' Anne recalled that, due to theological differences, the Archbishop of Paris had barred Épée from serving as a priest and prevented his institute for the deaf from moving into the more spacious rooms of an abandoned convent.

O'Fallon pointed to Ireland on the map. 'It's almost forty years ago to the day when I left, a lad of fifteen, to escape English oppression of Irish Catholics. The English king confiscated my family's estate and turned us out penniless. I found a new home in the French king's service.' His tone was nostalgic. Still he glanced at her with a hint of mischief in his eyes. They knew each other well enough to tease on the sensitive subject of religion.

O'Fallon was a tall, gaunt man and looked much older than his fifty-five years. In his youth he must have been strikingly handsome. His facial features still had a classic structure. His body, once robust, was now frail and bent. A plaster cast supported his badly damaged spine and stiffened his neck. This added to the impression that he was aloof in his manner and rigid in his convictions. Frequent pain had deeply creased his brow.

With the aid of his servant, the priest let himself down into a chair and went directly to the point. 'Madame, I'm seeking help for Marthe Boyer, a deaf woman in a difficult marriage. Her husband, Jacques Boyer, is a violent, domineering man, an impious atheist, and founder of a small radical political club, 'Citizens for Equality'. Yesterday, my servant heard of her distress and brought her to me. Unfortunately, I can't be helpful to her. I'm involved in public controversy with her husband. He would strongly object to a priest, especially me, becoming involved in his private affairs. He's also jealous and spies on her. I don't want to make her situation worse. He would surely beat her.'

'Poor woman! Tell me more.'

'She's twenty-five years old, the daughter of a prosperous butcher in Rouen. She had worked alongside her father until his death. He left the business to his son and provided a dowry for her. Five years ago, Monsieur Boyer married her for the dowry and to cook and clean. Two or three years into their marriage, a sickness took away her hearing.'

'What can I possibly do for her?'

'I'm not sure. However, you have often helped other deaf persons in distress. Would you look into this matter?'

'I'll try.'

'Be cautious. Avoid her husband. Today, my servant will contact the woman and arrange a meeting with you. Where should it be?'

'Tomorrow at mid morning, I'll be at the little puppet theatre in the Camp of the Tatars in the Palais-Royal. She'll be safe there. We'll get to know each other and I'll find out if I can help her.'

The next day, the Palais-Royal's ramshackle commercial gallery known as the Camp of the Tatars seemed busier than ever. Shoppers thronged through the narrow aisles between its wooden stalls and shacks. At mid morning, the puppet theatre was usually closed. Anne opened it now – she was its co-owner and a partner in its productions. She and her deaf artist friend Michou had arrived a few minutes early to observe Madame Boyer as she arrived.

At the door the woman threw a quick look over her shoulder, then slipped inside. A minute later, Anne and Michou introduced themselves and sat opposite her on a wooden bench. She understood their simple signs. Since she had lost her hearing only recently, she could still speak well. Anne detected a Norman accent.

The woman was petite and lively, and seemed resourceful. Her features were plain, her manner awkward. After all, she had spent much of her life before the marriage slaughtering chickens and chopping meat in her father's shop. She appeared ill at ease with Anne, a police colonel's wife. Her eyes had a wary look.

Michou leaned forward and offered her a sketchbook and a pencil for comments. She accepted them with a grateful smile and a conversation got under way. The woman was intelligent, could read and write, and was well informed. In the early years of their marriage – before her deafness – her husband was eager to educate her. They discussed books, heard lectures, and went to theatres. Now, she and her husband communicated rarely – and mostly by simple written notes and gestures.

'Alas,' she exclaimed, 'He treats me with contempt. I protest in vain that being deaf is not my fault. We haven't slept together in months. When he looks at me, his eyes are so hateful. I'm afraid of him. Sometimes he beats me.' She pointed to an ugly bruise on her cheek. 'I think that he would like to get rid of me. He says that he wishes he could live with a *real* woman.'

'How did you come to meet Patrick?'

'He's deaf, like me. Patrick and I used to see each other in our parish church, Saint-Eustache. I went there to pray when my husband was out of the house. We'd meet also in the garden of the Palais-Royal. Patrick always greeted me with a smile. His good humour put me at ease, cheered me up. Unlike my husband, Patrick was always patient and helpful even if I misunderstood his signing and gestures. With him I felt like a normal person again.

'On Monday, Monsieur Boyer beat me again. When he left the house, I went to Saint-Eustache and met Patrick. This time I confided in him and he brought me to the priest O'Fallon at the Oratory.'

'Do you have friends or family to whom you could turn?' Michou asked.

A sadness dulled the lustre of Marthe's eyes. 'I have few acquaintances in Paris, and no close friends. Since I've lost my hearing, my brother in Rouen regards me as a useless burden.'

'What's Monsieur Boyer's Christian name?' Anne asked.

'Jacques.' She explained that he was thirty-five years old, the illegitimate son of a brilliant, dissolute lawyer. 'My husband is very touchy about his birth. He claims it's as honourable as anybody else's. Even a hint of disrespect makes him angry and quick to strike back. He is proud of his father, who gave him a good education in languages, law, literature, and philosophy.'

Madame Boyer frowned. 'He has good manners, fancies himself a gentleman, and he's bright. But his character is another matter. He's conceited and headstrong. His ambition is one day to play a leading role in Paris. He claims to speak for the oppressed common people of the city.'

Anne raised a sceptical eyebrow. 'Really?'

'Yes,' Marthe replied. 'He can be persuasive and has a small following in his club. Some of the city's poorest, most ignorant and desperate people trust him. He can actually speak their jargon.'

Anne cast about in her mind for the right way to help this woman. Could her marriage be saved? Or was a legal separation the only reasonable solution?

Michou looked up from her sketchbook, wrote a quick note, showed it to Anne, and handed it to Marthe. 'How do you feel towards him?'

The woman's jaw stiffened, her eyes narrowed. 'I hate him and wish he were dead,' she exclaimed, then wrote it out in large, bold letters in the sketchbook.

Anne and Michou flinched together at the woman's vehemence. 'I must study your situation,' Anne said. 'Let's meet here again in two days.'

Madame Boyer shrugged agreement. Still there was a glint of hope in her eyes.

'Father O'Fallon mentioned that your husband spies on you. Could you tell me how? For safety's sake, I had better know.'

Marthe nodded. 'A month ago, Monsieur Boyer hired this little man. I call him, Monsieur Rat-face. He's very short and bandy-legged, with a long pointed nose and a small, receding chin, a thin grey moustache and narrow, squinting eyes. He wears a shabby grey coat, soiled grey breeches, and a grey knit cap. He usually stands across the street from our entrance. I can see him from our window. Whenever he thinks Boyer isn't watching, he tipples. By nightfall, he's often wobbling drunk.'

'Appearances can deceive,' Anne cautioned. 'He may only pretend to be drunk and may notice more than you think. He also may have associates whom you don't recognize.' Anne suspected that the spy's slovenly appearance and his apparent inebriation could be meant to lull Marthe into feeling safe and tempt her into careless, unguarded actions.

For a moment Anne's remark seemed to give Marthe pause. Then she signed, 'He just can't be that clever.'

It was time to leave. The women got up from the benches and Anne led Marthe to the door. 'By the way,' Anne asked. 'Where might we find your husband this afternoon?'

'He usually meets with acquaintances at a table in front of Café de Foy in the garden of the Palais-Royal.'

After she left, Michou and Anne remained in the theatre for a few minutes. Michou had sketched the woman. Now she showed the sketch to Anne. A toxic mixture of bitterness, desperation, and resentment seethed in her eyes.

'Her husband could indeed be the devil's nephew,' Michou signed. 'But she might exaggerate.'

Anne nodded. 'We'll gather more information about him and form our own opinion.'

Anne and Michou left the puppet theatre and walked across the garden of the Palais-Royal towards Michou's studio. She would put the finishing touches on her sketch of Marthe Boyer. Suddenly, Anne heard a man's voice calling out to her from a distance. At first she couldn't recognize him. As he came closer, she saw that it was Dr Philippe Pinel, the city's most respected expert in the treatment of mental illness. He seemed anxious to speak to her. Michou excused herself and continued on her way.

'Madame Cartier,' the doctor began, 'I'm sorry to intrude, but I need to speak to you.'

'Of course, doctor. I have time.' He rented a couple of chairs and they sat in the shade of a tree.

Pinel began. 'You surely recall Mademoiselle Renée Gros. I'm concerned about her.'

'I remember her very well, a small, wiry, clever young woman with a troubled spirit.'

A prostitute and petty thief, Renée was beaten by the police, imprisoned, and nearly died. Anne rescued her from the infamous Salpêtrière hospital and put her in Pinel's hands. He diagnosed her as suffering from mania and depression, brought her to his clinic and treated her according to his enlightened, humane views on mental illness. That was almost three years ago. Anne had recently wondered how she was doing.

'What has happened?'

'She ran off – about a month ago. I've lost touch with her.' Pinel explained that Renée had greatly improved under his regime of baths, good food, music, engaging work, exercise, and compassionate counselling. 'After a year, she was feeling healthy and became restless, so I found work for her as a maid in the hôtel of Marie Brignoles, the Princess of Monaco, on Rue Saint-Dominique. When the princess fled the country last year and leased the hotel to the British ambassador, I persuaded his steward to continue to hire Renée. I don't know why she left. Her work seemed to please her. The steward thinks a man lured her away.'

'That's likely,' Anne agreed. 'Old habits are hard to break, even vile, degrading ones like prostitution. I fear for her. I'll inquire among her former associates and let you know if I learn anything.'

'She's been a challenge,' said Pinel. 'I'd hate to lose her. That would truly be a pity.'

TWO
A Radical Agitator

1 June

Early that afternoon, disguised as domestic servants, Anne and Michou entered the garden of the Palais-Royal. On the way from Michou's studio, Anne had described her meeting with Doctor Pinel and his fears for Renée Gros. Michou had known her and had helped treat her illness with lessons in drawing. 'That's sad,' she signed. 'I'll tell my friends to look for her.'

They found Boyer drinking wine with acquaintances at a table outside Café de Foy, just as his wife had said. He was a short, stocky, intense man, his eyes deep-set and iridescent black, and his hair thick, black and curly. He wore a light buff silk suit, the product of an excellent tailor's hands. The suit had minimal embroidered decoration. Anne surmised that the leader of Citizens for Equality shouldn't look like a proud, self-indulgent aristocrat.

With each glass of wine the flush in Boyer's cheeks grew a deeper pink, his voice louder. He was a powerful speaker, vulgar and caustic, with a mocking wit. Anne and everyone else within twenty paces could hear distinctly what he had to say. Michou noted his vehement gestures and recorded them in her sketch-book.

For most of the time, he carried on a tirade against the clergy. 'Traitors all,' he shouted, 'They try to subvert the new constitution prepared by the National Assembly. The constitution is far from perfect – it still allows the clergy to control the people's moral instruction and pays them far more than they deserve. Still they object to the people's right to elect them and insist that the pope in Rome should have the last word in religious matters in France.'

Others at the table appeared annoyed and attempted to cut him short. 'Save your speech for tonight at Café Procope,' said one of them. They finished their drinks and left him sitting there, staring into his empty glass with frustrated fury. Michou seized the opportunity to finish sketching him.

Anne glanced at the sketch. It caught the strain of brutality in his character. Anne's hope for his wife diminished.

Late in the afternoon, Anne quietly opened the door to her husband's office. He was absorbed in reading an official document at his writing table. The room was warm. He had removed his blue coat and hung his sword on the wall behind him. A frown darkened his handsome face. The streaks of grey in his brown hair seemed to have grown wider. She hesitated at the door, reluctant to interrupt him. He sensed her presence and beckoned her in.

'Bad news, Paul?' She pulled up a chair facing him.

She knew that his job was in jeopardy. For seven years Colonel Paul de Saint-Martin had served as provost of the Royal Highway Patrol for the region around Paris. The new government had recently begun to reorganize the force. They renamed it the Gendarmerie Nationale, doubled its numbers and removed its judicial responsibilities.

Unfortunately, these changes offered certain reformers, chief among them Monsieur Jérôme Pétion, President of the National Assembly, an opportunity to give Paul's position to one of their own men. A sharp critic of the monarchy, Pétion argued publicly that Paul could not be loyal to the revolution since he owed his position initially to Baron Breteuil, the minister for Paris in the old regime. From exile in Switzerland, the baron was attempting to organize a coalition of Austria, Prussia and other European powers to overthrow the new French constitution and restore the French king's pre-revolutionary powers.

'It could be worse,' Paul replied, laying aside the document. 'I must appear before a committee to answer questions about my record of service these past seven years. What they really want to know is how close I am to the baron. I understand their concern. He's doing all that he can to undermine the new regime.'

'What will you tell the committee?'

'I'll say that I'm my own man and not beholden to the baron. He inquired a few months ago by mail about my views. I wrote back that I avoided political controversy and devoted myself to the work of the Gendarmerie in my district.'

'What would you do if they chose someone else for the post?'

'In these uncertain times I'd go back to my estate and think of ways to make myself useful.' His tone had become rather doleful.

Anne caressed his cheek and drew a smile from him. She led him from the table to the window overlooking the courtyard. 'Tell me about your day,' he asked.

'Father Denis O'Fallon came here this morning on a visit.'

Paul raised an eyebrow. 'A deep man, not given to social visits.'

'What do you know about him?'

'He comes from a distinguished Irish family. As a young man he entered French service and was a captain in the Dillon regiment under my father during the Seven Years War. In a skirmish with the British in Germany, he was thrown from his horse and landed hard on his neck. That ended his military career and nearly his life.'

'What can you say about his character?'

'I've heard that he had been worldly and pleasure loving, though not debauched. During a long, painful convalescence he underwent a profound conversion. When his health improved, he joined a religious society, the Oratory of France, and became a priest. For years, he taught English and theology at the society's much respected college at Juilly.'

'An unusual story,' Anne remarked. 'In the garden of the Palais-Royal they tell me that he's a combative man and argues against the new constitution.'

'I'm not surprised. He has the courage of his convictions. Since retiring to Paris, he has loudly condemned the National Assembly's reforms of the church. His enemies threaten to hang him. He doesn't seem to care – he taunts them to do their worst.'

'He appears at daggers drawn with Monsieur Boyer,' Anne said. 'However, at the institute I've seen a much kinder, gentler and generous side of O'Fallon. He would like me to help Boyer's wife, a deaf woman in distress, and I've agreed to see what I can do for her.' Anne went on to explain Madame Boyer's problem. 'I need to know more about her husband. Do you have time to help me?'

'Of course.' Paul smiled indulgently. 'I've heard the name Boyer, a radical agitator, I believe.'

'This is what he looks like.' Anne showed him Michou's sketch of Boyer.

Paul studied it carefully. 'A telling likeness. I'm sure to recognize his piercing eyes even before he opens his mouth.'

'Where is Café Procope?' she asked. 'He's going to speak there tonight.'

'It's on the Left Bank, where Rue Dauphine and Rue Mazarine intersect, across the street from the Comédie Française. I'll go there and observe him. My adjutant, Georges Charpentier, can speak with the servants outside. We'll come back to you with a fuller picture of the man.'

Shortly before Jacques Boyer was about to speak, Saint-Martin entered the Café Procope. He had brought along his adjutant Georges Charpentier and left him outside among the servants. Some of them were tippling from small flasks of brandy. 'Their tongues will soon be loose,' Georges had said with delight. 'Much can be learned here.'

As usual, the café had attracted a distinguished clientele. Saint-Martin recognized Earl Gower, the British ambassador. Some thirty well-dressed men had crowded into the room around small tables and were drinking coffee, tea, and brandy. Jérôme Pétion was among them and gave Saint-Martin a curt nod. He took a seat, ordered tea, and joined in the conversation.

His companions were concerned about the National Assembly's reforms of the church. Opinions divided sharply between those who thought the Assembly had gone too far and those like Pétion who thought it hadn't gone far enough. Boyer had asked for this opportunity to speak. To judge from remarks that Saint-Martin overheard, Boyer's views were extreme and he faced a sceptical audience.

As the clock on the wall struck eight, Boyer rose from his table and the others fell silent. For several minutes he systematically made his case for abolishing all organized religions that claimed a divine foundation. In fact, self-serving priests had fabricated them to exploit the ignorant and the gullible. The philosophers Helvetius and d'Holbach had demonstrated that there was no God, no Heaven, and no Hell. The universe was composed simply of matter.

Boyer was especially harsh towards the Catholic clergy whom he called parasites and loathsome insects that infected the naive,

common people with superstition. The ruler's duty was to rid
the country of such pests and ensure the people an authentic
civic education.

When the audience had heard enough, they began to object.
'The universe needs a Creator,' one man argued. 'Matter can't
generate itself out of nothing.'

Another man claimed that atheism failed to offer a moral
foundation for society. Without divine sanctions to deter men
from evil, they would descend into anarchy. He insisted, 'The
common people especially need moral guidance. An enlightened parish clergy must teach them their duties to each other
and to the nation as a whole.'

'Atheism,' a third man added, 'recognizes neither good nor
evil, only self-interest. That's a recipe for crime.'

Confronted by a rising tide of opposition, Boyer grew angry
and abusive. 'You blind idiots! You don't know the clergy.
They've also deluded you who fancy yourselves *enlightened*.'
He virtually spat out the last word and strode to the door.

Most of his audience responded with a chorus of hoots and
whistles until he was gone. Pétion and a few other radicals sat
rigidly still, frowning.

THREE
A Don Juan

1 June

Meanwhile, Georges Charpentier was across the street visiting with servants and coachmen of the gentlemen inside the café. Suddenly, Boyer burst out the door like a wild man, shaking both fists. He stopped for a moment and breathed deeply. Finally, he smiled, pulled the wedding band off his finger, and walked briskly away.

'He's up to some mischief,' Georges said to himself and followed Boyer at a safe distance.

Five minutes later, Boyer entered a tavern near Place Saint-Sulpice. As Georges walked in, he saw Boyer disappear up a rear stairway. A few minutes later, he came back down with a slender, dark-haired young woman. For a half-hour they ate bread and cheese and drank a jug of wine. The waiter appeared to know them.

Georges sat close to their table. They seemed fond of each other, perhaps lovers. She was barely seventeen at the oldest, but was attempting to act like a mature woman. Her deep-cut dress and her heavy use of rouge only made her look like an inexperienced tart. She used lively gestures but spoke feeble French with a heavy accent, probably Italian.

Boyer was quite gallant. He smiled kindly, paid her compliments, told her amusing anecdotes, and gave her a patently fictional account of his life as a lonely widower before meeting her. His wedding band was securely hidden in his pocket. After their meal, they went back upstairs, presumably to spend the night together.

As the waiter cleared their table, Georges said softly to him, 'I believe that we know each other.' He searched his memory for the name. 'Ah, you're Bernard Fontaine from . . .'

The waiter had discreetly raised a finger to his lips.

Georges nodded slightly and mouthed, 'The waiter from Café

de Foy.' Bernard's appearance was so self-effacing that it was difficult to recall him. He was one of the most skilful spies in Paris, with a group of associates at his disposal.

Bernard signalled another waiter to finish clearing the table. To Georges he murmured, 'Wait a minute, then go to the back room.'

It was a small office. Bernard gestured to a pair of chairs at a writing table. 'I've taken temporary leave of Café de Foy. Certain gentlemen have engaged me and my associates to gather useful information in a variety of public places. And what brings you to this tavern?'

'I'm interested in Monsieur Jacques Boyer and have followed him here from Café Procope. I suspected that he had a female acquaintance, perhaps a lover, who might work or be known in the neighbourhood. My suspicion has been confirmed.'

'Amazing!' exclaimed Bernard. 'You are right on the mark. He is also one of several objects of my interest. He's known here as Monsieur Robey. Tell me more. I might be of use to you.'

'My Monsieur Boyer is married but has put his wedding band in his pocket. I didn't know that he meets the young woman under an assumed name, an anagram in fact. I smell a rat.'

'Yes, among his many faults, Boyer is false towards women.'

'Could you tell me the name of the attractive young lady who was here with him tonight? I believe she's Italian and I've seen her before.'

'That's Mademoiselle Magdalena Diluna, an acrobat, a very good one. As a young girl she entertained with her brother in the Foire Saint-Germain nearby. Now she performs in small theatres wherever she can, sometimes on the Boulevard.'

'I must have seen her at the Foire. Where's her brother?'

'He has been away for months in the provinces with a troupe of Italian entertainers. We expect him to return any day now.'

Georges said, 'I must talk to Mademoiselle Diluna.'

'You might want to watch her first. She'll perform on Place Saint-Sulpice tomorrow afternoon.'

'Good. I'll be in the audience.' Georges paused with an afterthought. 'Bernard, are you acquainted with a spy whose nickname is "Rat-face"?' Georges described Boyer's spy.

Bernard reflected for a moment. 'That must be Jean-Paul

Filou, a clever swine, from a notorious dynasty of thieves, most of whom have ended badly. Jean-Paul left the family trade and is prospering as a spy. He usually recruits a small band of associates, often children, and gathers scandal for use in extortion schemes. He also works in marital disputes, supplying proof of adultery.'

Georges was intrigued. Why had Boyer hired Rat-face to spy on his wife? Had he good reason to suspect her? Madame Cartier should be alerted.

'What did you learn, Georges?' Saint-Martin led his adjutant into a quiet corner of a wine tavern near the Café Procope. It was about an hour since Boyer had quit the café. Saint-Martin signalled a waiter. He served them two glasses of wine and left for another customer.

Georges saluted his superior and swallowed a draught. 'While I was visiting with servants outside the café, Boyer left in a huff. So I followed him to a tavern near Place Saint-Sulpice.' Georges described his conversation with the waiter Bernard.

'Bernard doesn't come cheap,' the colonel murmured. 'Someone with money and authority has hired him, probably Mayor Bailly or General Lafayette. His employer is probably interested in customers from the nearby radical political club of the Cordeliers.'

'And why so much interest in Boyer?' Georges asked. 'He must be more dangerous than we think.'

'Well, it's two years since the revolution began. Most people are no better off than before – or worse. Agitators like Boyer might see an opportunity. Bailly and Lafayette are losing popularity and are worried. At the moment, Boyer is also our problem. Tomorrow, find out more about the young Italian woman and how she's connected to him. Anne needs to know. Come to think of it, she should go with you. She speaks Italian and could question the young woman. What did the servants outside the café have to say about Boyer?'

'Most of them had no opinion, or didn't even know his name. Some thought he's one of many agitators who talk a lot but achieve nothing. But he has a few admirers. They say he speaks their mind and means what he says. The people won't have a decent life until the king, the clergy and the aristocrats are swept away. One of the servants helps Boyer distribute his pamphlets. He gave me a couple.' Georges handed them to Saint-Martin.

As he read, a frown gathered on his face. '"Hang the priests by their entrails," Boyer writes. If he has his way, there will be a bloodbath in Paris.'

FOUR
Riskful Behaviour

1 June

Meanwhile that evening in Michou's studio, Anne and Michou agreed that they needed to know Boyer's wife better.

'Most people have secrets,' signed Michou. 'Why shouldn't Marthe?'

To observe her more closely they stood opposite her building on Rue Jean-Jacques Rousseau, a short distance to the east of the Palais-Royal. A few feet away from them was Rat-face. The door opened, Boyer stepped out, nodded slightly to the spy, and left for the Café Procope.

He was barely out of sight when the spy left his post and entered the nearby tavern. A few minutes later, Marthe Boyer sneaked out of the building, glanced left and right, then hurried through the streets. Anne and Michou followed her to the Louvre's entrance off Rue Saint-Honoré. She stopped to speak to the watchman and he waved her through.

'I know him,' Michou signed. 'He'll let us pass. We'll see where she goes.' A frequent visitor to the Louvre, Michou was engaged to a painter with a studio in the old palace and often worked with him.

As they entered the courtyard, they saw Madame Boyer approach the door to a suite of ground-floor rooms. She knocked, the door opened part way, and she slipped inside.

Anne signed, 'I can guess who lives in that suite.'

Michou nodded. 'Father O'Fallon and his servant.'

To make sure, the two women went back to the watchman at the entrance. 'Sir,' Anne asked, 'Could you tell me where Father O'Fallon lives?'

The watchman stepped into the courtyard and pointed to the ground floor suite. 'Those are his rooms. But he's not there now – he's at evening prayer in the church across the street. Could his servant help you? He should still be in the suite at least until the prayers are over and he must help the priest to return. That's their routine.' He paused. 'Is there an emergency?'

'No,' Anne assured him with a smile. 'We were just curious. The priest has been in the news recently.'

'And made a name for himself,' the watchman added. 'He stirred up a tempest when he publicly denounced the new constitution of the clergy. Our self-styled patriots called him a traitor.'

After thanking the watchman, the two women walked across the courtyard into a darkened entrance and waited. An hour later, Madame Boyer emerged, furtive again. She scurried through the courtyard and out into the street. A few minutes later, the servant left also and soon came back with the priest leaning on his arm.

When the men were inside their rooms, Anne and Michou stepped out of the shadows and stared at each other. Anne signed to Michou, 'What do you make of it all?'

'I have more questions than answers,' she replied. 'Why would Madame Boyer visit the servant Patrick, especially in such a secretive way?'

'And choose an hour for the visit when the priest isn't there,' Anne added.

Michou pondered for a moment. 'Perhaps she simply reports on her husband's movements and his plans. Patrick then passes the information on to the priest, who needs to know what his enemy is up to. She acts nervously because she fears that her husband or one of his followers might discover her betrayal.'

'That's plausible,' Anne agreed. 'But why choose a time when the priest isn't there?'

Michou hesitated, drew a deep breath, and signed, 'There's another explanation. Patrick and Marthe have something in common – they're both deaf. They may also be lovers. What do you think of that?'

'I agree. And they've been lovers for some time,' Anne replied. 'If her husband were to discover her infidelity, he could go to the police and accuse her of adultery. If there were sufficient witnesses, a magistrate might convict her. According to the old civil law that's still valid, the magistrate could give her dowry to Monsieur Boyer, the aggrieved husband, and sentence her to the Salpêtrière for a year or two.'

Michou added, 'That could explain why Boyer spies on his

wife. He's not so concerned that she might cuckold or dishonour him. Rather, he's scheming to get her dowry – the greedy bastard!' Michou's gaze drifted across the courtyard. She stiffened. 'Look at that young boy,' she signed, then pointed Anne's eye to an urchin sneaking past the watchman and out into the street. 'I saw him with Monsieur Rat-face.'

Anne's heart sank. 'Should our suspicions be correct, our attempt to help Madame Boyer could be much more difficult – and dangerous – than we thought.'

Anne waited up for her husband. It was nearly midnight when he and Georges returned. She served them a chilled cherry drink in the salon, and reported on Madame Boyer's visit with Patrick, the priest's servant.

'They may be romantically involved,' she concluded.

Paul frowned, 'Do you think the priest knows?'

'I doubt it,' Anne replied. 'True, he treats Patrick as a grown man – as he should. After all, he's thirty years old and virile. Women admire his curly blond hair and deep blue eyes, his well-shaped, muscular body and strong hands. But he's no saint. O'Fallon might allow him to sin occasionally with unmarried women. But adultery is a more serious moral as well as legal issue. O'Fallon wouldn't treat it lightly.'

Georges shook his head. 'Still there's really not much he can do about it, beyond scolding him. He's too fond of Patrick to disown him.' He paused, his brow furrowed. 'I'm more intrigued that Monsieur Boyer might be encouraging his wife's infidelity. On the one hand, he treats her brutally, prompting her to think of a happier relationship with another man; on the other, he lets her sneak out to an illicit assignation.'

'That's consistent with his sly, self-centred character,' Anne granted. 'However, doesn't his affair with the young Italian acrobat near Saint-Sulpice jeopardize his scheme?'

'Not at all.' Paul explained that the law wouldn't punish the unfaithful husband, unless he committed an aggravated adultery, for example, by installing his mistress in the family's home. But the law would take no notice of Boyer's affair with the young Italian woman.

Anne asked, 'Isn't the National Assembly even now discussing these issues concerning a woman's inheritance and her dowry?'

'That's true,' Paul replied. 'Boyer's scheme for the dowry requires that he bring his grievance to the magistrate while the old law is still valid. I expect a change by September at the latest, when the new constitution will go into effect. According to the proposed law being debated, an adulterous wife will not lose her dowry.'

Georges conjectured, 'Then Boyer is feeling pressure to conclude his scheme very soon. He must know about the proposed law. If he sees that he can't prove Marthe's adultery in time, he might be willing to compromise with her. Perhaps he would agree to a legal separation in return for a piece of the dowry.'

'How big a piece?' Anne asked doubtfully.

'Much too big,' Paul replied.

'Then why should I help Marthe negotiate that compromise? It's not realistic.'

'Perhaps,' granted Paul. 'So let's consider a different possibility. Boyer may be motivated more by lust than by greed. The Italian girl may have infatuated him. He might want to divorce Marthe and marry her. The National Assembly is also discussing legislation that would permit divorce in cases of adultery. I think it will be approved next year. Boyer is surely aware of the discussion.'

Georges nodded. 'We should look into that possibility. At the least, his affair with the girl appears to increase his brutality to his wife and makes her life unbearable.'

Paul turned to Anne. 'Would you help Georges speak with the Italian girl tomorrow? She's performing acrobatics at Saint-Sulpice.'

'I'm willing. It might take me back to somersaults on stage at Sadler's Wells. I'll try to be helpful.'

FIVE
An Angry Brother

2 June

Late the next afternoon Anne joined Georges on Place Saint-Sulpice in front of a temporary stage divided by a curtain. The great church provided a monumental background. A small crowd had gathered. Street vendors were selling fresh fruit and fruit drinks, cheese and baguettes, and a variety of sweetmeats. Street musicians were at work as well. Anne searched for Boyer. He was not in the crowd. Good, she thought. It should be easier to talk to the young woman.

A trumpeter blew a flourish, the curtain parted. Mademoiselle Diluna strutted forth, chin high, arms akimbo. Then she cartwheeled across the stage. Her slender, supple body was clothed in tight, yellow breeches and a chequered green and yellow blouse. A soft green cap with a yellow tassel covered her thick black hair. Her lips were bright red, her eyelashes long and black.

She launched into a series of back flips and somersaults, and walked around on her hands. Meanwhile a slack rope was being erected. Finally, she sang and danced on the rope to a fiddler's lively Italian melody. All the while, she gave the crowd an engaging smile. At the end of her performance she bowed profoundly and blew kisses to them. They responded with loud applause and a shower of small coins. She scooped them into a purse and danced back through the curtain.

A few minutes later, Anne and Georges went behind the stage and found Magdalena, still in her costume, resting. She would probably repeat the performance in fifteen minutes or so.

'Could we have a few words with you?' Anne asked in the Italian she learned several years ago from friends at Sadler's Wells near London. She had later spoken the language during a lengthy stay in Nice on the Mediterranean.

'Here? Now?' Magdalena replied in Italian. 'I'm tired and must rest for the next show.'

'We understand.' Anne introduced herself and Georges. 'Could we set a time and a place to speak? What we have to say has great importance for you as well as for others.'

The urgency in Anne's request seemed to persuade the young woman. Her brow creased with apprehension. 'I'll meet you in the church in an hour.'

Inside, Saint-Sulpice was vast, only slightly smaller than the Cathedral of Notre Dame. And it was cool, even on a warm late spring day. Anne shivered. She had dressed in a light pink muslin gown. She found a quiet side chapel where there were a few chairs and they could be alone. Magdalena was now nervous, her eyes flickering between Anne and Georges.

'Would you tell us what Monsieur Robey means to you?' Anne began.

'Why do you ask?' the young woman replied, her tone growing testy.

'We fear that you are likely to be hurt. For Monsieur Robey is not what he professes to be.'

'What are you saying? Jacques is a charming, honourable man. True, he's much older than I, but we enjoy each other's company and agree on almost everything. He said his wife died a few years ago, and he was lonely until he met me.'

'Has he proposed marriage to you?'

The question took the young woman by surprise. Flustered, she stammered, 'Not exactly, but we are close to reaching an agreement. I had told him that we should get to know each other better before making a lifelong commitment. He said he understood.'

Anne met the young woman's eye. 'I'm sorry to have to inform you, Magdalena, that he has lied to you. Monsieur Charpentier will tell you that Robey is known at the Café Procope as Monsieur Jacques Boyer.'

'Last night,' Georges said, slowly and carefully for the young Italian's sake, 'I saw him at Procope where he spoke to a group of thirty men. As he left the café, he took off his wedding band and put it in his pocket. Afterwards, I followed him to the tavern where he met you. If you need more proof, visit the garden of the Palais-Royal. He is well known there as Boyer.

Or, you can find his wife in their rooms on Rue Jean-Jaques Rousseau.'

Anne took a paper from her bag and handed it to the young woman. 'This document states that Monsieur Jacques Boyer is legally married to Marthe Boyer. She has signed it in the presence of a notary.' Anne pointed to his seal. 'Therefore, Monsieur Boyer is not free to marry you.'

The young woman reacted with anger. 'You are wrong. You hate Jacques and are trying to separate us and to ruin him. He will certainly be able to explain everything.' Her eyes grew dark with fury. 'If he discovers that you are trying to undermine his reputation, he will punish you.' She rose, shook her head, and stalked out of the church.

'We've planted a seed of doubt,' Georges remarked. 'She may inquire in his neighbourhood or take a walk in the garden of the Palais-Royal and chance upon one of his tirades. Then she should change her tune. In any case, she will likely bring us to his attention.'

'I'm concerned for her safety in case she confronts him.'

Georges nodded. 'I'll alert Bernard to let me know if there's trouble. He already suspects that Boyer is preying upon the young woman.'

That evening at home on Rue Saint-Honoré, Anne sat alone in the salon. Paul was at the Hôtel de Police in a meeting with the mayor. She debated with herself. Should she tell Madame Boyer about her husband's Italian lover? Would that be helpful? She was still undecided when Georges appeared.

'I have news,' he said. 'I've just heard from Bernard at Place Saint-Sulpice. A woman next door to Mademoiselle Diluna had reported loud screams and shouts coming from the Italian girl's room. Her brother Antonio had returned from his trip. The neighbour thinks that the brother had discovered that Magdalena was pregnant. Afterwards, the neighbour said, they had come to her and explained that they had had a fight but were reconciled. Would she give them warm water and clean cloths to treat their wounds. The left side of Magdalena's face was red and swollen. He had bloody scratches on his left cheek.'

'If she is truly reconciled with her brother, she is most likely safe from Boyer.'

Georges nodded his head. 'Presumably she identified Boyer

as the father. I wish I were a fly on the wall while they discussed what to do about him.'

Anne ventured an opinion, 'I would imagine that brother Antonio would lie in wait for him, perhaps try to force him to pay the costs of this pregnancy. That confrontation might be violent. Should Boyer be forewarned?'

'Bernard thinks not. Boyer would run away and try to hide. Antonio would be angered, chase him into a dark alley and puncture him with a stiletto. It's better that he meets Antonio at the tavern, where the risk of violence is less. Antonio's French is poor. He often confides in Bernard who understands some Italian. If Antonio were to consult him in his sister's case, Bernard would urge him to negotiate a settlement.' Georges rose from the table. 'I'll go to the tavern and observe what happens. Bernard might need support.'

'I'll go with you,' said Anne. 'Mademoiselle Diluna might need support as well.'

Anne and Georges were at a table when Boyer arrived in the tavern. Bernard greeted him as if nothing untoward had happened. He seemed unaware that he was walking into a storm. Bernard persuaded him to take a seat and engaged him in conversation. Meanwhile, a servant ran upstairs to inform Mademoiselle Diluna.

A few minutes later, she arrived, the damage to her face only partially concealed by powder. A few steps behind her came her brother Antonio, grim-faced, a patch on his cheek. They walked towards Boyer's table.

He sat up, instantly alert. He had not expected to see the brother and even less the anger in his face.

Bernard signalled the barman, a burly army veteran. He moved swiftly into the confrontation. 'I believe that you three have important business to discuss. You may use the room in the rear.'

Boyer glanced over his shoulder towards the front door, as if about to make a sudden exit. But the barman took a step and blocked the way. Apparently resigned, Boyer got up and headed for the rear, followed by Antonio and his sister.

Before entering the room, Magdalena glanced at Anne and Georges, then whispered in her brother's ear. Antonio stopped, thought for a moment, and walked back to them.

'My sister has told me that you tried to warn her about Monsieur Boyer. Now she's sorry that she rejected your advice and wants you to help us deal with him. He's very slippery and could trick us. We don't understand or speak French well enough. You, Madame Cartier, speak Italian. You shall also bear witness to our cause.'

Anne and Georges exchanged glances and nodded. In Italian Anne added, 'We think our presence might foster a good outcome.' She and Georges followed the others into the room.

Like two pugilists, Antonio and Boyer stood in the middle of the room, glowering at each other. If it came to physical combat, the lithe, athletic Italian would have the advantage. Magdalena moved nervously in between Anne and Georges. Anne put a hand on the young woman's shoulder. She was trembling.

Antonio pointed a finger at Boyer and spoke in rapid Italian, Anne translating for him. 'You, sir, have deceived my sister, pretending to be a widower and free to marry. Then you took advantage of her youth and her *naiveté* in order to seduce her. She's now carrying your child. As an honourable man, will you acknowledge your responsibility and pay the costs of the child's birth and upbringing?'

Boyer sneered, 'How can you prove that I'm the father of her child? She could have slept with any number of men besides me. You've offered no evidence against me, just an unfounded accusation. No magistrate in France would prefer her word to mine. So, I'm not obliged to acknowledge or pay anything.'

The Italian's jaw tightened. He took a step towards Boyer. 'You gave her a false name and insinuated that you would marry her.'

Boyer stepped back. Beads of sweat gathered on his brow. 'My actions could be considered dishonest but not illegal. In love as in war, any trick is fair. Your sister was foolish to believe me. Indeed, she wanted to believe. All that really matters is that we gave pleasure to each other. What's wrong with that? I don't claim to be an honourable man. For what it's worth, I leave honour to aristocrats. It's a foolish affectation.'

'You *will* pay!' Antonio shouted.

Boyer smirked and said softly, 'Your threats are nothing but hot air. You shall not receive a single sou from me. Good day.'

He walked briskly to the door. No one moved to stop him.

By now, Antonio's voice was low and ominous. 'This isn't the end of the matter. You must give me satisfaction or one day you'll be sorry.'

Boyer didn't look back. He slammed the door behind him. Suddenly, Anne felt limp; her hands trembled. Translating this exchange had drained her.

SIX
Lethal Confrontation

3 June

Early next morning, while walking in the garden of the Palais-Royal with Michou, Anne described last night's confrontation with Boyer near Saint-Sulpice.

Michou remarked, 'He has made a dangerous enemy in Antonio Diluna, and he doesn't seem to care. Does he have a powerful mentor to look after him?'

'Monsieur Jérôme Pétion of the National Assembly seems to share his views and smiles kindly upon him. Like Pétion, Boyer is hostile to the church and to religion in general and obsessed with the Civil Constitution of the Clergy. In his club, Citizens for Equality, he calls for the overthrow of the monarchy and the establishment of a democratic republic. Most reformers think he goes much too far and they're afraid of his influence among the poor of Paris.'

'How can you reason with such a person?' Michou remarked, taking a sketchbook from her bag. She hoped to record Boyer's daily ritual and any significant persons that he met.

'Point well taken, Michou. He's a clever, wilful man,' Anne replied. 'Nonetheless I should try to persuade him that a fair separation from Marthe would be in his own interest. The dowry would be the sticking point. He would claim it all, leaving Marthe penniless. I would urge him to share the dowry and avoid a lengthy, expensive legal process.'

Michou shrugged her doubt at that idea.

As they reached the Camp of the Tatars, a placard tacked to a post caught Anne's attention. 'DEBATE,' it screamed in bold letters: 'Monsieur Jacques Boyer dares the traitorous priest, Denis O'Fallon, to argue against the new Civil Constitution of the Clergy. Nine o'clock in the garden of the Palais Royal near the Circus.'

Anne signed to Michou, 'It's nearly the time. Let's go.'

About fifty men and women of various ages and descriptions had already gathered in front of a low wooden platform. The hulking mass of the Circus served as a backdrop. Boyer sat behind a podium off to the left, smiling confidently, nodding to acquaintances. He wore a simple, pale blue silk suit. His hair was lightly powdered.

He occasionally glanced at the vacant podium to the right. At a few minutes to nine he glanced again, this time impatiently. He said to the crowd, 'Perhaps the priest is a coward as well as a traitor.' Most of the crowd shrugged off his remark. They had probably come merely out of curiosity and were chattering about trivia. But in the front benches a knot of men in the dress of artisans began to chant, 'Death to the priests.'

Promptly at nine, the tall, gaunt figure of Denis O'Fallon, clad in a long black soutane, appeared on the edge of the crowd. His servant Patrick cleared the way for him and he shuffled towards the platform leaning on his cane. Patrick, a powerful man, lifted the priest on to the platform and placed him behind his podium. He looked out over the people with an expression of serene confidence, his eyes brimming with passion. This spectacle of an infirm and unpopular man braving his enemies quieted the crowd, even the artisans.

The debate began with O'Fallon. He granted that the church in France needed reform. The male monastic orders in particular lacked vitality. The wealth of the church was unfairly distributed. The common, parochial clergy were poorly paid, while many prelates like Rohan of Strasbourg lived in princely splendour. But the solution that the National Assembly conceived was mistaken. It didn't just reform the male monastic orders; it abolished them and went on to close down the nuns as well, though they were performing useful services to society in schools and hospitals. He admitted that the Assembly rightly prescribed a more equitable salary scale for clergy. But, nationalizing all church lands without cause was simply theft on a grand scale and violated a citizen's basic right to his property. And, finally, the requirement of an oath to uphold these spurious reforms violated a priest's conscience.

O'Fallon's brief analysis of the Civil Constitution of the Clergy was cogent, his tone was reasonable. Many years teaching at Juilly, one of the most respected colleges in France, had sharpened his mind, even while his physical strength ebbed.

For the few minutes of his speech Anne set aside her Protestant bias and her resentment towards the church that had persecuted her family. In the end she had to respect O'Fallon's point of view.

His audience, however, was less open-minded or respectful. Most simply heard him out while looking forward to Boyer's rebuttal. The artisans standing near the platform tried to distract O'Fallon with taunts, rude gestures, outbursts of laughter, and whistles.

The priest appeared to recognize their leader and treated his behaviour with contempt.

'Do you know the fellow?' Anne pointed discreetly to the bold, slope-browed man.

'I've seen him before,' Michou replied. 'Armand Flamme, an unemployed carpenter by trade and a clever thief. He's a dangerous agitator and has a following among poor artisans. Recently, they have joined Boyer's club.'

As O'Fallon stepped away from the podium, Flamme and his men surged forward, as if to assault the priest. Alarmed and angry, Boyer confronted Flamme and ordered him to let the debate continue. Flamme said something under his breath that caused Boyer to flinch. An insult? Anne wondered.

Flamme retreated with his men back to their places, un-repentant, muttering to each other.

Boyer stepped up to his podium and launched into a list of crimes against the state, inspired by the clergy, from Ravaillac's assassination of Henry IV to Damien's attempt on the life of Louis XV. The lesson of history, he argued, is that 'Priests are a nest of vipers who pursue their own corporate interests rather than those of the nation. The Civil Constitution of the Clergy is just the first step towards bringing these pests under control.'

'Where do the reforms fall short?' asked a well-dressed man in the crowd.

'I welcome the citizen's question,' said Boyer with an earnest smile. 'Unfortunately, in the new regime, as in the old, priests are assigned to be our teachers. But history shows that they are corrupt.' Boyer went on to titillate his audience with tales of immorality among priests, monks and nuns. And at the end he asked, 'Should we trust our children's education to such hypocrites?'

Led by their leader Flamme the artisans shouted a resounding

'No!' Some of the crowd drifted away to the shops in the arcades and were soon distracted. Anne supposed that others would gather in the cafés to discuss what they had heard.

Throughout Boyer's anticlerical diatribe the priest had listened impassively. When it was over, he shuffled across the platform and faced his opponent. The priest drew himself up to his full six feet and glared down at the much shorter Boyer with contempt. 'To you, sir, nothing is sacred; you defame the church and her servants. May you burn in Hell.'

Boyer smirked. 'Before I journey to that improbable place, I hope to see a republican court convict you of treason and send you to the gallows.'

Anne and Michou walked to a table in the garden terrace in front of the Café de Foy. Anne ordered chilled fruit drinks and filled in details of the debate. Meanwhile, Michou idly drew in her sketchbook. She had understood little of what was said. But she had accurately discerned the attitudes of the speakers and the crowd.

She put down her pencil and signed, 'The old priest believed in what he said; Monsieur Boyer did not.'

Anne looked askance.

Michou showed her nearly finished sketch of Boyer, then explained. 'He's full of himself, enjoys his own wit, and ignores the opinions of others. He also rejects any authority other than his own will. That's why he speaks badly of the king and the church.'

The drinks arrived and Michou put aside her sketchbook for the moment.

'Look who is here,' Anne observed. Boyer had appeared on the terrace, sat at a table with a few acquaintances, and was quickly engaged in an animated political conversation. From Paul's description, Anne recognized one of the men as Monsieur Pétion, the politician.

Soon, Armand Flamme's ragged band of coarse-looking artisans also arrived at the terrace. Laying down a challenge, they wore the scuffed aprons of their profession rather than the proper dress for the Palais-Royal. In their hands were bundles of pamphlets. Men and women at nearby tables stiffened, anticipating trouble. Flamme led the way, boldly thrusting his pamphlets upon people at the tables. Many were clearly annoyed, but they accepted the pamphlets under the menacing glare of his ruffians.

Anne asked for a pamphlet and scanned it. On the front was a crude sketch of a prosperous-looking businessman stealing money from the pocket of a starving artisan. On the back was a detailed list of artisans' complaints of their masters' unjust practices, followed by threats to expose certain financial crimes.

Flamme threw an impertinent glance at Boyer and Pétion, and then approached the table next to Anne's. A well-tailored, robust, middle-aged man of business was conversing with an attractive young female companion. The rogue rudely forced his way in between them and slapped a pamphlet on to their table. As he withdrew, he glared at the businessman and muttered 'bastard' under his breath. The older man stiffened and turned red in the face. 'Villain!' he shouted. He glanced at the pamphlet, lifted it with two fingers and grimaced as if it stank. '*Merde!*' he said loudly and threw it to the ground.

The rogue uttered a vulgar curse, stooped, and picked up the pamphlet. While he was rising, he 'accidentally' tipped the table. Coffee spilled over the gentleman and his companion.

He jumped to his feet in a fury, fists clenched, about to thrash the offender. The woman seized her friend's arm; a waiter cautioned him. For the rogue's companions had quickly formed a phalanx around him. Sunlight glinted off steel blades, half-drawn from sheaths beneath their aprons.

Boyer left his chair, an expression of horror on his face, and seemed about to intervene. But Pétion cautioned him.

Anne asked Michou, who had watched the politician intently, 'Did you catch any of that?'

'I think he said, "Let it be. We'll deal with Flamme later."'

The victim backed off, stood rigid and still for a moment, and stared intently at the rogue, as if committing his features to memory. Finally, the victim and the woman followed the waiter into the café.

Michou leaned over to Anne and signed, 'I recognize the victim. He's Monsieur Jean Guiscard, a wealthy master builder in the city. He employs dozens of workers and often takes his coffee here. The woman is his mistress. I've sketched both of them.'

Anne finished her drink. 'Guiscard and the rogue appeared to know – and hate – each other. They have clashed before.

After today's episode, there will surely come a severe reckoning.'

'No doubt,' Michou signed.

In the meantime, the priest, O'Fallon, in his black soutane, had walked into the scene, leaning on his cane. His servant Patrick followed close behind. The priest pointed to the coffee-soaked man on his way into the café, and then challenged the guilty rogue.

'You, sir, are a cowardly, arrogant bully,' he said and shuffled on.

From a distance Flamme's followers mocked the priest's lofty, cultivated speech, his noble bearing and manner. They shouted insults at him and cursed him for refusing to take the oath in support of the new constitution, Flamme leading the pack.

O'Fallon gave them a look of withering scorn and turned to leave. At that moment, Flamme dashed up behind the priest and threw a stone that hit him on the back of the head. He crashed to the ground. The rogues closed in on the prostrate priest, loudly threatening to hang him from a street lamp.

A frantic Patrick tried in vain to push them back. Finally, desperate, he clenched his fists and knocked two of them senseless to the ground. The others seized him, shouting, 'We'll hang you too.'

Meanwhile, as soon as the scene had begun to turn ugly, a waiter from the café had gone in search of watchmen. They arrived just in time to drive the ruffians off.

Anne and Michou left their table and knelt by the priest. Unconscious, he appeared to have suffered a concussion. Patrick and the women lifted him on to an improvised stretcher, carried him to his rooms in the Louvre, and made him comfortable.

Did he need more care than his servant could provide? Anne asked herself. The city hospital, the Hôtel-Dieu, had a poor reputation for care and could not be trusted to keep the priest safe from his enemies. She hurried to the nearby convent of the Oratory and explained to the porter what had happened.

'Couldn't your priests at the Oratory look after Father O'Fallon?' she asked. 'There must be an infirmary in this building.'

The porter shook his head. 'There's an infirmary but no one to tend to it.' He explained that only a few old, infirm priests were left. The government was closing down religious societies.

Most of the Oratorians in Paris had already dispersed. Some, especially the young, had taken the oath to the new constitution and left the Congregation weeks ago. Others had returned to their families or to areas in the country where priests who refused the oath would feel safer.

Discouraged, Anne turned to leave.

The porter called out to her, 'The Louvre is guarded. The priest will be safest there. His servant can care for him with help from a medical doctor.'

Back at the Louvre, Anne sent for a doctor, then asked Patrick, 'Shouldn't we summon the police? They must arrest the man who threw the stone.'

Patrick swore a silent oath. 'That's a waste of time. They don't dare to pursue Flamme and his men. You call the police if you like. They won't pay attention to a deaf man like me anyway.' He paused, then added in rapid, angry signing, 'But the villain who threw that stone is going to be punished. I've seen him before in the garden. I know his name and will find out where he hides.'

Tears streamed from Patrick's eyes. His face was flushed and bruised. The knuckles of his hands were bleeding and blood had spattered his shirt.

Anne found a clean cloth and wrapped his hands. For a moment, he came out of his rage and gave her a faint smile.

She wondered about his grief. It seemed more heartfelt than she would expect even from a devoted servant to whom the priest had given his name.

He seemed to discern her mind. 'He's my father, my *real* father.' He went on to explain that he grew up in a remote village believing that his father had died in battle. Several years ago, this tall priest came to the village and declared they were father and son. The fact was apparent in their likeness. Over time, he adopted his father's views on life, and on religion in particular, and he condemned those who publicly reviled him. 'They are the devil's agents attempting to destroy the Catholic Church, but they will be destroyed.'

At a loss for words, Anne and Michou returned to her studio and sat quietly at a table. The violent incident had badly shaken both of them. Finally, Michou opened her sketchbook and showed a page to Anne. Patrick was there in all his grief and anger. On another page was Flamme, the thickset rogue, drawn in a few swift, sure strokes of Michou's pencil.

She signed, 'I'll make a more detailed copy for the police. Who knows, they might find the courage to arrest him. By the way,' she added, 'Boyer frowned when the rogue threw the stone. I wonder why he disapproved.' She sat at her easel, propped up the sketchbook off to one side, and set to work.

Anne also thought Boyer's reaction seemed out of character in view of his wish that the priests be eliminated. Could there be dissension within his following?

Mid afternoon that day, a pair of National Guardsmen appeared at Anne's residence asking for Madame Cartier. She met them in the parlour by the entrance on the courtyard. With the collapse of the old royal system two years ago, the Guard had taken over ordinary police work. From a chaotic start, they had improved. But in criminal investigation they lacked experience and training, and perhaps even sufficient intelligence. The two men standing awkwardly before her didn't inspire confidence.

The senior of the two began to speak. 'We're investigating this morning's incident outside the Café de Foy. An old priest was seriously injured. You were present. Tell us what you saw.'

While she described what had happened, the officers observed a stony-faced silence. They didn't seem to pay close attention.

At her conclusion, the younger officer remarked, 'You've failed to mention that the priest's servant, Patrick O'Fallon, struck two patriots. One of them suffered a broken jaw and a smashed nose; the other received a blow to his temple resulting in a severe concussion. We've taken the servant into custody and charged him with assault.'

For a moment Anne couldn't believe what she was hearing. Then she rallied. 'Patrick was defending his father and himself. Your "patriots" threatened to hang both of them.' Anne sensed that the officers were attempting to excuse or at least mitigate the rogues' attack on the priest.

The younger officer ignored her protest. 'The old priest is an aristocrat and a notorious enemy of the people. He has also refused to take the oath in support of the constitution. Our eyewitnesses declared that he provoked the incident. So I say that he got what was coming to him.'

Anne could see no point in quarrelling with the officers. As members of the National Guard, they were approaching this incident from the so-called patriotic point of view. So, she asked

instead, 'Have you questioned Monsieur Jean Guiscard? The
rogue who attacked the priest also deliberately tipped a cup of
coffee on to Guiscard and his female companion. I believe he
will tell you that the rogue and his friends were a band of
ruffians masquerading as patriots.'

The mention of Guiscard caused the officers to exchange
puzzled glances. Either they hadn't heard of him, which was
unlikely – he was well-connected to the revolutionary elite –
or they realized that the incident had just become more complicated than they had expected.

The older officer cleared his throat and adopted a more
professional attitude. 'At this time, we are focusing our attention on Patrick O'Fallon and his part in this incident. We've
attempted to question him but he refuses to cooperate.'

'He's deaf.' Anne felt her patience with these men nearing
its limit.

'We know that, Madame. We speak to him loud and clear.'

'Sir, he's not hard of hearing. He's completely deaf and
couldn't hear cannon fire from a foot away. Have you written
your questions for him?'

Both officers averted their eyes. Anne realized that they were
effectively illiterate and ashamed to admit it. If Patrick were
to get a fair hearing, she would have to help him. He would
refuse to cooperate with persons, like these police officers, who
couldn't or wouldn't understand him or treat him with respect.

On her way to the police bureau near the Palais-Royal, Anne
picked up Michou and her sketches from the incident. The
bureau was on the ground floor of a decrepit building, its walls
propped up by scaffolding. Inside the main room was a sham-
bles of mismatched old furniture and crumbling plaster walls.
File boxes and piles of paper lay pell-mell on the broken tile
floor. The several guards on duty leaned over a low table in a
game of dominoes. Others seemed engaged in idle conversation. Anne and Michou silently shared their impressions that
this was a poorly motivated, undisciplined body of men.

The women were led to an inner office where at least the
plaster had been repaired. The captain in charge of the bureau
appeared more intelligent than the officers who had accompanied the women, but also more intimidating. He had the face
of a bulldog. His nose was flat; his neck was so thick and

short that his bald head appeared to sit directly on his massive shoulders.

He looked up from a paper on his writing table and glared at the women approaching him. 'What do you want?' he growled.

Anne showed him her identification papers and introduced Michou. 'We witnessed the incident this morning at Café de Foy in the Palais-Royal. We hope to give you an honest account of what happened.'

The captain glanced at his officers. They shrugged in a gesture of helplessness.

'Well, be quick about it. As far as I'm concerned, it was a brawl about politics. Some men were hurt. I've got one of the culprits in custody, and I have to decide what to do with him. The others have disappeared.' He pushed back from the table and stared at Anne with narrowed, sceptical eyes.

She repeated the story of the incident that she had given to the officers an hour earlier, speaking as briefly and clearly as possible. To judge from his grimace the captain was more disturbed by the coffee spilt on Guiscard than by the rock that struck down Father O'Fallon.

'The chief instigator of the entire incident,' Anne concluded, 'is this man.' She nodded to Michou who presented her sketch of the slope-browed, thickset leader of the pack of villains, Armand Flamme.

The captain studied the sketch for a moment, stroking his chin. Suddenly he cried out, 'Aha! I've seen Flamme before, a clever rogue. So, he spilt coffee over Guiscard. Well, that wasn't very bright. My men had better pick up Flamme or he'll soon be a bloody corpse and I'll have a murder to solve.' He showed the sketch to the two officers. 'Commit that face to memory and bring him here.'

The officers glanced at each other, shrugged, and left with remarkably little enthusiasm.

Anne continued, 'I'd like to speak on behalf of my deaf student, Patrick O'Fallon.'

'He's charged with assault. What about him?'

'False witnesses have accused him. Michou and I will testify under oath that he merely defended himself.'

The captain studied Anne's identification papers again, then looked up at her. 'I've heard of you, Madame Cartier, years ago, when I was serving in the French Guards. Your husband is a colonel in the Gendarmerie Nationale. I'll release the deaf man officially to him. That will look better on the record. He writes that you're acting on his behalf. So you can take custody of the deaf man.'

Anne signalled to Michou that it was time to leave. At the door Anne remarked, 'In any case, Captain, you may have a murder to solve. I don't expect Father O'Fallon to survive the blow that Flamme gave him.'

'Thank you for the warning, Madame,' he said, his voice dripping with irony. 'But I'll not lose a wink of sleep over that treacherous priest.'

'Oh, is that so, Captain?' Anne spoke softly and with an ironic smile. 'You may not realize that, unlike many of today's self-proclaimed patriots, Father O'Fallon as a young man actually fought for his country and suffered a grievous injury.'

For a brief moment, the captain looked thoughtful, then he remarked brusquely, 'Thank you, Madame. I'll try to think better of him for that.'

A guard brought Patrick to the captain's office and handed him over to Anne. On the way out, he stopped at the door, bowed politely to the captain, and gracefully signed to him, 'Swine!'

Anne flinched inwardly but tried hard not to show it.

In return, the captain gave him a brief blank stare, followed by an irritated nod, and then turned to other business.

Outside on the street, Anne was about to scold Patrick, but he signed, 'I'm sorry, Madame Cartier. I shouldn't have risked provoking the captain and embarrassing you. I couldn't help it. He's such a beast.' He glanced at her and smiled. 'I do appreciate the help you've given me. Now I'm hungry. Shall we eat something quickly in the Camp of the Tatars and then return to my father? I'm anxious to find out what the doctor has learned.'

The doctor, who had examined the priest, was waiting at his bedside in the Louvre when they arrived. He gestured towards the unconscious man and told Anne, 'There is serious bleeding in the brain and it will soon prove fatal. Moreover, the fall has broken his neck and paralysed him.'

When Anne passed the news on to Patrick, he signed, 'Death will be a mercy.'

* * *

It was now late in the afternoon. A show was just ending at the little puppet theatre in the Camp of the Tatars and a dozen smiling patrons were filing out the door. Anne's partner in the theatre, Victor the puppeteer, came out last and looked around. When he saw Anne, he greeted her with a smile and a wave. They went into the theatre together and opened windows to air out the room. The benches were strewn helter-skelter. She helped rearrange them for the next show. Then she explained that she wanted to use the storeroom for an hour.

'That's not a problem,' he said. 'I have all the equipment that I need.'

He seemed curious, so she said, 'I'm meeting Madame Boyer – privately. We made the appointment two days ago. Monsieur Boyer isn't supposed to know.'

Victor seemed to understand. Anne had known him for more than five years, ever since she arrived in Paris. He had a wide knowledge of life in the arcades of the Palais-Royal and often helped her investigations.

'I've heard Boyer, and dozens like him, speaking in the garden. He's fond of his own opinions and is harsh towards others. I pity his wife.' After thanking Anne, he left for a bite to eat.

Soon Marthe arrived and followed Anne into the storeroom. Surrounded by puppets, Anne described this morning's incident in front of Café de Foy.

Anne asked, 'What do you make of your husband's critical attitude towards the violence done to the priest?'

'I'm not surprised,' Marthe replied. 'Violence is in his scheme of things. The republic of his dreams will destroy the royal family, the clergy, the nobles and other enemies of the people. But he rails against vulgar brawling in public that discredits his cause. He thinks that artisans and others of the lower class should follow leaders, like himself, who are more enlightened in their strategy and more judicious in their tactics.'

As Marthe signed, Anne recalled the debate with O'Fallon and Boyer's scurrilous attack on the clergy. To Anne's mind he seemed to encourage precisely the vulgar violence that he claimed to condemn.

'Father O'Fallon isn't expected to survive his injury,' Anne reported, trying to observe Marthe's reaction.

She appeared sympathetic. 'He has been kind to me and to Patrick.'

'Furthermore,' Anne continued, 'the National Guard arrested Patrick for injuring two of the rogues.'

At the mention of Patrick's brush with the law, Marthe turned pale. 'But he was only defending himself and his father,' she exclaimed. 'How is he?'

'For the time being, he's safe in my custody,' Anne replied.

Marthe appeared to relax. But her reaction had confirmed Anne's impression that a romantic bond had formed between Marthe and Patrick.

SEVEN
A Malicious Placard

5 June

Early Sunday morning, Michou asked Anne to join her for a walk in the garden of the Palais-Royal. Without smiling, she had added, 'I want to show you something.' Anne didn't ask her to explain. In any issue concerning the Palais-Royal Michou's judgement was dependable. Nearly every day, and for hours at a time, she sketched life there, low as well as high, with a keen observant eye.

As the two women entered the garden, a brisk westerly wind whistled through the trees and raised wispy clouds of dust from the ground. Debris from last night's carousing and boisterous political arguments swirled about aimlessly. Then the wind suddenly subsided and an eerie quiet hung in the air. In the distance church bells pealed, calling the faithful to the early mass.

Though subdued, there was activity. Servants in aprons were cleaning the outdoor cafés and collecting stray tables and chairs. Workers were tearing placards from trees and street lamps and collecting rubbish. By mid morning, the garden would regain its exotic vitality for Sunday visitors. Ladies and gentlemen would come in their most fashionable costumes to see and be seen in the cafés and promenades. Also on Sunday, families of modest means would enjoy puppetry, sweetmeats, song and dance in the garden and the adjacent arcades.

Traditionally, the only entrance requirements were decent clothes and a few copper coins. But in the recent, troubled years, the rules were bent for poorly dressed, coarse men like Armand Flamme, who were useful in political confrontations. He must have a patron, Anne thought.

'The colonel's name came up often last night,' signed Michou, a frown on her face. 'My friend Sylvie and I walked in the garden to see what was going on. According to Sylvie, people were excited about the incident on Friday outside Café de Foy. They told her that the priest O'Fallon was your friend and was seen visiting your house. I must show you one of the placards, if it's still posted.'

She led Anne to a tree near the Valois arcade opposite Madame Lebrun's brothel. Michou pointed to a placard fastened to the tree at eye level. 'I drew close enough to read it. Some of the text was too complicated for me. What I could understand was enough to make me want to tear it down. But that would have been dangerous. Many rogues were standing nearby.'

Anne glanced at the placard, felt her gall rising, and looked over her shoulder. No one was watching. She pulled the placard from the tree and walked rapidly away to her puppet theatre, the only place in the Palais-Royal where she could feel safe now. Trembling with apprehension and anger, she laid the placard on a table and read, signing for Michou.

Attention: Citizens and Patriots

You all know that the traitorous priest, O'Fallon, provoked a quarrel in the garden yesterday outside Café de Foy. Two patriots were injured before the priest was subdued. At the scene, aiding and abetting him, was Madame Anne Cartier.

Michou broke in with heat to sign, 'Whoever wrote this placard didn't even notice me. But of course he's not trying to tell the truth.'

Anne gave her a weak smile and continued.

She and her husband, the Colonel Paul de Saint-Martin, are the priest's closest friends. He was observed visiting their house on Rue Saint-Honoré shortly before the incident. Patriots will recall that the colonel has long consorted with enemies of the people. He owes his position in the Gendarmerie Nationale to that arch-traitor, the Baron de Breteuil who now organizes counter-revolutionaries from his lair in Switzerland. Four years ago, the colonel helped former Lieutenant General Thiroux de Crosne arrest the patriot Hercule Gaillard who still languishes in the naval prison in Brest. Two years ago, the colonel also attempted to save the royal intendant, Berthier de Sauvigny, from the people's righteous wrath.

Do you think Colonel Paul de Saint-Martin should be chosen to command the Gendarmerie Nationale in the Paris region? All true patriots must shout together, loud and clear: NO! And they should do whatever it takes to stop him and his English consort from undermining our liberty.

From the Patriotic Committee on Place des Victoires

Anne took a deep breath. Her heart was racing. Michou put an arm around her shoulder until she calmed down. Then her reaction began to irritate her. She shouldn't have become so upset. She was familiar with scurrilous publications that had long disgraced the Palais-Royal. Several years ago, when she was still a newcomer in the city, a malicious sheet circulating in the garden had branded her a promiscuous English whore. Its author was a disgruntled, corrupt police inspector whom Anne had exposed.

But this placard's attack was much more ominous because of its thinly veiled physical threat aimed at Paul as well as her. And the threat was all the more serious in that the city's forces of public order and safety had weakened. Demagogues could rather easily draw the wrath of a confused and angry populace towards convenient scapegoats like her and Paul.

'Who do you think wrote the placard?' Michou signed, as they left the garden. 'He has to be someone involved in the incident at Café de Foy, either Armand Flamme or Jacques Boyer.'

'Boyer, most likely,' Anne replied. 'The language in the placard reads like the work of a cultivated man. He must resent that I'm helping his wife.'

She folded the placard and put it into her bag. 'Paul will want to read it,' she signed. 'I'll walk you to your studio and then go home.'

Anne found Paul in the garden. He had cut a dozen red roses and removed the thorns. While she watched, he arranged the roses in a vase and held them up for her to smell. Their scent was strong and fragrant.

'These are for you,' he said and placed the flowers on the garden table.

Anne embraced him. 'That's sweet of you, my dear. But I must show you something that will dampen your spirits.' She laid the placard out on the table. 'It comes from the Palais-Royal. I'll fetch tea while you read it.'

When she returned, he was seated at the table rubbing his chin, thoughtfully staring at the placard. She placed a cup in front of him and quietly took a seat.

'Boyer?' asked Anne.

Paul nodded. 'We must be alert and watch our backs.'

'But,' Anne cautioned, 'we should continue to help Madame Boyer and to seek justice for Father O'Fallon.'

'Right.' Paul paused for a moment. 'I'm concerned that the placard raises the issue of my loyalty to the new regime. How shall I respond? With a placard contradicting Boyer's?'

Anne shook her head. 'You must ignore his slander. Your record as Provost of the Royal Highway Patrol proves that you respect legitimate authority and oppose mob rule. Mayor Bailly and General Lafayette will support you. So will the king, for all that's worth.'

'At this point, Bailly, Lafayette, and Louis XVI, King of the French, have become slender reeds. I'd better not depend on them.'

Anne was becoming anxious. She asked, 'What's the attitude of the gendarmes under your command? Can you count on them?'

Paul shrugged. 'Those who previously served under me in the old Royal Highway Patrol are trustworthy. But more than half of the new gendarmes come from the former regiment of French Guards and other old royal military units. Revolutionary ideas have undermined their discipline. Some of them demand the right to elect their officers. So they probably share the sentiments in Boyer's placard. I'm not even sure I can count on the rest.'

'Then,' concluded Anne, 'we'll have to rely mostly on our own wits.'

That afternoon, Monsieur Augustin Savarin, formerly Count Savarin, arrived with his wife, Paul's aunt Marie de Beaumont. Anne and Paul had invited them to music in the salon. A string quartet would play new works by Joseph Haydn, the Viennese composer. An excellent amateur cellist and especially fond of Viennese music, Savarin had eagerly accepted the invitation. But on entering the house, more than music seemed on his mind. He murmured in a confidential tone to Anne and Paul that he had something to discuss with them after the concert. This was intriguing. Savarin was usually a reticent man, averse to gossip.

Since recently becoming the husband of Paul's aunt, Savarin had grown from a respected acquaintance to a trusted friend, as well as a valued confidant. He had much to offer. For many years he had worked in the royal palace at Versailles, overseeing the royal archives. He also researched documents pertaining to the French nobility, chiefly claims to titles and privileges, and resolved disputes. A widower, he had divided his leisure hours between the cello and the science of cryptography. The Foreign Office often asked him to decipher certain difficult codes.

In August 1789, the abolition of noble status and its privileges made Savarin's function at the court largely redundant. In October, when a mob forced the royal family to move from Versailles to Paris, the Foreign Office followed and settled into new quarters in the city. Savarin let them know that he was available. Since several experts had retired or gone into exile, the Foreign Office gladly engaged Savarin as a cryptographer and assigned him to spy particularly on the correspondence of Baron Breteuil and other disgruntled nobles at home and abroad. A prudent man, he masked his work as much as humanly possible. Officially, he was merely an elderly clerk with a nominal stipend.

The musicians took their places before a dozen guests. The cello passages in Joseph Haydn's String Quartet in D Major transported Savarin into a near-heavenly universe. His eyes closed, his lips parted slightly. After the Quartet's last difficult, riotous movement, the guests moved to a buffet table and were served a fine white wine and an assortment of cheeses, followed by fruit tarts. Savarin seemed preoccupied again, but he was a good guest and mixed with the others.

When the party ended and most of the guests left, he and Marie stayed behind. She chatted with Anne in the salon; he went with Paul to his office. As the door closed behind them,

Savarin remarked, 'This is more drama than I'm used to. But what I need to tell you is both important and delicate.'

They sat facing each other at the writing table. Paul inclined his head slightly in expectation.

'Paul, how well do you know Count Axel von Fersen?'

'*Le beau Fersen,* as the ladies call him, is a handsome Swedish army officer, thoroughly familiar with French language and manners. His father was once Sweden's ambassador to our court at Versailles. Fersen and I served together for three years in the American War. Since then, we've seen less of each other. He bought an army regiment, the Royal Swedish, for 100,000 *livres* and entered into court society at Versailles.'

Savarin asked tentatively, 'Is it true that the queen has taken a fancy to him?'

Saint-Martin shrugged. 'No doubt she regards him as a particular friend. Four years ago, their relationship tempted a hack journalist to devise an extortion plot. I defeated him and put him in prison. Fersen is in my debt.'

'I've enquired about him,' Savarin began, 'because lately I've been reading his correspondence with Baron Breteuil. It's always couched in a difficult, shifting code. The exchange that I'm currently deciphering became clear to me just before coming here.' He paused and met Paul's eye. 'Fersen writes that he's preparing the royal family's flight from Paris. It will take place this month, depending on conditions. He urgently asks the baron to prevail upon you to hold back the gendarmes in the area around Paris under your command.'

'I'm not entirely surprised,' Paul remarked. 'For the past few months, rumours of such a flight have circulated widely. Lafayette has greatly increased the guard at the Tuileries. The royal family are virtually imprisoned there. I can't imagine how Fersen could expect to free them. I'm troubled that he would even think that I could be persuaded, enticed, or cajoled into his scheme. My gendarmes know the law. The royal family may not leave Paris without the government's permission. I expect gendarmes to do their duty. Fersen will have to outwit them – and do it without my help.'

'I'm pleased to hear you say that, for I think Fersen has set out on a fool's errand. I suspect that the queen is pushing him. He must be infatuated, or he'd see that the scheme is bound to end badly.' Savarin paused again, smiling wryly. 'And now for

the baron's reply. He tells Fersen to speak in his name and urge
you in the strongest terms to cooperate with the scheme. You
will have to choose sides, for or against the king. If the flight
is successful and the king returns to Paris at the head of a victorious army, he will reward his loyal friends and punish those
who failed him.'

Paul reflected for a moment dolefully. 'Since I came back
from the war in America, the baron has been a most helpful
patron, in fact more like a concerned uncle. I would not be an
officer in the Gendarmerie Nationale without his support. But
I fear that he intends to put our relationship to the test. And I
must refuse him.'

He went to the window overlooking the courtyard and stood
there rapt in thought. Then he turned to Savarin. 'I thank you,
sir, for warning me. I'll keep this conversation strictly confidential.'

'You may share it with Anne as I have with Marie. They can
be trusted.'

The two men shook hands and returned to the salon, where
their wives were waiting.

'The music was superb and the food was tasteful,' said
Savarin, as he and Marie said goodbye at the door.

Paul added, 'And our conversation offered much food for
thought.'

EIGHT
Death of an Irish Priest

6 June

Three days after the attack, Father O'Fallon was near death. Anne sat at his side, relieving Patrick who had nursed him through the night. He had been unconscious since his injury. The bleeding in his brain would soon kill him, probably today or tomorrow.

Over the past few days, the priest occasionally had visitors. A National Guard officer had come while Anne was there. She gave him a report on the priest's condition.

The officer thanked Anne and added, 'The priest's servant Patrick has written down information about the incident and given it to us. We're searching for the rogue Flamme. He has left his home and is in hiding. The sketch helps.' Anne sensed that the officer was merely going through the motions.

A few elderly priests remaining at the Oratory also visited. One of them brought the holy oil and anointed O'Fallon. But he remained unconscious and they left without speaking to him.

Late in the afternoon, the room became warm. Anne had almost nodded off when O'Fallon suddenly opened his eyes and began to speak with surprising vigour. 'This is near the end, Madame Cartier. Thank you for coming. May I ask a favour of you? The religious society to which I belong has collapsed. I have no one else to turn to. Would you and your husband kindly look after my affairs when I'm dead? Patrick's experience with the world is limited; he might need help. Death is coming sooner than I had expected.'

'My husband and I shall certainly do whatever we can.'

He told her where his will and other papers were kept and described financial arrangements he had made for Patrick and for various charities. 'I've arranged to be buried in the crypt of the Oratory church. The sexton has a key and another is

hanging to the right of the door. I've shown Patrick the crypt
and where I'm to be laid.'

His eyes shone with gratitude and relief. 'I'm pleased that
you're here. I'll not die alone or abandoned. Otherwise, I look
forward to death and hopefully to a new life beyond pain and
suffering.' He paused for a few moments, apparently struggling
with a thought. 'I must tell you about Patrick. He's my son –
he knows. His mother and I have told him. Thirty years ago,
I was a worldly, carefree young soldier. His mother was a gentle
domestic maid. I went to war without knowing that she was
with child. I was badly injured, she thought I was dead, and
we lost touch.

'Many years later, gravely ill, she learned that I was still
alive. A friendly village priest wrote on her behalf and told
me about Patrick – a deaf man who was likely to go adrift
in a cruel world. I went to her immediately, gave him my
name, and promised to look after him. I was with her when
she died.

'Until then, Patrick had lived with her, a poor young man,
largely isolated from society and with little formal education.
He might appear to be simple. However, he's intelligent, as
well as normal in every respect but his hearing. When I retired
from teaching and moved with him to Paris, my plan was to
put him in contact with the Abbé de l'Épée's institute. Thanks
to you, he's now learning to sign. Perhaps he will enter the
printer's trade. I hope that, when I'm gone, you will offer him
encouragement and guidance.'

'I'll surely do my best. Now you should rest.'

His voice was becoming so faint that Anne had to draw close
to hear him. His eyes were almost closed, a smile spread over
his face. He mouthed the words, 'Thank you and God bless,'
and fell asleep.

That evening at home while Anne was at supper with Paul, a
servant approached with a message from the Louvre. She read
it to Paul.

> *Please come. My father is dying.*
> *Patrick O'Fallon*

'I'll go immediately. Would you accompany me, Paul?'

'Of course. It's late and dark and the streets aren't safe. Besides, although we disagree on points of theology, I respect his courage and integrity.'

At the Louvre, the atmosphere in Father O'Fallon's room was heavy with Patrick's grief. The priest was awake, his breathing shallow, his eyes glistening and fixed on his son. Patrick knelt by the bed, sobbing.

As Anne and Paul approached, O'Fallon's eyes shifted towards them. He smiled a faint welcome, and then looked up. For a few minutes he seemed to stare at a flickering light that the lamp cast on the ceiling. His lips moved soundlessly. Anne could make out a simple prayer that he repeated again and again. Finally, his breathing ceased and life left his eyes.

Patrick's sobs rose to a wail and filled the room. Paul and Anne placed their hands on his shoulder and comforted him for several minutes. He gradually calmed down, rose from his knees and faced his benefactors. With tears still flowing down his cheeks, he began to sign his grief. His father had saved him from hopeless circumstances. Now he was alone again.

Then rage set in. He turned towards his father's body. Fists clenched, he signed furiously, 'The devil that did this to you must be punished.' He leaned over the bed and stroked his father's brow. He signed farewell, stepped back and nodded to Anne and Paul. 'I'll make the burial arrangements now.' Then he stalked out of the room.

NINE
An Uncertain Future

7 June

Early in the morning at the Louvre Colonel Saint-Martin waited in an anteroom to the mayor's apartment. He had come to inform Bailly of the Irish priest's death last night and to discuss its implications. When he had requested a meeting, the mayor proposed this private place. He apparently anticipated that their conversation would touch on sensitive issues.

Bailly played his various roles in three different residences. As a private person he had a home in Chaillot and as mayor of Paris, an official office in the Hôtel de Police, a short distance north of Place Vendôme. The king gave him the Louvre apartment as a member of the Académie Française and a scholar – he was one of the leading astronomers of the age. When he became mayor, he kept the apartment for its fine view overlooking the Seine. Free from spying eyes and ears and centrally located, it was also more suited for intimate conversations than his official office.

Saint-Martin didn't have to wait long. The mayor himself ushered him into his study and seated him comfortably at the writing table. Nothing had changed since his last visit a few years ago. The large, well-lighted room was still a scholar's den. His books covered one wall, maps and astronomical charts hung on another. An impressive celestial globe, as tall as a man, stood in a corner.

A slender, dignified man, Bailly dressed as usual in a plain black silk suit. Black, his preferred colour, enhanced his grave appearance and simple manner. Two strenuous years as mayor of the metropolis had left him outwardly unchanged – for the most part. Perhaps his eyes had lost their lustre. Faint lines of care creased his forehead.

'Colonel, you told my clerk that you wished to talk to me

about a murder. To which one are you referring? There have been several recently.'

'The killing of Father Denis O'Fallon, sir. He died late last night of the injury he had received three days earlier.'

'Oh?' The mayor appeared surprised. 'I hadn't realized that his injury was so serious. I suppose I should feel sorry for O'Fallon. Shortly after the incident, a National Guard officer described it to me as a disgraceful quarrel outside the Café de Foy. The priest and two other men were injured. A prominent businessman, Guiscard, was insulted – coffee spilled on him, I believe.'

Saint-Martin felt that the mayor would be happy to leave the incident and its consequences in the hands of the National Guard and the district magistrate. He remarked evenly, 'The officer did not witness the incident. His account was drawn uncritically from the rogues who were its chief instigators.'

'How do you know what really happened, Colonel?' The mayor's head tilted at a sceptical angle.

'My wife Anne and her friend Micheline du Saint-Esprit were there, eyewitnesses to the event.' The colonel went on to give the mayor a detailed description of Flamme's assault on the priest and Patrick's defence.

The mayor shifted in his seat, his brow furrowed, and he said without emotion, 'Frankly, the priest O'Fallon brought the assault upon himself. I can have little sympathy for him.'

Saint-Martin allowed his tone to grow testy. 'Folly is not a crime, sir. I'm embarrassed to have to remind you of the rule of law. Sympathy for the victim, or the lack of it, is irrelevant. The law should protect especially the most unpopular persons among us. In the shifting winds of public opinion we can never know when we too might become "unpopular".' Saint-Martin was alluding to the mayor's own declining popularity.

'*Touché!* Colonel. Still, you paint the priest's death in a lurid light.'

'Murder *is* ghastly, sir, and a hanging offence. In the eyes of the law, the priest's death raises Flamme's crime from an assault to a murder. That's a crime we cannot ignore. Flamme's companions are guilty of aiding and abetting the crime.'

The mayor sighed, perhaps chastened and a little weary. 'What do you want of me, Colonel?'

'Justice for the priest, sir, and respect for the law. As a nonjuring priest and an aristocrat, O'Fallon was deeply unpopular – at least in this city. I might add that he will be regarded as a hero and a martyr in other parts of the country, where traditional religion is still strong. True, his behaviour that day was provocative, but it was a protest in reaction to his opponents' attempts to silence him. In any case, they had no right to use violence and should pay for their crime.'

'You are speaking to the wrong man, Colonel. Officers of the National Guard, not I, carry out criminal investigation.'

Saint-Martin met the mayor's eye. 'I've come to warn you, the city's chief magistrate, that the National Guard will not seriously investigate this matter unless they are forced to do so. You and General Lafayette together should hold them to their duty.'

Bailly sighed again. 'Colonel, I applaud your commitment to justice and the rule of law. Unfortunately, when we overthrew the old regime almost two years ago, we opened a Pandora's box of genuine grievances and powerful, destructive passions that we have struggled to control. In O'Fallon's case, and others like it, we lack the power to intervene. The police and the army obey us only if they choose to. The mob often rules this country, especially Paris. Its *bêtes noires* at this moment are priests like O'Fallon who denounce the new constitution. Many have been assaulted, a few killed.'

Saint-Martin felt irony creep into his voice in spite of himself. 'So, should I be content that the National Guard will make a pathetic minimal investigation? There will of course be no convictions.'

The mayor smiled wistfully. 'I hope you will not think too badly of me, Colonel. I fully share your sentiments. Mired in the unseemly politics of this country for two years, I have fallen short of my civic principles and aspirations. I frankly feel tainted.'

Saint-Martin gently waved a dismissive hand. 'My remarks haven't sufficiently regarded your circumstances and hence seem unfair. I shouldn't wish any friend of mine to be mayor of this city. It's an impossible, thankless job.'

Bailly poured a fine brandy into two small glasses.

'Let's drink to better times,' he said.

'And to the rule of law,' added Saint-Martin.

*   *   *

Later that morning, Saint-Martin went by coach to Fersen's residence on Rue Matignon. The Swede had written that he wanted to discuss 'matters of mutual concern'. Saint-Martin had agreed even though he suspected that Fersen might probe into his political views, perhaps to persuade him to support the royal family's interests.

That their meeting would take place in Fersen's house on Rue Matignon strengthened Saint-Martin's suspicion. It was one of the few places where the Swede could feel free to speak his mind. At the Tuileries, or almost anywhere else in Paris, he would be spied upon as the queen's confidant. His words, his facial expressions, and his gestures had always to be guarded.

On the way, Saint-Martin found himself still reflecting on his conversation with Mayor Bailly. What struck him most was the corrosive effect of politics on the conscience of such a high-minded, morally rigorous man as the mayor. This experience steeled Saint-Martin's resolve to avoid taking sides in the debate over the new constitution.

At the door, he had a strong feeling that his resolve was about to be tested.

'The count is expecting you, Colonel,' said Mademoiselle Jeanne Degere and gave him a broad smile of recognition. Four years ago, she had helped him investigate the Duc d'Orléans' plot against the queen. A loyal family retainer, having served the count's father, she was Fersen's most trusted servant and probably understood the count better than almost any living person. A strong, large-boned, square-faced, sharp-eyed woman, about thirty-five, with a direct, unpolished manner, she seemed out of place in the urbane Swede's household. But the rustic impression that she gave was deceptive – and useful. A skilful, courageous observer, she moved easily in markets and taverns, and among grooms, artisans and soldiers. Thanks to her, Fersen was unusually well informed.

Jeanne led Saint-Martin through the house into the study. Fersen was standing with his back to the window, his face shadowed in the backlight – deliberately, thought Saint-Martin, who couldn't discern the count's expression. He must be studying his guest as he entered.

'It's been a long while since we've had a serious conversation,' he remarked to Saint-Martin and gestured towards a tea table set for two. For a few minutes, the two men exchanged polite remarks and recalled mutual acquaintances. Fersen complained that, during the past two years, many of their senior officers in the American War had been driven from their posts or had gone into exile.

The Swede went on to decry the present desire for equality that had sapped military discipline. Common soldiers demanded the right to elect their officers and were often insubordinate.

'War with Austria is approaching,' Fersen declared, 'And our army is in no condition to fight.'

Saint-Martin agreed but thought to himself that Fersen had often left his regiment unattended on the frontier, despite the complaints of his junior officers. Still, Saint-Martin encouraged him to speak freely. It was a way to take the measure of the man and, more to the point, to gauge the counsel that he offered to the Court.

An ardent conservative, Fersen repudiated the revolution's aims and achievements, argued that it was the work of a disgruntled minority, and claimed that the king could and should rally the people and restore his authority over the country.

'But I dwell too much on politics,' said Fersen. 'When did we last meet?'

'Four years ago,' said the colonel. 'We thwarted an extortion plot against the queen. To judge from a recent placard in the garden of the Palais-Royal, the perpetrators have not forgotten, nor forgiven me.'

Fersen seemed confused. 'I pay no attention to that sort of rubbish.'

Saint-Martin described the placard and its charges against him. 'In brief, I'm said to be an enemy of the people and no patriot.'

'The charges are patently false,' Fersen asserted. 'Why bother about them?'

'Because in today's overheated, poisonous public atmosphere, such charges can be a death warrant.' Saint-Martin mentioned Father O'Fallon's death. 'In the not too distant future, many nonjuring priests will face the same fate, as will anyone who defends the rule of law, like me.'

Jeanne Degere came with the tea and poured, then withdrew. She and Fersen exchanged cryptic glances. Perhaps she was supposed to eavesdrop on their conversation.

Saint-Martin seized the initiative and asked Fersen, 'Is there any substance to the rumours that the king is planning to escape from Paris?'

Fersen slowly, deliberately sipped his tea, then replied, 'His Majesty has voiced disapproval of certain aspects of the new proposed constitution, especially the measures concerning the church and royal authority. But he has publicly assured the National Assembly that he nonetheless will support the constitution and faithfully perform the duties that it assigns to him. That doesn't sound like a man about to flee the country.'

'His critics claim that he dissembles.'

'Then they presume to read his mind. Those who know him say that his character is not devious but simple, almost to a fault.' Fersen tilted his head in an inquisitive gesture. 'Let's just suppose for the sake of discussion that the critics are correct. What if the king were about to escape from Paris? Where would he go and what would he do there?'

'He might go to Rouen,' opined Saint-Martin. He understood where Fersen was about to lead the conversation. 'It's a pleasant day's journey. The people of Normandy are said to be more sympathetic to him than the Parisians. He could rally support. Then from a position of strength he could perhaps bargain with the Assembly for a constitution that would be more to his liking, particularly where royal authority and the church are concerned.'

Fersen stared into his cup for a moment before commenting, 'Some critics say that he might flee instead to the eastern frontier, draw together a coalition of foreign powers and impose his will on Paris.'

Saint-Martin shook his head. 'That would be a desperate gamble and certainly lead to civil war. I hesitate to predict the outcome but it would certainly be bloody and destructive. I can't believe that he would be so reckless. The king I know is a gentle, peace-loving man. In the past two years he has already rejected several opportunities to use force against the National Assembly and his other enemies in Paris. Of course, I must admit that clever, self-serving or imprudent advisors might persuade him to act contrary to his better nature.'

Fersen's gaze grew intense, his voice insistent. 'Any major worthwhile project is a gamble. Good planning can greatly improve the odds of success. In the king's case, he would need full, energetic support from all those who believe that the

National Assembly is on the wrong path. Its measures undermine the basic pillars of authority: the aristocracy, the church,
and the army. Only a strong, enlightened royal government can
save France from anarchy at home and from its enemies abroad.
Your patron, the Baron Breteuil, is struggling manfully to forge
a united royal force to save the country. What do you think of
his efforts?'

Saint-Martin replied, 'As the powerful, competent minister
for Paris in the old regime, the baron achieved significant
reforms. In exile he is virtually powerless and dependent on
the whims of foreign powers that do not have our country's
best interests at heart. I'll grant that the Assembly inspires little
confidence. Its quarrelling factions too often lose sight of the
common good. Their new constitution creates an executive and
a legislature too weak and divided to govern effectively. But,
for decades prior to the revolution, the old regime failed to
solve the nation's problems and instead made them much worse.
Why should we think that it would do any better now, even *if*
it could be restored?'

Fersen's expression turned severe. 'You seem to think that
you could stand between the two camps, the Assembly and the
King. In the upcoming struggle there wouldn't be any middle
ground. The baron would expect you to stand at his side together
with the King.'

'And if I stood in his way?'

Fersen's bluish-grey eyes turned an icy-blue. 'You would be
crushed.'

Anne was in the garden when Paul returned home at noon. The
tone of his greeting was flat. He slumped into the chair by her
side. 'You look dispirited, Paul,' she said to him gently. 'What's
the matter?'

'I've had two distressing conversations this morning, the first
with Mayor Bailly, the second with Count Fersen. Right now
I'd rather not think about either of them, perhaps later.'

'Good, then we'll go for a ride in the Bois de Boulogne.
Afterwards, when your spirits have lifted and your mind has
cleared, we'll find a private place and talk.'

It was a cool, sunny afternoon. Spring had arrived; trees were
in full leaf. For a couple of hours Anne and Paul rode leisurely

on paths through the great wooded park west of the city. Though she preferred to ride astride, and did so in less public places, today she sat side-saddle in the conventional manner of women. She wanted to avoid notoriety where at all possible, for it hampered her work as well as her husband's.

Occasionally they urged their mounts to a gallop through meadows lush with wild flowers. Many other riders had seized the same opportunity. This was a pleasant and popular release from the dirt and stench of the city, from its fretting cares and ugly bustle. In the park nature was joyfully alive. Spring breezes whistled through the trees. Birds twittered mysterious melodies to the beat of horses' hooves on gravel and on dirt paths. The sounds of riders and their mounts seemed deliberately muted out of deference to this special occasion.

After a couple of hours of riding Anne and Paul stopped for a light meal at a familiar inn, Le Grand Canard. It was a large, old, rambling structure, its exterior walls covered with ivy. Thick, rough wooden tables and chairs, and a low ceiling of rough-hewn beams, gave the interior a charming rustic appearance. Anne selected a small table in a secluded corner where they could speak privately.

While waiting for the food, Paul described his conversations with Bailly and Fersen. Then he concluded with a sigh, 'This morning, Mayor Bailly confirmed my opinion that the new regime is too weak to give justice to all. Count Fersen taught me that representatives of the old regime have learned nothing from its catastrophic failure to solve the problems that led to the revolution. Both sides demand my allegiance. So, what am I to do?'

The food arrived while Anne was about to reply. She waited until the servant withdrew. 'Go with Mayor Bailly and General Lafayette. They may be fading stars. But, at least for now, they are the country's best hope for peaceful, constructive change. Fersen and Breteuil would certainly bring us war and an end to reform.'

Paul smiled wryly. 'A thought just occurred to me. Going with Bailly and Lafayette may jeopardize my commission as a colonel in the new Gendarmerie Nationale. It depends on the king's approval, one of the few powers that he retains. Up to now, I've enjoyed his favour, largely I suppose due to Baron Breteuil's influence. Fersen will report my views to the queen and to Breteuil. They will most likely turn against me and persuade the king to appoint a more compliant officer.'

Anne tried to gather all these thoughts in her head and make sense of them. Finally, she concluded, 'The future is simply too obscure to judge. The king may or may not try to escape from Paris. If he stays, he may recognize your many years of excellent service and give you the commission, regardless of whatever Fersen and the baron may say. If he leaves, he will lose any power to help or to hinder you.'

She raised her glass. 'So I say, let's drink to this moment together. It's all we really have.'

Paul joined her in the toast, then asked, 'And how is Patrick?'

'I'm worried,' she replied. 'I've thought of him often this morning and made a point to see him briefly in his Louvre rooms. He was about to finish the customary arrangements for his father's burial. He refused any help.'

'Could you determine his state of mind?'

'I asked him but got only a shrug of his shoulders in reply. To judge from the frown on his face, he was preoccupied with dark thoughts. So I left him alone. If the police fail to apprehend Flamme, I fear that Patrick will seek justice on his own.'

'Then we must prod the police to do their duty. But how?'

'Magistrate Roland might be able to help. We'll speak to him tomorrow.'

TEN

A Grieving Son

8 June

Early next morning, Anne and Paul went to the local magistrate's bureau and asked for Pierre Roland. A young enlightened lawyer, he had joined the new revolutionary judiciary at its chaotic birth. More often than not, he led the court's criminal investigations and was responsible for Father O'Fallon's case. Five days had passed with no further word from the National Guard.

Anne and Paul had worked with him on previous occasions to good effect. Two years ago, he had helped Anne posthumously restore the rights and reputation of an unfortunate baker. A mob had wrongly accused him of profiteering and hung him from a street lamp. That was a trying time for Roland. He had barely survived a brutal beating at the hands of the Duc d'Orléans' agents, an experience that challenged his idealistic hope for a new system of justice, one that was better than the old royal despotism that it had replaced.

The outcome was still uncertain. But the young magistrate appeared to have become more self-assured and less sanguine. His reputation for honesty and competence had grown, and his opinions enjoyed respect. He welcomed Anne and Paul into his small, plain office. Its furnishings were meagre. Still, he did his best to be gracious and offered them tea.

When they had finished the tea, Saint-Martin inquired into the investigation of the attack on the priest.

'I'll see if the police have found anything recently.' Roland left to consult the files.

A few minutes later, he returned, shaking his head. 'The National Guard claim that they can't locate the suspect. It's true that he must have gone into hiding as soon as he heard that the priest was seriously injured. But, frankly, I believe the

Guard shares Flamme's point of view, approves of what he did, and won't seriously try to find him.'

Paul frowned. 'Then, tell me, how are the new police of Paris superior in criminal investigation to that of the old regime?'

Roland smiled wryly, 'We have twice as many police, more than seven thousand, but they are less than half as good. Most are soldiers with no training or experience gathering and evaluating evidence or interrogating suspects. Many are connected to the political clubs and share their biases. At its best, the old regime equipped its inspectors, men like Quidor or your Georges Charpentier, with a strong network of informers. We've lost most of them. And our police also lack effective leadership – we have no one even remotely comparable in ability to Lieutenant General Sartine in the old regime.'

'Is the National Guard's commandant, General Lafayette, aware of the situation?'

Roland shrugged. 'Perhaps. But there's little that he can do. His authority is limited, and his popularity has plummeted. The police are mainly responsible to local elected councils.'

'Must you be both inspector and magistrate, at least until someone devises a better system?'

'For difficult investigations, I hope to turn to you –' he glanced at Anne as well as Paul – 'and to Monsieur Charpentier. You've already been helpful. With the sketch you gave us, the Guard at least found their way to Flamme's apartment on Rue Bouloi. His mistress was there but refused to say where he's hiding. She was so obnoxious that she's now in the Châtelet. A taste of prison should encourage her to cooperate. For what it's worth, I've issued an arrest warrant for him.'

Anne had a sick feeling in the pit of her stomach. Rumours were circulating in Palais-Royal about Flamme's 'friend'. 'What's the name of his mistress?' Anne asked.

'Renée Gros,' the magistrate replied. 'We have a dossier on her from years back. She's a prostitute and a thief. The police found silverware and other stolen goods in the apartment.'

'I know her,' Anne said. 'She's not just a prostitute and a thief. She's been abused since infancy and is mentally ill. Could you arrange for me to talk to her?'

Roland instinctively turned to Paul.

He waved a hand. 'My wife is fully competent and doesn't need my permission.'

Anne was annoyed that the question had come up but pleased with Paul's response.

Roland turned apologetically to Anne. 'I'm happy to oblige, Madame. Perhaps you can talk sense to Mademoiselle Gros. We can't.'

Later that morning Anne presented Magistrate Roland's permission to the chief bailiff at the Châtelet, the city's prison on the Right Bank of the Seine. It was a grim, forbidding stone building, much of it an ancient fortress. The bailiff scowled as he read Roland's message. He thrust the paper back to Anne and said brusquely, 'Follow me.'

He showed Anne into a small, plain room with a battered table and two wooden chairs. 'I'll bring her to you,' he said and left. A few minutes later, he returned with Renée, shackled hands and feet. 'Here she is. Take care, she bites and spits. I'll be outside in the hallway.'

Renée looked much the same as the last time they had met – perhaps her face was a bit fuller. She was still a small, wiry young woman. When she recognized Anne, she blinked, then rattled her chains. 'Look, Madame Cartier. I've done nothing wrong and they've shackled me.'

'The magistrate thinks you know where Armand Flamme is hiding but you refused to tell him.'

'Armand has been good to me. I must not betray him.'

'But he killed a harmless old priest and should face justice.'

'The priest was a traitor, an enemy of the people and deserved to die.'

Anne realized that this line of inquiry was fruitless. Flamme had a firm grip on the young woman's heart and had implanted his view of the incident in her mind. She wouldn't reveal his hiding place, even to Anne. She tried a different tack. 'How are they treating you here?'

'They don't beat me,' she replied with a grimace and rattled her chains again.

'It's been a long time, Renée, since we last met. Tell me what prompted you to live with Armand Flamme.'

'Doctor Pinel healed me, and then got me a job in the Princess of Monaco's house. Later when the British ambassador leased the house, he kept me on. Armand was working there on the roof. We took a fancy to each other. He said he could help me do better than work as a maid.'

Anne had grown suspicious. Before coming here, she had read the police report. Armand and Renée were living in a large, well-furnished apartment. She had good clothes and shoes, silver tableware and pieces of jewellery. The police believed that some of these items had been stolen and were trying to find the owners. In a neutral tone Anne asked, 'What kind of work has he found for you?'

'I'm a merchant. I sell all kinds of goods.'

'The police say you're a thief.' Anne met her eye. 'Is that true, Renée? You can't lie to me. I know you too well.'

The young woman shifted uneasily on her chair. 'We take only from rich people, especially from those who are leaving the country. We give some of their things to the poor and keep some for ourselves. What's wrong with that?'

Anne saw no point in pursuing the moral issue. 'What's sad, Renée, is that the magistrate is going to put you in prison for a very long time.'

Renée stared silently at Anne for a long moment. Then she slowly, deliberately shook her head. 'I won't let him. I know what it's like in prison. I've been there before. I'll kill myself first.'

Anne groaned inwardly, recalling a bruised, emaciated Renée, three years ago, lying naked and near death on the stone floor of a cell in the Salpêtrière. Later, when freed and healthier, she had declared that she would rather die than face a similar experience. Since then, her conviction had grown even stronger, if possible. Anne felt at a loss how to help her.

Early in the afternoon, Anne returned to the Louvre to see how Patrick was doing. He wasn't in his room. From the watchman she learned that the priest's body was privately buried early that morning in the crypt of the Oratory's church. Only Patrick and a pair of elderly priests from the Oratory were present. Since then, Patrick had disappeared.

Anne had a nervous feeling about him. He was supposed to be in her custody and keep her informed of his whereabouts. What would he do after burying his father? Anne wrestled with the question for a minute, then concluded: he would meet

Marthe Boyer at a safe distance from her husband's jealous eyes. She might know where he was likely to be.

Anne hurried home and put on the shabby wig, scuffed black shoes, and plain grey woollen suit of her male servant's disguise. It would give her more freedom than female garb. Parisian cafés often welcomed men only.

The church of Saint-Eustache was still open. Anne found the sexton. Yes, he had seen Marthe and Patrick that morning. After a lively exchange of signs and gestures, they had separated, as if in disagreement, and gone off in different directions.

It was late in the afternoon as Anne hastened to the Boyer residence on Rue Jean-Jacques Rousseau. Boyer's spy, Monsieur Rat-face, was loitering outside the tavern across the street, already acting slightly tipsy. Anne concluded that Monsieur Boyer had left the apartment a few hours ago for his customary political discussion. This evening, as often, it would be in The Red Rooster, a tavern on Place des Victoires.

From a distance Anne studied the spy but couldn't determine whether he was truly drunk. So she hired a street urchin to carry a message to Marthe. She should meet Anne in a neighbourhood wine shop. A few minutes later, Marthe came out of the building with a jug. Rat-face glanced at her but didn't follow.

Anne waited a minute, and then approached her in the wine shop. At first, Marthe didn't recognize Anne in the male servant's disguise, not until she began to sign. They sat at a table in a corner out of sight from the street. Marthe seemed nervous and unhappy.

Anne probed gently. 'What's happened to Patrick?'

'He's nearly mad with anger. This morning I tried to calm him, but without success. He was still angry when he left me, still insisting on revenge. He wants to beat Flamme to death.'

'Does he know where he is hiding?'

Marthe shook her head. 'But he's confident that he will go to The Red Rooster for the evening's political discussion.'

'Yes,' Anne agreed, 'Flamme will feel safe there among his comrades and the police will look the other way. Patrick probably intends to wait outside for an opportunity to attack.'

'You must stop him, Madame. If the rogue is killed, the police will certainly suspect Patrick. His desire for revenge is no secret. He has mentioned his plan to several of his deaf friends. They tried to dissuade him but failed. The police will easily convict him – and hang him.' By this time, Marthe was close to tears.

Anne reached across the table and gave her a comforting hand. 'I'll go to The Red Rooster and try to intercept him.'

It was growing dark by the time Anne reached the tavern. During the day, Place des Victoires was a busy commercial centre. The square served as a hub for several intersecting streets. Traffic in coaches and carts was continuous and heavy. In the evening, the square was still lively. The Red Rooster and the other taverns and cafés were doing a brisk business. But most vendors had closed or left by sundown and there was less traffic.

Anne had kept her male disguise in case she might need to enter the tavern and observe the political discussions. Her face darkened with powder, wearing the breeches and coat of a male servant, Anne walked about the square with a man's gait, searching for Patrick. Under a street lamp near the tavern she approached a man of Patrick's size and shape selling roasted chestnuts. As she bought a few, she stared him in the face. Despite a deliberate effort, she shuddered – his eye sockets were empty.

She moved on past a darkened arcade. A large, bent woman stood there with flowers for sale. Eyes fixed on the tavern's entrance, she made no effort to solicit passers-by as a street vendor usually would. Anne hid behind a pillar, retrieved her opera glass and discovered that she was Jean Guiscard in disguise. Anne snickered. He looked ridiculous. But this wasn't a boulevard farce. Most likely, murder was on his mind.

Under another street lamp young artisans and maids loitered around a fiddler playing Italian country tunes while his young female partner juggled brightly coloured plates. Both were wearing harlequin masks.

For a few minutes Anne watched, intrigued, until they stopped to rest and took off their masks. Antonio Diluna and his sister Magdalena stared at the tavern's entrance. Their faces were hard, rigid, pinched with hatred. They exchanged a few curt words, donned their masks and resumed their performance.

By this time, Anne was thoroughly puzzled. Guiscard was interested in Flamme who had insulted him. Antonio Diluna hated Boyer who had deceived and seduced his sister. But what could this charade outside the tavern hope to achieve? If Flamme were to leave the tavern, he would surround himself with guards. Boyer could be more vulnerable, but he probably was armed.

Anne entered the tavern in search of Patrick. On this late spring night, it was crowded, noisy, and hot. In the front of the room was a typical tavern's evening clientele: men drinking wine, playing at cards or dice, or engaged in conversation. Patrick wasn't among them.

Anne moved to the back of the room where political discussion was in full swing and studied the forty-odd participants. She couldn't see Patrick among them. To judge from their sober woollen suits, they were mostly of the middling sort of commoners, small shopkeepers and the like. A few artisans, still wearing work clothes, sat together up front, intent on making their views heard. In his fine blue silk suit, Jacques Boyer was speaking in favour of a secular, democratic republic of equals under the rule of law. His ideas were lofty but his speech was simple and he sprinkled it with common profanity to suit his audience. Most of them seemed unconvinced but respectful. Flamme sat in the front row among the artisans, his head tilted at a sceptical angle.

Anne's ears picked up when Boyer began to argue in favour of the National Assembly's proposed legislation permitting divorce in cases of adultery. His tone became much more personal. He almost certainly had his own wife in mind.

'If the wife is adulterous,' he claimed, 'her husband should take her dowry in compensation for her injury to his honour. If he were to discover her and her partner in the sex act, *in flagrante delicto*, he could kill her as well as her accomplice.' Anne shuddered. Most of the audience, including Flamme, instinctively nodded in agreement.

The artisans raised the city's pressing issues of unemployment and rising prices. Soon it was Flamme's turn to speak. He rose, squared his shoulders, and spoke out in a loud, shrill voice that it was time for action rather than talk. The city's poor should join together, gather arms, and force the rich to share their wealth, most of it stolen from them. The bakers and other shopkeepers must also be forced to lower their prices or be flogged. Priests in any case were of no use to the country and should be banished. If traitorous, they should be killed.

The clique of artisans loudly cheered him on. The shopkeepers grew increasingly restive, then irritated. When Flamme mentioned price control, some stamped their feet; others shouted rebuttals. Boyer appeared to seethe with anger. Finally he left his seat, walked to the back of the room, and spoke to the barman. For a few minutes they glared at Flamme, shaking their heads and exchanging remarks. Their familiarity intrigued Anne.

When Boyer left, she moved closer and studied the barman – Aristide Blanc was his name – a nervous, pockmarked, stout man with thick, fat fingers. Blanc must have sensed her eyes on him. He glanced at her, a frown gathering on his face. Thereafter, he looked frequently in her direction, probably suspecting that she was a spy. Before he could confront her, she slipped quickly from the room to the fresh air outside.

Directly in front of her, in the centre of the square, loomed a huge, gilded bronze monument to the great king, Louis XIV. Standing tall in regal robes, he gazed imperiously over the square and beyond. In the ghostly light of several street lamps, he looked menacing and nearly alive. A female figure behind him held a laurel wreath over his head. Anne's gaze dropped down. Beneath the king, sitting in the shadow of the monument's white marble pedestal, was a beggar, dressed in rags.

Anne drew closer. The beggar was staring at the tavern. A pair of National Guards approached him from behind. In a loud, booming voice one of them ordered him to get up and move along. The beggar didn't stir. The guard poked him rudely with a club.

The beggar leaped to his feet, fists raised. When he recognized the guard's uniform, he dropped his fists. But it was too late. The guard's club was already halfway to the beggar's head. An instant later, he lay sprawled out on the pavement. He struggled to rise. The guard raised the club for another blow, but Anne leaped between him and the fallen man.

'Stop, sir, the beggar's deaf. He didn't hear you. I'll take care of him.'

The guard hesitated, waving the club above his head. Eyes narrowed, he glared at Anne. Then he slowly lowered the club. 'Get him out of here. Put him to honest work.'

The guard and his partner backed away a few steps, while Anne helped Patrick to his feet and studied him. He wobbled. His arms hung loosely by his side. In his rags he looked like a battered, discarded puppet. But his eyes focused properly.

Apparently the blow hadn't damaged his brain. Anne hailed a
cab parked on the square. The coachman helped lift him and
they drove off towards Rue Saint-Honoré.

Anne signed, 'How are you, Patrick?' He appeared to quickly
revive. His eyes searched her features until he penetrated her
disguise.

'Better,' he replied, his signing nearly normal. 'Thank you.
The guard was about to give me a severe beating.'

'Why were you there in beggar's rags, staring at The Red
Rooster?'

'Two of the men that I hate most in this world were inside.'

'Did you plan to kill them?'

'Yes!' he signed vehemently. 'If I found an opportunity, I'd
beat them to death, one at a time.' His expression was hard-
ening. A powerful passion appeared to grip him.

'Don't you care that the police would arrest you – and
certainly hang you?'

'I don't mind. My mother and my father, the only two persons
who ever loved me, are dead. When I've avenged my father's
murder, and released Marthe from her husband's tyranny, what
else do I have to live for? Who would marry me? Who would
hire me? It's cruel being a deaf man in a hearing world.'

The coachman reined in the horses and called out, 'Rue
Saint-Honoré. Where should I go from here?'

'Come to our house, Patrick. It's not good for you to be
alone. We can offer you a guest room until these dreadful feelings subside.'

For a moment, a hint of tenderness filled his eyes. 'You are
kind, Madame,' he signed. 'But I'll leave you here.' He leaped
out of the coach, waved to her, and stalked rapidly away into
the darkness.

The bells of Saint-Roch struck midnight as the coachman let
Anne off at her house on Rue Saint-Honoré. Paul had waited
up for her. He knew she could fend for herself, but he grew
anxious anyway when she was out late at night. He had prepared
sweet Champagne wine and mixed fresh fruit for her in the
garden. The air was mild and fresh. A majestic array of stars
filled the sky. An oil lamp on a tree branch above them gave
off a flickering, golden light. Roses in bloom lightly scented
the air. The raucous sounds of the city were muted.

As they sipped the wine, she related to him the evening's story from Place des Victoires.

Paul smiled wryly at her description of Guiscard. 'Why didn't he send one of his men to spy for him?'

Anne bit into a cherry. 'Perhaps he took the insult so personally that only he could avenge it. He also couldn't trust any of his men to keep his secret.'

'Hmm.' Paul gazed at Anne. 'You are suggesting that he had come not simply to observe Flamme but to kill him – if he had the chance. That's plausible.'

'I'm not sure why Antonio was there observing Boyer. What could he hope to achieve? He wouldn't kill the man while Magdalena was present, would he?'

'I doubt it. Perhaps he was studying Boyer's movements, preparing for an opportunity to strike. Still, I'm now most concerned about Patrick. Tell me about his confrontation with the National Guardsman.'

Anne described the incident at the monument. 'Patrick's behaviour shouldn't come as a surprise. He reacts vigorously to gestures of disrespect from persons in authority. He's also taking his father's death in a bad way. I think he may have become suicidal as well as vindictive. What can we do for him?'

'He's a grown man, Anne, usually of sound mind, and hasn't committed any crime. Still, in his present condition, he probably should be held in protective custody, as a danger to himself and others. Under the old regime I could have asked the king for a *lettre de cachet* to confine him in a royal prison until he came to his senses. But that was an arbitrary procedure and our enlightened reformers have abolished it along with other vestiges of despotism.'

Anne drained her glass and reflected for a moment. 'Perhaps tomorrow I could persuade Marthe Boyer to try again to bring him to a healthier attitude.'

Paul nodded. 'And I could assign a spy to follow him and to warn us if he appears about to cause harm. Then we would have to intervene.'

Anne cautioned. 'But he might not act for several days, if at all. He's also clever enough to detect a spy and evade him.'

'Then we must simply hope for his better nature to assert itself.'

'And for Flamme and Boyer to guard themselves well.'

ELEVEN
A Gathering Storm

9 June

The next day, during breakfast conversation with Paul, Anne returned to the events at Place des Victoires.

'Can you imagine such a weird sight?' she remarked. 'Guiscard, a painted woman, dressed as an old fruit vendor, and Antonio Diluna and his sister performing in harlequin masks.'

Paul smiled with a hint of irony. 'Passion deprives men of their senses.' He paused and reflected. 'I assume that a government spy was in the audience taking mental notes.'

Anne shrugged. 'Perhaps, though I didn't notice him. Why would the government pay that much attention to what Flamme and Boyer were saying?'

'It does seem odd,' replied Paul. 'At the present moment, they have few followers. But if conditions in the country continue to deteriorate, as I believe they will, then their radical ideas of a democratic republic of equals will sink roots among many desperate people. Our leaders, General Lafayette and Mayor Bailly, have good reason to dispatch a spy to The Red Rooster. His reports should disturb them.'

This morning, Anne had planned to work at the institute until mid afternoon. A paid staff of priests, former nuns, and laywomen cared for most of the children and taught the bulk of the curriculum. An unpaid helper, Anne took on special students like Patrick as well as children who were falling behind or having emotional problems. Their progress was her reward.

Shortly after breakfast Anne set out for the institute in a coach. Previously, it was within walking distance but it had moved to a distant location. Following the death of the founder, the Abbé de l'Épée, and the appointment of a new director, the Abbé Sicard, a disciple of l'Épée, the government provided shabby, but larger quarters in a former monastery near the Arsenal.

During the ride, Anne thought of Patrick. He didn't fit well into the institute's programme of instruction or mix easily with its much younger students. He and Anne were nearly the same age and had in different degrees experienced similar discrimination and rejection, he as a deaf man, she as an actress. In a word, they could understand each other. He appreciated Anne's instruction and made slow but sure progress in signing. The articulation of words and the reading of lips – beyond the most simple – seemed nearly impossible. The fact that he lost his hearing as a very young boy was probably to blame. Fortunately, he was highly motivated and never missed an appointment.

Upon arriving at the institute, Anne was surprised and disturbed to find that he hadn't come this morning. Last night, during the coach ride from the Place des Victoires, he hadn't cancelled. He was probably still in the grip of that blinding, consuming rage that she had witnessed.

She couldn't think of any way to help him, so she set to tutoring her other special students. The memory of his angry face, however, continued to distract her.

At about three in the afternoon, she left the institute and hurried towards the Boyer residence. She calculated that Monsieur Boyer would soon go out for another evening of politics, and his spy would begin to drink, or pretend to. On the way, Anne checked at the Louvre. The watchman said Patrick had left his room early in the morning and had not returned.

At the Boyer house on Rue Jean-Jacques Rousseau, Rat-face was still loitering across the street. Nonetheless, Anne sent an urchin again with a message to Marthe. In a few minutes he returned. Marthe had written simply 'Saint-Eustache.'

She soon emerged with a shopping basket. This time the spy signalled a young boy to follow her while he entered the tavern. When Anne saw him order a drink, she hastened after Marthe and the boy. In the Central Markets, the boy lost interest in her and began to work on his own, stealing fruit and vegetables from inattentive vendors. Marthe quit the markets and hastened to the church.

Anne met her again in a quiet side chapel. They sat side by side and began signing. Anne inquired about Patrick.

'He hasn't tried to contact me this morning,' Marthe signed. 'We had a disagreement here yesterday. I warned him against pursuing Flamme. "What good could come of it?" I asked.

He insisted that he was duty bound to kill the villain. "That's a stubborn and foolish thing to do," I signed. To sneak up on a man in the dark and club him to death, even if he were a villain, didn't seem honourable.'

Marthe paused with hurt in her eyes.

'He retorted that I was only a butcher's daughter and knew nothing about honour. I left him then, afraid I might sign something that I would later regret.'

In the evening Anne returned to Place des Victoires and The Red Rooster in her male disguise. Warm spring weather drew people from their small, stuffy rooms out into the vast open square. It would be difficult to detect Flamme's enemies. Throughout the day, she had searched in vain for Patrick. His deaf friends and acquaintances had not seen him either. And she was hoping that he wouldn't be here.

Guiscard had returned to the arcade, dressed again as a woman and pretending to sell flowers. But, with a weary shake of his head, he left the square long before the Citizens for Equality club concluded its meeting. Boyer also left early – and he appeared indignant. Anne edged as close to him as she dared and overheard someone ask why he was leaving.

He replied for all to hear. 'Flamme's men have turned the club's meeting into a shouting match. They demanded an immediate uprising of the people, then insulted me when I called them lunatics. Nothing worthwhile can be accomplished at The Red Rooster tonight. I'll find more congenial company at Café Marcel and later at Madame Lebrun's brothel.'

After nearly an hour searching the square, she could still detect no sign of Patrick. At eleven, the discussion in the tavern ended. Many participants left but some lingered over wine. Anne slipped into the room, sat at a table by herself, and ordered a glass. She had a view of Flamme at a table drinking with Aristide Blanc, the barman, as if the two were old friends. Blanc smiled, nodded his head, and was pouring generously from a large bottle of brandy on the table. That seemed odd, she thought, recalling the barman's critical attitude last night as he and Boyer observed Flamme.

The clientele gradually diminished to the point that Anne began to feel exposed. As she rose to leave, Flamme seemed relaxed and clearly tipsy. The brandy bottle appeared half empty, though the barman had barely sipped from his glass. Flamme pulled a gold watch from his pocket, glanced at the time, and shook his head. 'The night is still young,' she heard him say.

Outside, Anne couldn't see any of his enemies lurking on the square. She was tired and frustrated. Nothing would happen tonight, she thought. Patrick couldn't hurt Flamme as long as he was with someone. She also had begun to suspect that Flamme would be armed.

As she left the square, she cast a glance over her shoulder at The Red Rooster. She shivered, and then shook herself. But that sense of foreboding that had dogged her since Father O'Fallon's death refused to go away.

Back home, Anne found Paul and Georges in the salon nervously waiting for her. A bottle of white wine and three glasses stood on the table.

'We were beginning to worry,' Paul said, embracing her.

Georges poured while Anne cautioned him, 'Just a little, please. I've already had my quota at The Red Rooster.' They raised glasses and toasted each other.

'It was a long day,' Anne said and went on to report on Patrick's quarrel with Marthe in the church. 'His obsession with killing Flamme is worrisome. I had hoped that she could have persuaded him to give up the idea.'

'Did you see him on Place des Victoires?' asked Georges.

'No, perhaps Marthe's counsel had later changed his mind. I hope so. Boyer took part as usual in the political discussion in the tavern but left early. Flamme acted as if he hadn't a care in the world. The barman was looking after him – I don't know why. Guiscard was outside again on the square, disguised as before, and also left early with his flowers. The danger of violence there appears to have subsided,' she concluded. 'The men who would harm Flamme must have concluded that, guarded and possibly armed, he was too dangerous to attack.'

'There's time yet for serious mischief,' cautioned Georges.

'And Flamme might grow careless,' added Paul.

A half-hour later, Anne and Paul went to bed. Soon he was sound asleep. But Anne tossed and turned. Gruesome images of the guard clubbing Patrick roiled her mind. Finally, a distant church bell struck midnight. She fell into a troubled sleep.

TWELVE
A Rogue's End

9–10 June

I n the deep shadow of an arcade a hooded figure watched the tavern's entrance. It was near midnight. He had waited for an hour. Armand Flamme had been drinking, drowning his troubles. The police were keeping him from his home. He had made many enemies and few friends. But the tavern's barman had listened patiently to his complaints and filled his glass.

The tavern would soon close. Flamme was the only customer. All the other members of the club had long gone, including those who usually guarded him. Flamme was carrying a double-barrelled pistol and must think he was safe. Perfect. He was too drunk to shoot straight and would have to walk alone to his hiding-place.

A distant bell tolled midnight. The door opened. The barman held Flamme under the arm, drew him through the square to a narrow street, and shoved him off in the direction of his room.

He staggered into the darkness, blindly feeling his way by touching the walls to the left and right. The hooded man followed, stepping softly. He had studied every inch of the street. At its darkest point, where a passage to the left offered a way to escape, he pulled a club from beneath his cloak, moved up close, and struck his victim on the back of the head.

Flamme fell to the pavement like a sack of stones and didn't utter a sound. The hooded man hit him again and again. Felt his pulse. None.

The hooded man found his victim's money purse and emptied its coins into his own pocket. From the man's vest he took a pocket watch, from his coat, the pistol. Then he shoved the body to the edge of the street, pulled a pile of rubbish over it, and fled along the passage to safety. He leaned against a wall and drew deep breaths, exhaling slowly. He felt enormously relieved and satisfied. The rogue was dead, and no one had witnessed the incident. The body wouldn't be discovered until dawn, if then.

THIRTEEN
Suspects

10 June

Early in the morning, Anne was at the table in the garden, finishing breakfast. The porter's terrier came out from under a bush, lapped water from the fountain, and approached the table tentatively for a treat. As she was about to feed him scraps, a servant came from the house. 'Monsieur Pierre Roland is at the front door, Madame. He asked to speak to you. Shall I show him into the parlour?'

'Yes,' Anne replied. 'I'll see him in a few minutes.' She added a silk scarf to her gown and tucked a wayward lock of blond hair into her bonnet. She thought it odd that the magistrate would visit so early and would want to speak to her rather than to Paul.

Roland stood hat in hand and bowed as she entered. She motioned for him to sit. He laid his hat aside on a nearby chair. His courtesy seemed a little strained, as if he was uncertain how to relate to Anne. Was this a social or a professional visit? she wondered.

'We've found Monsieur Flamme,' Roland began. 'Early this morning in the Saint-Eustache district, a girl delivering bread noticed his body under a trash pile.'

Anne was surprised and shocked. Late last night Flamme had seemed safe. His enemies had given up and left the Place des Victoires. 'How did he die?'

'He had been beaten to death several hours earlier, most likely on his way home from The Red Rooster. The barman told the police that Flamme was drunk and alone when he left the tavern near midnight. He was also carrying a pistol in his coat pocket.'

'Do you have any idea why he was killed?'

'We aren't sure. He could have been the victim of a carefully calculated robbery. His watch and his pistol were missing. His pockets were empty though he had paid for his drinks with a silver *écu* and had received a handful of copper coins in change.'

'That's far more money than a common labourer would usually carry and certainly enough to tempt a thief even to murder.'

'That's true, Madame. We've learned that Flamme did common labour but he was once a skilled carpenter and lived well. In recent years he added to his income by thievery. At the tavern he had shown the gold watch to the barman who told us it was a fancy one. So Flamme must have earlier picked a rich man's pocket, perhaps in the crowd outside a theatre. It happens frequently. But we haven't heard of one lately.'

'Flamme had reason to celebrate,' Anne suggested.

Roland shook his head. 'That would have been unusual – and unwise. Most professional thieves, like Flamme, are careful to conceal evidence of sudden prosperity. They would rather avoid the envy and greed of their comrades or the attention of the police. Still, strong drink could have undermined his prudence.'

Anne offered a thought, anticipating the magistrate. 'A violent, disreputable ruffian like Flamme must have made many enemies. I can think of two. Could one or more of them have killed him?'

'Frankly, I believe that's what happened. He was clubbed from behind. The blow was heavy. He fell to the pavement, almost certainly unconscious. A common thief would have immediately taken the victim's money, pistol and watch and would have fled. Instead, the perpetrator of this crime beat the fallen man several times, as if his chief intent was to kill him. Then he piled rubbish on him. That looks to me like anger, or revenge, or other personal motives were at work.'

'I agree. A stronger motive than thieving is possible.' She hesitated to say more. At some point she would have to tell the magistrate that she had spied on Flamme and his enemies on Place des Victoires. She wasn't sure that he would approve. The police tended to frown on private citizens, especially women, usurping their responsibility or acting without their authority in criminal investigations. But it would be better to tell him now rather than later when he might suspect her of having wrongly withheld useful information.

Anne explained, 'Four days ago, as Father O'Fallon was dying, he asked me to look after his son, since I was his teacher. As a deaf man in a hearing world, he needs counsel and training, especially now while grieving for his father. During the past two evenings I've gone in disguise to the Place des Victoires in hopes of observing Patrick as well as Flamme and his enemies.'

Roland didn't seem surprised and nodded for her to continue.

She went on to describe her experience on those nights. At her reference to Guiscard in female dress, Roland raised an eyebrow.

'After several nights without incident,' she concluded, 'Flamme must have felt safe enough to walk to his room alone. He was also armed. One of his enemies apparently outwitted him.'

Roland met Anne's eye. 'Among Flamme's enemies *is* the same Patrick O'Fallon, the dead priest's servant, alleged to be his son. We know that they were close. Flamme had killed the priest. So it's safe to assume that Patrick had a strong motive for this crime.'

Anne nodded reluctantly. 'If he felt a need for revenge, I wouldn't be surprised. That feeling seems entirely natural to me. But I doubt that Patrick had the will or the opportunity to act upon his feeling.' She paused for a moment. 'Perhaps I should clarify the relationship between the priest and his servant. Denis O'Fallon fathered Patrick as a young soldier *before* he became a priest. Many years later, he adopted Patrick and gave him the family name.'

'I stand corrected. I knew that you were familiar with both father and son. I'm also aware that you can communicate with the deaf. That's why I've come here.' He gave her an ingratiating smile. 'With your help I would like to question Patrick myself, rather than ask the National Guard. I fear that they would intimidate him and produce a useless, coerced confession. Would you bring him to my office in the magistrate's bureau, say, this morning at eleven?'

Anne was uneasy with Roland's request. She had come to enjoy the challenges of criminal investigation but had always reminded herself that her husband was the only policeman in their partnership. She had no authority to order anyone into interrogation and didn't want it.

'I'm willing to tell him that it's in his interest to meet you voluntarily and answer your questions. And I'll say that I know you to be a fair-minded magistrate. I'll also offer to accompany him. Hopefully, he'll be available this morning and will agree to a meeting. That's not certain.' Anne was quite unsure if she could even find Patrick. He seemed to have disappeared.

'That's what I hoped you would do.' Roland smiled. 'I personally feel that citizens of our young democracy should be persuaded rather than forced to do their duty – as much as humanly possible.'

He picked up his hat and rose to leave.

Anne stopped him with an afterthought. 'Isn't Monsieur Guiscard, the wealthy master builder, a potential suspect? Like Patrick, he has a strong motive. Flamme deliberately spilled coffee on him and his mistress. Guiscard was as angry a man as I've ever seen. Had the other ruffians not intervened, he would have strangled Flamme on the spot.' Anne smiled dryly. 'I believe, however, that a man as wealthy and powerful as Guiscard is not used to anyone, even a magistrate, questioning his actions or his motives.'

Roland appeared to flinch at the prospect of confronting the master builder. 'You're correct, Madame Cartier, he will be difficult. Like other powerful men in these tumultuous times, he can call upon ruthless supporters. Nonetheless, he should be questioned.' Roland hesitated. 'I think the man to do it is your husband's adjutant, Monsieur Georges Charpentier. He's the most experienced and skilful interrogator that I know. I'll ask him. By the way, Madame, would you have time today to visit Flamme's mistress in prison? It would be a humane thing to do. She probably hasn't heard about his death. You know her better than anyone else.'

'Thanks for reminding me,' said Anne. 'I'll go immediately.'

Anne was brought to the same plain visitor's room as before. Renée soon entered, again shackled. She glanced at Anne, read the expression on her face, and asked, 'What's wrong?'

Anne held the young woman's hands and spoke gently. 'Your friend Armand Flamme is dead. Someone killed him with a club early this morning. His body was found at daybreak.'

Renée's eyes widened, her lips began to quiver, and soon she was sobbing. Her whole body began to shake.

Fearing that the young woman might fall into a manic attack, Anne got up and consoled her.

In a minute or two, the grief subsided and Renée said, 'We got on well together. I'll miss him. Who did it?'

'The police can't say. No witnesses. He was walking to his room in the dark and was hit from behind. His money, his pistol, and his watch were taken.' Anne paused to gather Renée's attention, then tested her. 'Would you describe the watch for me?' Flamme had most likely stolen it.

Renée suddenly became wary – she was an inept liar. 'I didn't pay attention to it. Don't know where he got it.'

Her suspicion sufficiently confirmed, Anne tucked the watch into her memory and moved on. 'The police think that his killer's chief motive wasn't robbery. Do you have any idea who might have had a personal reason to kill him?'

Renée reflected for a moment. 'Do you remember that trouble in the garden of the Palais-Royal a week ago? At the time, I laughed when Armand told me about tipping coffee all over Monsieur Guiscard. Now I think it wasn't funny. Guiscard is a mean bastard and he's powerful. He would try to kill Armand.'

'Did you ever notice him, or anyone else, stalking Armand?'

Renée began to bite her lip, trying to recall suspicious persons loitering in the neighbourhood. 'There was usually a police spy outside our house. There were other suspicious characters. But our apartment on Rue Bouloi is near the stagecoach station. We see many strangers coming and going. I saw Monsieur Guiscard in disguise once or twice and I told Armand. He knew that, among his enemies, Guiscard in particular would try to kill him. He also thought he saw him in disguise on a couple of occasions. So he arranged for an escort when he was out on the street especially late at night.'

'It was a week since he insulted Guiscard. Do you think Armand might have let down his guard?'

Renée nodded. 'Armand used to say that the bastard had more important things on his mind, like making a lot of money. "He won't waste his time on me forever," he said. Yesterday, he told me that he no longer thought the escort was necessary. Besides, he was carrying a pistol. I warned him that the pistol would do him no good if an enemy caught him by surprise. But Armand laughed and called me a silly goose.'

From the Châtelet Anne set out to find Patrick. In an hour the magistrate would expect to interrogate him. He wasn't in his Louvre rooms. The watchman at the gate had seen him briefly last night but not since then. He added, 'Why don't you talk to the sexton at the Oratory? He says the young man often visits the church.'

At the main entrance to the Oratory Anne rang for the sexton. No response. An elderly man, the sexton had to serve also as porter. Anne rang again, telling herself to be patient. The poor man might be working in a distant part of the convent. Finally, he opened, breathless. He recognized her and invited her in.

'I'm sorry to keep you waiting, Madame Cartier. How can I help you?'

Anne asked him about Patrick.

'I think he's in the crypt of the church. He insisted that he didn't want to be disturbed. But I think someone should look after him. Since his father's burial he seems to spend many hours there.'

'Do you know when he goes in or out?'

'Not really. I have to look after the entire building and can't watch all the doors. You have to ring to fetch me.'

'So, can Patrick come and go as he pleases?'

'Yes. No one is really in charge here but me. I trust him with a key to a side door. It's good to have him in this big, empty building. He helps me sometimes move heavy things – he's a strong man.'

'Would you show me to the crypt? I have to bring him to a magistrate.'

'Follow me, Madame.' The sexton led her across the court-yard, through the church and down a flight of stairs. 'There he is,' whispered the sexton, pointing to a seated figure midway in the room. 'Will you be all right, Madame?' the sexton asked, a hint of anxiety in his voice.

'Yes, thank you. I'll be fine. I know him well.'

The sexton left. For a minute Anne stood there, growing accustomed to the room. It had a low, vaulted ceiling and was damp and mouldy. Thin streams of light came through small high windows, leaving much of the crypt in darkness. When her eyes were ready, she walked towards Patrick, careful not to startle him. He took no notice of her, until she sat on a stool by his side. He pointed to the stone slab covering his father's grave. It was illuminated by light from one of the high windows.

At the head of the slab was a Celtic cross. Beneath it were the dates of his birth and his death: 1736 Dublin and 1791 Paris.

'He can finally rest in peace,' Patrick signed.

They sat together silently for a minute or two. Then Anne told him about Flamme's murder. Patrick merely shrugged, 'I know. A watchman told me.'

Anne signed, 'The magistrate Monsieur Roland wants to question you, like everyone else who was involved somehow with the victim.'

'Just tell him that I know nothing.' Patrick's face was set in an obstinate expression.

Unwilling to use threats, Anne cast about in her mind for a way to move the young man. Finally, she asked him, 'What would your father have wanted you to do?'

He stared at the grave and visibly struggled with the question for a long moment. Tears welled up in his eyes. Finally, he replied, 'I'll go with you to the magistrate. That's what father would want.'

Promptly at eleven, Anne brought Patrick to the magistrate's bureau. A National Guardsman showed them into Roland's office. He was standing at his writing table, waiting. Anne drew him to one side. 'I've spoken with Armand Flamme's mistress and must warn you that she's suicidal. Could you do something for her?'

'Thank you for the information, Madame. I'll put her under constant watch for a while and try to improve her situation.'

Anne pressed further for Renée. 'Her guilt seems minor. Because of her illness, she's emotionally vulnerable. Flamme seduced her, and then exploited her in his schemes. Doctor Pinel is willing to take her back. She needs more treatment. He'd keep her under close supervision.'

'That sounds like a reasonable plan. I'll speak to the doctor.'

Roland turned to Patrick, smiled kindly, and gestured him to a chair at the writing table. When Anne and Roland had worked together on the deaf baker's case, she had instructed him in the basic techniques of communicating with deaf people. He now remembered to face Patrick across the table and to speak slowly and enunciate clearly. Anne sat alongside Roland, also facing Patrick.

Roland began by offering condolences to Patrick for the loss of his father. 'You know,' he went on, Anne translating, 'that the man who caused your father's death was killed last night or early this morning. Flamme was a bad man – we were searching for him at the time. Had we found him alive, we would have put him on trial. Still it was wrong for a private person to take upon himself the role of judge and executioner. Since you had good reason to hate Flamme, I must ask, are you responsible for his death?'

Patrick showed no emotion and signed simply, 'No.'

'What did you do last night?' Roland asked.

'I read a book in my room at the Louvre until ten. Afterwards I walked outside for a few minutes in the courtyard. Then I went to bed and slept through the night.'

'Can anyone vouch for your movements?'

'The watchman saw me in the courtyard.'

Roland's voice grew more insistent. Anne's signing did as well – to her growing distress. He met Patrick's eye and asked, 'Was anyone with you during the night?'

The young man's cheeks coloured. He hesitated for a fraction of a second, then signed, 'No.'

Roland noticed the hesitation and glanced at Anne, a hint of scepticism in his eyes. He shifted to Patrick. 'That will be all for now. You may go. I'll need to ask you a few more questions later.' He turned to Anne. 'Would you stay with me, Madame?'

She agreed with a feeling of trepidation. Patrick might well lack an alibi.

When Patrick had left, Roland asked Anne, 'Do you think he had a companion during the night?'

'Yes, I do, though I'm not certain.'

'If he didn't, he lacks an alibi.'

Anne nodded reluctantly. 'He may not wish to compromise a certain woman.'

Roland looked at her with a mixture of surprise and curiosity. 'Would you give me her name?'

Anne found herself in a quandary. 'I understand why you would have to question her. However, if it were made public that she was with Patrick that night, the consequences could be disastrous. Her husband is a jealous and violent man, though he is unfaithful himself.'

Roland reflected for a moment. 'Then could you question the woman for me – so I might not have to do it myself? While I wait to hear from you, I'll ask Monsieur Georges Charpentier to pay a visit to Monsieur Guiscard.'

FOURTEEN
Failed Deception

10 June

Early in the afternoon, Anne and Marthe met again outside the little puppet theatre in the Camp of the Tatars. This would be Anne's best opportunity to test her suspicion that Patrick had spent the night of Flamme's murder in bed with Marthe. In such an intimate matter, success depended on having a trusting relationship with the woman.

For the past ten days, Anne had seriously tried to cultivate that trust. She and Marthe had met in various informal settings, including Michou's studio on Rue Traversine. They carefully avoided hours when Monsieur Boyer might come home. He would object to these meetings, fearing that his wife might escape his control. Thus far he seemed unaware of his wife's apparent infidelity. But Anne was nervously unsure. Boyer could be pretending ignorance while he watched for an opportune moment to expose or even kill her.

Michou was teaching her sketching as well as the basic signing that deaf people used in Paris. Anne was trying to determine if she had any talent for reading lips and if it could be developed. For amusement Anne had also introduced her to hand puppets. She had gained sufficient skill for simple skits. Trust between them had grown so that they now used their Christian names, Anne and Marthe. A delicate conversation seemed possible.

Before coming to the puppet theatre this afternoon, Anne had spoken to the watchman on duty at the Louvre during the night of Flamme's murder. He confirmed that Patrick had walked around the old courtyard at about ten in the evening, and he hadn't left the Louvre later. Females had come and gone during the night, but the watchman hadn't recognized Madame Boyer.

Anne felt that his statement couldn't be trusted. Louvre watchmen notoriously napped on and off through the night.

Strong drink sometimes blurred their vision. They could also be bribed. Marthe might have easily slipped past him into Patrick's rooms. He could have as easily left the Louvre in order to kill Flamme.

After glancing left and right for possible spies, Anne unlocked the theatre and the two women hurried in. This was the hottest time of the day, and the puppet theatre was uncomfortably warm. Anne opened the windows, latched the door, and began today's session with the hand puppets for 'Punch and Judy'. Afterwards, she drilled Marthe through a few simple exercises in reading lips, complimenting her when she did well.

When Marthe seemed at ease, Anne remarked, 'A man was killed last night near the Place des Victoires. I'm gathering information for magistrate Roland, an acquaintance of mine. Perhaps you can tell me about the victim, Armand Flamme. He was one of your husband's followers.'

'I seldom see Monsieur Boyer's friends or acquaintances. If he brings them home, he never introduces them to me. I usually don't know what they're talking about and he never tells me.'

Anne showed her Michou's sketch of Flamme.

'Oh, that one! I recognize him. Frankly, I think he's not quite sane. When he comes to our rooms, he and my husband soon argue and become angry. Flamme shouts, pounds the table, and stamps his feet. I think he threatens my husband. Monsieur Boyer keeps his anger inside. Still, I can see it in his eyes, but I don't know what he's thinking.'

'What do they argue about?'

'I think Flamme wants to kill all the priests now. Boyer says it's not yet time – he'll decide.'

'Any other issues?'

'Church property,' she replied. 'Money from the sales is going into the pockets of rich business men and politicians. Flamme thinks it should be divided among the poor, so they wouldn't have to starve.'

'How did Patrick feel about Flamme's death?'

'He was pleased and said justice was done.'

'How do you know that?' Anne studied Marthe's face. She had begun to look uneasy.

'He told me this morning.'

'Do you think Patrick did it?'

'Of course not! He's a kind-hearted, gentle man.'

'The police suspect him. Since Flamme had killed Patrick's father, Patrick had a powerful motive for revenge. He also has no alibi for the night of the murder.'

Marthe was now struggling. 'Patrick would never kill anyone! Not even Flamme!'

'The police can't read Patrick's heart. They look at the facts.' Anne pressed on. 'Patrick claims he was alone in his room that night. The police think he might have slipped out of the Louvre and killed Flamme.' Anne now carefully measured her words. 'No one can vouch for Patrick.'

Tears welled up in Marthe's eyes. 'I can. I was with him until dawn.' In a tone of reproach she added, 'The watchman promised not to tell anyone.'

'He kept his promise, Marthe. And I will use your confession only if necessary to protect Patrick. Do you agree?'

She nodded and breathed a sigh of relief. Then she reconsidered and signed desperately, 'Monsieur Boyer must not find out, or he'd kill me. That's legal in this country.'

'That's true,' Anne admitted, 'if he were to catch you and Patrick in the sexual act. So, you must be careful. Now let's clean up the theatre for the next performance.'

They rose from the benches and picked up the puppets. They were about to put them away when someone banged rudely on the door.

Anne gestured urgently to Marthe to play with her puppets. Then she hastened to the door with a puppet in one hand. With the other she unlatched and opened the door. A dark, glowering Jacques Boyer stood there.

Anne put on her most innocent, joyful smile and held up the puppet. He stared at her, mouth agape, eyes confused. For a few seconds he sputtered nonsense. Finally he asked, 'What's going on here?'

Anne put her hand puppet to work in front of him. Marthe came forward and did the same. 'We're learning "Punch and Judy".'

'I see,' he muttered, deflated. He scowled at his wife. 'I was wondering where you were. Leave a note when you go out.' He hesitated, momentarily uncertain, then walked away.

Anne wondered how he had found them. Rat-face or his young spies must have followed them. She and Marthe would have to be even more cautious in the future. Then a question surfaced in her mind. As they put away the puppets, she asked, 'Where was your husband last night when Flamme was killed? If he was at home, didn't he miss you or ask where you had been?'

'He wasn't at home. For several months, he has rarely spent the night with me – only if he's not feeling well. Then he wants me to take care of him. Otherwise he returns home early in the morning to change his clothes and unlock his study. He goes inside, closes the door and reads and writes. After dinner, he locks his study and goes out again, usually to the Palais-Royal to talk to people and read the newspapers, or visit a printer about his pamphlets. In the evening, he goes to speeches and meetings at The Red Rooster or other political clubs. He spends the night with his young mistress near the Foire Saint-Germain. If she's indisposed, he goes to a brothel. I don't see him again until the next morning.' She signed her story without agitation, as if she were talking about a stranger. But her lips were thin, her jaw tight.

'Do you remember what he wore that morning when he came home?'

She took a moment to recall. 'He had on his plain pale blue silk coat. His breeches looked soiled. I asked if he wanted them washed. He seemed distracted and didn't hear, but he gave them to me. As I was about to wash them, I found some copper coins and a gold pocket watch in the coat. He seemed upset that I found them.'

Anne's heart beat faster. 'Can you describe the watch? Could it have been his own?'

'I couldn't inspect it closely or even open the case. Boyer was looking at me. But I could feel that the gold casing was smooth. He does have a pocket watch that he keeps in his study. The one I found could have been his own, but why would he have become upset?'

'Do you know what he did with the watch?'

'He put it in his pocket. I haven't seen it since.'

Anne met Marthe's eye. 'You must know his secret hiding places. See if you can find it.'

Marthe shook her head. 'He probably hides things in his study and he keeps it locked.'

'You haven't mentioned seeing any pistols. Were there any in his coat pocket?'

'I didn't find any.' Marthe paused. 'But he has had pistols in the apartment for as long as I've known him. Since he's often out late at night, he needs protection. Or, so he says.'

Anne returned immediately to Magistrate Roland's office and described her conversation with Marthe Boyer though without mentioning her name. 'It's true, as we suspected, that Patrick was in bed with a woman at the time when Flamme was killed.'

'May I have her name for the record?'

Anne expected and feared that question. 'How can we protect her? If her husband were to discover her infidelity, he would certainly beat her, or quite possibly find a way to kill her, as law and custom permit. And we would lose a key witness in this case.'

Roland nodded thoughtfully. 'I'll need her name if I'm to take the case to trial. At this point in my investigation, it's enough to know that a credible witness has given Patrick an alibi.'

Anne relaxed.

Roland met her eye. 'Nonetheless, Patrick O'Fallon remains a possible suspect. The alibi from a lover might be false, as I'm sure you realize.'

Meanwhile early that afternoon, Georges Charpentier introduced himself to the porter at Monsieur Guiscard's residence on Rue Colbert, east off Rue de Richelieu. They chatted briefly about the residence, the weather, speculation in bread, and growing crime in the city. Georges said he had come on business and asked for directions to Guiscard's office. As they parted, he gave the man a generous tip – a prudent investment.

Georges proceeded through the portal and into the courtyard. There he stood for a few moments and studied Guiscard's property. Buildings could often yield clues to the character of their inhabitants. Guiscard had built for himself a large stone mansion that was more pretentious than pleasing to the eye. Especially offensive was a pair of thick, tall columns on either side of the portico, too large in relation to the narrow, cramped facade.

Georges had learned from the porter that the master's living quarters were in the upper floors, his office on the ground floor. Behind the mansion, instead of a garden, was a large workshop employing at least a dozen artisans. They were mostly

involved in renovating, enlarging or repairing his many properties throughout the city.

Georges entered a display room, its walls covered with
engravings of the Roman Forum and other ancient architecture.
A large-scale model of the Hôtel de Monaco on the Left Bank
stood prominently on a table. As he bent over the model to
examine its fine details, he became aware that a clerk was
regarding him with a sharp eye.

Could he possibly think I'm about to steal the model? Georges
asked himself. Or, does he have a reason to be concerned why
I'm here? Georges moved around the model in order to face
the clerk. A middle-aged man of unassuming appearance and
deferential manner, he could easily be dismissed as dull. Still
his eyes betrayed a cautious, keen, searching intelligence.

He told Georges that Monsieur Guiscard had built the hôtel,
one of several major accomplishments in the city. Georges
received the information politely, though he knew the building
almost as well as Guiscard did. Years ago, in the course of a
secret criminal investigation Georges had studied it closely.

He gave his card to the clerk who knocked on an elegant
oak door and announced the visitor. Guiscard's big voice called
him in.

Upon entering the spacious room, Georges felt disoriented
for a moment. The left third was furnished as a salon. Richly
embroidered upholstered chairs were arranged around a tea
table. A pair of tall, elaborately gilded porcelain vases framed
a large fireplace. A long couch covered with dark green silk
stood against one wall. Two life-size marble nude females
lurked in the corners behind leafy potted plants. Heavy dark
green velvet drapes hung on either side of the half-opened
windows. A thick Turkish carpet lay on the floor. Gilded sconces
on the walls and a chandelier of faux crystal served to light
the room. Everything about these furnishings reminded Georges
of an expensive, tasteless brothel.

The space to the right of the entrance had a much simpler
aspect. Georges noted shelves of file boxes, rolls of architec-
tural drawings, sketches and engravings of ancient and modern
buildings, and a few plain chairs and tables. This was the
builder's working area.

In the central section of the room stood an enormous writing
table, twice as wide as any Georges had ever seen. Constructed

of speckled brown mahogany and oak, it rested squarely on eight thick tapered legs. In the middle of the table's surface was an inlaid slab of white veined marble. A single row of locked drawers served for storage. An abundance of gilded, chased bronze ornaments offered partial relief from the great bulk of dark wood. Nonetheless, the table had a heavy rather than a graceful appearance. Georges' mind raced to detect the hand of its maker and the character of its owner.

The latter stood behind his table, legs apart, thick chest thrust out, and a quizzical expression on his broad, ruddy face. 'To what do I owe the honour of this visit?' he asked with a hint of irony in his voice. He sat down at the table, gestured Georges to a chair facing him, and brusquely waved the clerk away.

When the door closed, Georges introduced himself and explained that he had a few questions. Guiscard leaned back, his head tilted at a sceptical angle. A few years ago, at the height of his powers, that would have been an intimidating posture, but not any more. Recent self-indulgence had taken a toll. Loose flesh hung from his cheeks, his eyes had a jaded look.

'You may have heard, sir, that Armand Flamme, the rogue who spilled coffee on you outside the Café de Foy a week ago, was found dead early this morning.'

'In fact, I had not heard. Business has kept me from the Palais-Royal and its gossip today.' He chuckled malignly. 'I thank you for bringing me the good news.'

Georges went on. 'Someone had beaten him to death and covered his body with trash.'

Guiscard nodded sagely. 'That was an appropriate conclusion to his worthless life. Paris is a better place without him. I realize, however, that the police must find his killer. We can't allow just anybody to go about the city killing its human vermin.'

Guiscard's contempt for the murdered man appeared to reflect a high degree of familiarity as well as resentment. Georges asked, 'Sir, did you know Flamme personally prior to this incident?'

'Indeed I did! He's been a thorn in my side for years. I've taken him to court.'

Georges cocked his head to encourage Guiscard to elaborate.

He seemed pleased to do so. 'The rogue was a journeyman carpenter by trade – a good one – but a demagogue by inclination. He worked for me on several buildings – the Hôtel de

Monaco on Rue Saint-Dominique is the best known. That was fourteen years ago.'

'I've seen it,' said Georges. 'A magnificent building, worthy of the princess who paid a fortune for it.' As a police spy, unknown to Guiscard, Georges had investigated labour unrest at the site of the building and secretly reported to the authorities that the master was cheating his workers. Sympathetic to Guiscard, the authorities ignored the report and punished the workers.

Guiscard acknowledged Georges' compliment with a nod, then scowled. 'Flamme wasn't satisfied with what I paid him. He also accused me of blocking his application for the Master's grade. We had a hot argument. In the end, I threatened to dismiss him. Then he organized the other workers and they tried to force concessions from me. That was too much. I persuaded the police to put him in prison for a couple of years and I dismissed the rest of them. Since leaving prison, he could not find work. I made sure that no master builder would hire him. I hear he had to steal for a living.'

'Then you must realize, sir, that you are among those with strong reasons to hate Armand Flamme. So, my first question must be, did you or one of your men kill him?'

Guiscard smiled sardonically. 'Monsieur Charpentier, I can assure you that I did not kill Flamme. I'm a busy man and must make better use of my time. Furthermore, I didn't hire anyone to do it. That would have been a waste of money. Why don't you question Flamme's companions? They had probably robbed a wealthy man and Flamme had tried to cheat them out of their fair share. Was he himself robbed?'

Georges nodded. 'Your theory has merit, sir. I'll keep it in mind.' Guiscard's guess was intriguing. What would prompt him to think that Flamme was probably killed for his valuable objects, a gold watch and change from a silver *écu*? Could Guiscard have merely pretended not to know that Flamme had been robbed?

For the time being, Georges kept these musings to himself. 'I must ask you, sir, where you were the night of Flamme's death?'

Irritation flashed in Guiscard's eyes. 'If you must know, I was in the arms of my mistress.'

'I suppose she will confirm your statement, but I must ask her. I'll need her name and address.'

Guiscard's irritation rose to a higher level, but he said, 'Yvonne Barcome, Rue Saint-Marc, near the Théatre des Italiens. She's an actress.'

'I've heard her name and may have seen her on the stage.'

'Then, if that's all you have to ask me, I have work to do.'

Georges rose and walked at a slow, measured pace to the door. He turned to Guiscard and said, 'I may have more questions later.' As he closed the door, he heard the businessman mutter an obscenity. Georges smiled – he loathed the man.

While waiting in Mademoiselle Barcome's antechamber, Georges learned that she had risen late and was still dressing for an afternoon of social engagements. She was also scheduled for a minor role in a farce that evening at the theatre. Georges countered that he too had engagements and a schedule. He would speak to mademoiselle now.

Her maid turned pale, and her lips quivered as she said, 'Then follow me please.' She led Georges into the mistress' boudoir, a large, densely furnished room. An elegant pianoforte occupied one corner. Two huge Sèvres vases flanked the fireplace. Several small Sèvres vases crowded together on the mantel. They appeared to be rare and expensive. A rack of embroidered silk evening gowns stood against a wall. No two were alike. A glance assured Georges that they, like everything else in the room, were expensive gifts from Guiscard and striking evidence of his lack of taste, as well as his infatuation with the young actress.

The maid broke into Georges' observation. He would have to speak to mademoiselle through a folding screen. Playing the gentleman, he agreed.

'How seriously does Monsieur Guiscard take offence?' Georges addressed his question to the curly black hair moving above the screen.

'Once at a gambling den, a man made a snide remark to me. Guiscard threw him through a large glass window.'

'Then he would have severely punished the man who poured coffee on you, had the others not defended him,' Georges remarked.

'Indeed. The rogue was fortunate to have escaped alive.'

'Mademoiselle, someone murdered him early this morning.'

Georges heard a gasp from the other side of the screen. She had apparently not yet heard the news.

'May I ask where were you at the time?' When Georges asked that question, the maid was walking across the room towards the screen, carrying a gown in her arms. She stumbled, nearly losing her balance. It was as if the words had physically struck her.

Behind the screen, Mademoiselle Barcome stammered incoherently. Finally, she said in a halting voice, 'I was with Monsieur Guiscard here.'

Georges deduced that Guiscard had told her what to say but had not mentioned the murder. She now seemed fearful that Guiscard might have killed Flamme and had implicated her in the crime.

Georges raised his voice. 'Mademoiselle, put on a dressing gown and come out here. We must have a serious conversation.'

A minute later, she emerged in a bright red silk gown, her face not yet larded with cosmetics, her hair still tousled. She was about eighteen, pampered, but still very pretty. Her dark eyes were now wide with anxiety.

Georges pulled up chairs. 'Sit down,' he commanded. 'I want the truth. Did Monsieur Guiscard tell you to say that he had been with you last night? Am I right?'

She nodded and said weakly, 'Yes, he said it was an excuse he needed in his business. It was too complicated to explain.'

Georges wrote out a deposition and had the young woman sign it. Two maids were witnesses. As he was about to leave the house, he met Guiscard at the door, his face flushed from exertion and anxiety. He started when he saw Georges.

'Ah, Monsieur Guiscard!' Georges exclaimed. 'You have arrived just in time to learn that you were not here with your mistress the night of Flamme's murder. Step into the parlour and you may tell me exactly where you *were*.'

Guiscard walked stiffly to a window and looked out, his hands clasped tightly behind his back. After a few minutes he turned around to face Georges and began softly. 'I was alone in my office. The clerk had left. It was late. I was very tired but still had work to do. I lay down on the couch for a tenminute nap. Hours later, I woke up with sunlight pouring into the room. My clerk soon arrived and mentioned Flamme's murder. I realized I'd be questioned and would need an alibi. So I fabricated one – badly.'

'Could anyone in your house give you an honest alibi? Your wife? Your servants?'

'My wife resides at our country estate. We lead separate lives. My servants have no reason to come to my office unless I call them.' Guiscard's chin jutted out. 'I have no alibi and I don't need one. You have no evidence that I killed Flamme.'

Georges returned to Guiscard's home on Rue Colbert. At the porter's door Georges called out. The porter appeared, recognized Georges and smiled. Georges whispered, 'I believe we knew each other, years ago. May we speak privately.'

The porter nodded. 'But this place is too busy, carts and men going in and out constantly.'

'Are you free this evening?'

'Yes,' the porter replied, his eyes glittering with interest.

'Then come to The Nimble Heifer at about seven. I'll make it worth your while. It's a café nearby on Rue Sainte-Anne. The owner is a friend.'

'I know her. I'll be there.'

FIFTEEN
At the Red Rooster

10 June

That afternoon at dinner, when the servants had withdrawn, Anne reported to Paul the death of Flamme and Magistrate Roland's investigation. Paul had just returned from inspecting his country estate south of Paris with a view to improving its efficiency. A steward managed the property. A rich banker leased the château for his mistress. If Paul were to lose his position in the Gendarmerie, he might have to retire there. He hadn't heard the news about Flamme.

'I'm surprised, Anne. I thought he was taking sensible precautions. Who does Roland suspect?'

'Patrick O'Fallon, of course, since he had openly declared his intention to kill the man.' Anne described her conversation with Marthe. 'She gave Patrick an alibi – they had slept together in his room at the Louvre. She's terrified that her husband might discover her infidelity. He could beat or even kill her.'

'A reasonable fear, I'm sorry to say. Who are the others on Roland's list?'

'Jacques Boyer and Jean Guiscard are there. In our conversation Marthe appeared to implicate her husband. He seemed disturbed that she found a gold watch and a few copper coins in his clothes. They might be items taken from Flamme's body.'

'I'm sceptical, Anne. What motive could Boyer have to kill a man of his own political faction?'

'His wife witnessed them quarrelling bitterly but couldn't fully understand the issues between them.'

Paul reflected for a few moments. 'That's slim evidence but reason enough for a conversation with Monsieur Boyer. Georges and I must meet him privately. Can you suggest a way?'

'I'll ask Marthe. This evening, she'll sneak out again to meet me at the puppet theatre. In the meantime, she'll search for the watch, but I doubt that she'll find it. He most likely has locked it in his study.'

'Georges and I will wait here until we hear from you.' He paused. 'By the way, has Roland put Georges to work?'

'Yes, he's investigating Monsieur Guiscard, a task he seems to relish. He admits that Guiscard is clever, but at heart he's a greedy brute and a sham patriot.'

A few minutes before six o'clock, Anne walked through the Camp of the Tatars looking out for Rat-face or any of Boyer's men who might be trying to spy on her. She wore the plain, grey woollen gown and the worn shoes of a poorly paid seamstress. Hunched to add age to her disguise, she shuffled ahead painfully. In the crowded gallery it was difficult to discern who might be a spy. At least in the vicinity of the theatre she could see none.

She had closed the theatre for the hour of this visit. At six she stood near the entrance waiting for Marthe. Several minutes passed. Finally, it was obvious that she wasn't coming. Anne began to worry. Was Marthe ill or had her husband kept her at home? One way to find out was to ask Patrick.

He came to the door of his rooms at the Louvre, let her in, and then slouched in a chair, pale and listless.

'How are you?' she signed.

'Exhausted,' he replied. 'I can hardly bear to stay in these rooms. They are so empty.' He sighed. 'Anyway, I'll soon have to leave and must find another room somewhere. Then again, Magistrate Roland may save me the trouble and put me in prison.'

Anne shook her head. 'Marthe has given you an alibi.'

He sat up, his signing agitated and choppy. 'No! She shouldn't have done that. Think of the shame. Her husband will kill her.'

Anne encouraged him to carry on.

'It isn't true, Madame Cartier. Marthe is trying to protect me. We didn't sleep together the night Flamme was killed. Now the police will punish her for giving me a false alibi. I'm so sorry for her.' He appeared on the verge of tears. 'Yesterday, I had treated her with contempt at Saint-Eustache, called her a butcher's daughter who didn't understand honour. This afternoon, I hoped to meet her again in the church and apologize, but she didn't come. I wondered what had happened.

But I didn't think I should inquire at her home. I don't know what to do.'

Anne raised her hands in a calming gesture. 'Her alibi isn't public. I warned the magistrate about the danger from her husband. The magistrate agreed that he didn't need to know her name, at least not for a while. Trust me to straighten out this problem. I'll leave you now and try to find her.'

At the wine shop near the Boyer residence, Anne explained to the barman that she was an old friend of Madame Boyer. 'Do you expect her to come to your shop later in the evening?'

'I don't think so,' he replied. 'Late this morning she bought wine for dinner.'

'How did she look?' Anne asked, putting a concerned expression on her face.

The barman glanced to the left and right, then spoke softly. 'She looked dreadful, as if she had been beaten. When I inquired, she said that she had fallen down the stairs and had bruised herself.'

'Does she have these *falls* often?'

'From time to time, but this is the first one recently. I thought she had learned to be more careful.'

Anne expressed her regrets, thanked the man and left with the feeling that something was going very badly for Marthe Boyer. Could her husband's spies have exposed her affair with Patrick?

A few minutes before seven, in advance of meeting Guiscard's porter, Georges took a seat at a secluded table in The Nimble Heifer. To avoid attention he had also put aside his gendarme's uniform and dressed in a plain brown woollen suit. He needed to talk to Cécile Tremblay, a strong, handsome woman who owned and managed the café. He had met her four years ago.

A recent, impoverished widow, she had gone through rough patches in life and was anxious and dispirited. Since taking over the café, she had prospered, grown more self-confident and had helped him as an informer in various investigations. He could trust her judgement.

'Are you here on business or pleasure?' she asked with a welcoming smile and sat at his table.

'It's always a pleasure to see you, Cécile.' He leaned forward and lowered his voice to a whisper. 'I have a question. Are you acquainted with Monsieur Guiscard's porter? We've arranged to meet here. I may want to do business with him.'

Cécile wrinkled her brow, recalling the porter while calculating the possible costs of becoming involved with the police. Georges understood and didn't press her.

Finally, she said softly, 'Luc Thierry is an honest man. But when he has had a glass of wine, he might speak more freely and loudly than is wise. I suggest that you carry on your conversation out of earshot of my other customers. Some of them also work for Guiscard and could carry tales to him. He would retaliate brutally. You may use the back room.'

She rose from the chair, leaned over Georges and kissed his bald head. 'I'll tell Thierry that you're a good man, Georges, and send him to you.'

'You wanton woman!' he whispered to her back as she walked away.

Georges had barely settled into the room when the door opened and Luc Thierry walked in. Cécile followed him with a bottle of red wine and two glasses. She poured, then with a wink to Georges, she withdrew. Georges raised his glass and saluted his companion. The porter responded in kind.

Georges began by prodding Thierry to speak about himself. Their paths must have crossed somewhere in the past.

'Where could we have met?' asked Georges.

The porter related that he came from Normandy, Georges' province. For years he had served in the royal army, as had Georges. During the Seven Years War, he had taken part in several battles.

'Were you at Minden in Germany in 1759?' Georges was then himself a young soldier. The dreadful carnage of that battle had imprinted on him a lasting dark view of life and a sceptical outlook on the political follies of kings and their witless ministers.

'Yes, I was near General Saint-Martin when he fell.'

'I was too, and now I work for his son, the colonel, in the Gendarmerie Nationale.' Georges studied his companion closely. 'It's all coming back. After the war, we were both agents of the Lieutenant General of Police, Monsieur Sartine, the master of criminal investigation.'

'I remember now,' Thierry exclaimed. 'We searched a marquis' town house and discovered an illegal distillery in his basement.'

They raised their glasses in a toast to Sartine and to the bitter-sweet memories of their youth.

Georges set his glass down on the table and met Thierry's eye. 'So besides opening and closing the gate, what else are you doing on Rue Colbert?'

The porter hesitated, suddenly a bit wary.

'I understand your need for caution,' Georges assured him. 'Your master is ruthless, but vulnerable. His great, powerful body stands on feet of clay, if you perceive my meaning. If we are careful, we can safely share our interest in him to our mutual advantage.'

Thierry relaxed, apparently intrigued, and nodded Georges on.

'I need to know if your master killed Armand Flamme. What are you investigating? Don't worry, I'll be discreet.'

'My eye is on his secrets, especially his money,' Thierry replied. 'Madame Guiscard hires me to spy on him. She has me gathering evidence for a divorce or legal separation and wants a fair piece of his wealth – she'd gladly take every bit of it. In the mansion on Rue Colbert a maid helps me. His office clerk tells me about his business.'

'What have you learned?'

'Guiscard is speculating heavily in confiscated church property, buying large pieces at auction from the government. I don't know how much profit he makes, nor exactly how he makes it.'

'Given his greedy character,' Georges observed, 'you can be sure that he expects to make huge profits any way possible.'

'His clerk thinks that Guiscard must bribe unscrupulous politicians and officials in the finance offices to buy the properties cheaply at fraudulent auctions. He also buys monastic and other church buildings, probably in the same crooked way. His workmen convert them into commercial properties, fitted out with rental apartments and various shops, or adapt them for public use by schools or municipalities.'

Georges stroked his chin thoughtfully. 'Your ally, the clerk, lacks proof. Am I right?'

Thierry nodded. 'The clerk works mostly in an antechamber adjacent to his master's office and is called in when needed.

Guiscard gives him no opportunity to search for incriminating material.'

Georges raised his glass and took a long draught. 'Then Monsieur Guiscard has much to hide. For a start, he must keep two different account books. The one that he shows to the public makes him look like a great patriot. Much of his modest net profit seems to go to charity or public works, either his own or those of certain influential politicians, especially Monsieur Jérôme Pétion.'

The porter emptied his glass and filled it again. 'And he secretly records the real profit elsewhere.'

'So, your problem,' said Georges, 'is to discover his secret correspondence and his hidden account book.'

Thierry added, 'And that discovery would almost certainly convict him of fraud. His estranged wife wants to put him in prison as much as to take his money.'

Georges pushed his glass aside and rested his arms on the table. 'I think I can help you, Luc. We must figure out how to search Guiscard's office. But now you can help me. Did you observe him leave his house last night?'

'Yes, he passed through the main gate,' replied Thierry. 'He had tried to disguise himself as a woman, a common vendor, in black frock and bonnet, carrying a basket of flowers. He's been going out in different garb for a week. One night he was a coachman with a short cape and high boots. Still, I recognized him by his swagger and stride.'

Georges shook his head. 'His behaviour is bizarre. How do you account for it?'

'I think his mistress fits him out, trains him, and probably plays him for a fool. But he seems to enjoy the challenge and may fancy himself a great actor. His disguise works well enough, especially in shadowed or dark places. He's not been exposed.'

'The man could play Falstaff on the stage. Where did he go?'

'I followed him twice to the same place, a house on Rue Bouloi near the Messageries Générales, the royal stagecoach company. At sundown, Guiscard kept watch on the door. When a certain man came out, Guiscard followed him to The Red Rooster, a tavern on Place des Victoires. It's in one of Guiscard's buildings.'

Georges showed him Michou's sketch of Flamme.

The porter nodded. 'That's the man. I've heard about his

earlier, failed attempt to organize Guiscard's men. Lately, he dumped coffee on Guiscard, reason enough to hate Flamme and to harm him. At The Red Rooster he joined the club, Citizens for Equality, and discussed politics. Guiscard hid outside until they left. Then he followed Flamme back to his home on Rue Bouloi. Two or three men escorted him, as if he didn't feel safe in the dark. That was his routine.'

'I see,' said Georges, 'Guiscard apparently hoped to catch Flamme alone, late at night when the streets were dark and empty. But Flamme realized that he was in danger. His escort frustrated Guiscard's scheme.'

'That's right,' said the porter. 'But last night was different. I was tired and assumed the escort would take Flamme home as usual. Guiscard must have given up a little later for the same reason. He passed through the portal just before eleven o'clock and went directly to his office.'

'Are you sure of the time?' Georges asked. 'We know for certain that Flamme was alive and leaving the tavern at midnight.'

Georges might have looked disappointed for Thierry replied, 'I'm sorry, Georges. You seem to have lost a strong suspect. But I'm sure of the time – I looked at my watch.'

'Could he have gone out again without you noticing?'

For a long moment, the porter pondered the question. 'There's a small locked entrance in the rear of the property. He would have the key. I suppose he could have gone out that way. But why would he?'

'He made sure you noticed him at eleven, his disguise notwithstanding. That gave him an alibi, if he needed one. Later, he could kill Flamme and sneak back through the rear entrance. Guiscard is too promising a suspect to surrender. I'm intrigued that he also owned the building and speaks in a familiar way with the barman. Something else to look into.'

The porter added, 'By the way, Monsieur Guiscard wasn't the only person following Flamme. I noticed one or two others in Place des Victoires like wolves stalking their prey.'

Georges finished his drink and thanked his companion. 'Last night, Flamme must have figured that his enemies had lost interest in him and that it was safe to go without an escort. The barman told the police that Flamme left the tavern alone. One of those wolves must have pounced on him.'

*   *   *

Georges glanced at his reflection in a window, tugged at the thin lapels of his coat and entered The Red Rooster, Flamme's favourite tavern on Place des Victoires. He had asked Madame Cartier and Michou to precede him and observe the place. Out of the corner of his eye he saw them at a table with a clear view of the bar, both of them in the plain dress of housemaids. Michou gave him a brief discreet smile, wrote a line in her sketchbook and showed it to Anne. She nodded without looking at Georges.

The tavern was on the ground floor and consisted of a large, plain hall. The rear portion was L-shaped. On this evening at about nine o'clock, in the front or main section, the tables were half-occupied. For the most part, the men and women appeared to come from shopkeepers' families. There was a sprinkling of single apprentices and journeymen. Their clothing was well worn but decent.

Conversation was subdued. The snatches that Georges heard concerned last night's brutal killing of Flamme. The section at the back of the room could be curtained off for meetings but was open and empty tonight.

A single waiter tending tables gave Georges a sidelong glance, then ignored him. Behind the bar, Aristide Blanc was serving drinks. He looked peevish.

For several seconds, Georges stood there, tapping on the bar, while Blanc filled a customer's jug of wine. Finally, when the customer left, Georges introduced himself politely as a gendarme out of uniform and received a sour look. 'I need to ask you a few questions privately.' He gestured towards a table near Anne's.

The barman shook his head. 'I'm busy until midnight. I might give you a minute then.'

Georges put a little ice in his voice. 'That won't do. Would you prefer that I summon the Guard? We could have our conversation at the police bureau.'

The barman's jaw tightened. He beckoned the waiter. 'Tend the bar for a few minutes.'

Georges led him to a chair that offered Michou a good view for sketching.

The barman glared at Georges, 'The National Guard pestered me all day with stupid questions. I couldn't help them, so they left here none the wiser. They succeeded, however, in scaring away my customers. This has been a bad day for business. And to make matters worse, the political club that usually meets here didn't come this evening, out of respect for their murdered comrade.'

Georges expressed his sympathy, said he wouldn't be long, and asked who had been present on the night of the murder. The barman gave him a list that he had prepared for the police. It included Flamme and Boyer.

'Tell me what you remember about the meeting.'

The barman explained that about forty men gathered in the back section of the room. At first, they complained about the high price of bread, the low wages for artisans and the lack of work in the city. Then they moved on to politics and what the Assembly was planning to do for them. Not much, they concluded.

'I was running back and forth, serving them wine, so I gathered only scattered impressions. Flamme and Boyer talked the most and argued with each other about the new constitution and the clergy. Flamme's opinions seemed popular with the artisans. They shouted down Boyer. He became angry and left early.'

'Did he make any threats?'

'None that I know of. Flamme called out the word "bastard" as Boyer left. I didn't hear his response but I could imagine. His face was purple with rage. I've often heard him swear by Satan and all that's evil.'

'Really?' Georges remarked. 'That sounds odd, coming from a declared atheist.'

The barman shrugged and went on. 'The meeting ended at about eleven and everyone but Flamme soon went home. He stayed until I closed at midnight. By that time he was tipsy. I had to help him leave the tavern and send him off towards his room.'

'When you were out on the street with him, did you see anyone loitering nearby?'

He shook his head. 'It was dark. I had a lantern, but I didn't look around. I was in a hurry to clean up.'

'Really!' Georges' head reared back in mock disbelief. 'You sent him off alone in the dark! Every night for a week he had left this place with an escort. He needed one badly, for God's sake. He had insulted Guiscard the master builder, his bitter enemy for years.' Georges glared at the man. 'You must have understood that Flamme's life was in danger. What was he drinking?'

'Brandy.' Hints of anxiety began to show in the barman's eyes.

Georges looked askance. 'His usual drink? Did he pay for it?'

The barman hesitated. 'No. In a friendly way, I asked if he'd like to try it.'

Georges studied the barman's hard, narrow eyes. He didn't look at all like a kindly, generous person. 'Why did you keep him at your table and then let him walk off in the dark alone and drunk? His friends, even the police, are sure to wonder.'

Georges' sceptical, lightly menacing tone seemed to unnerve the barman. He flustered, 'I owed him some free drinks. He helped found the club and had brought in his artisans. That was good for business.' The barman appeared to push back against Georges' insinuations. 'I'm not Flamme's keeper,' he muttered, 'and I'm not obliged to tell him what he should drink or how much. Anyway, after the meeting, he told his escort that they were free to leave. "I'm armed," he said and showed them his pistol. Then he said, "Guiscard must be bored by now and won't bother with me."'

Georges pressed on. 'You're still in trouble. You should have stopped serving Flamme and sent him home while he still could defend himself. His friends will think you're greedy and encouraged him to buy drinks long after he should. They may punish you.' Georges paused and said slowly in a low voice, 'Or, perhaps his assassin paid you to send him out drunk and alone. Perhaps he spoke only of beating, not killing him. Am I right?'

By this time, the barman's brow was dripping sweat. 'You're leading me on. I'll not say another word. You can't prove anything. You should leave now.'

Georges nodded. 'I'm going to have to check a few points. I'll be back.' He took a last look around, then met the barman's eyes. 'By the way, I understand that you lease this room from Monsieur Guiscard. Has he spoken to you lately about Flamme?'

The barman was breathing heavily, and he gripped the table for support. His complexion turned livid. He stammered, 'You must go. I've nothing more to say.'

SIXTEEN
A Hidden Past

11 June

The next morning, Anne and Paul were at breakfast in the garden, when Georges arrived. She had invited him to join them. While spooning sugar into his coffee, he asked Anne, 'How well could you and Michou observe the scene last night at The Red Rooster?'

'Perfectly,' she replied and handed him a folder at her side. 'Here are her sketches of the barman and the plan of the tavern. She finished them in her studio afterwards. I've kept copies.'

He scanned them and smiled. 'Excellent image of the barman, a man with troublesome secrets on his conscience. The sketch should help connect him to other suspects involved in Flamme's death.'

'Was the killing a conspiracy?' asked Saint-Martin, raising an eyebrow.

'Possibly,' Georges replied. 'The killer might have had a partner, most likely the barman, to signal that the victim was leaving the tavern. A third person could have ordered the killing and paid for it.'

'And who would want to do that? Monsieur Guiscard?'

'A strong suspect,' Georges replied. 'He had both the means and the motive. But his behaviour on Place des Victoires tells me that he would have preferred to kill Flamme with his bare hands. He could have done it. But I have to admit that he has a strong alibi. His porter, Luc Thierry, a reliable witness, saw him return to the house on Rue Colbert before midnight.'

Anne groaned. 'He was my chief suspect. His evil deeds richly deserve punishment.'

'But not for this particular crime,' cautioned Paul.

Georges sipped his coffee, bit into a piece of bread, and then addressed Anne. 'You may still suspect Guiscard. He could have slipped out of a rear door with time enough to kill Flamme and to return. No one saw him.'

'How deeply involved was the barman at The Red Rooster?' Paul asked.

Georges thought for a moment before replying. 'I suspect that the killer might have paid him to set Flamme up for the assassination by plying him with brandy. The barman was probably led to believe that Flamme would be beaten rather than killed.'

Anne mused, 'Then, wouldn't the barman know the killer's identity?'

'Right,' Georges replied. 'And he'll keep it to himself. He's terrified that the killer might silence him.'

As they finished their coffee, Paul said, 'The investigation goes on. We need to find out what Boyer did with the rest of the evening. He's still a possible suspect.'

Georges added, 'We should also question Marthe Boyer and Patrick O'Fallon.'

Anne must have grimaced. Georges met her eye. 'Sorry, Madame, but your Patrick is a potential suspect. Though you didn't see him last night among those lurking outside that tavern, he could have arrived after you left. If so, he probably was clever enough to arrange with Marthe Boyer for an alibi. She could even have been his partner in the killing.'

'I'll start my investigation today with Marthe,' said Anne. 'She knows both men, loves the one and hates the other. It will be a challenge to get the truth from her.'

Anne put on her disguise as a maid, hid Michou's sketches in a shopping basket, and went to the Boyers' apartment. By asking around, she learned that Marthe Boyer regularly walked to the Central Markets at about nine in the morning to buy food for dinner. Anne waited for the woman to appear, scanning the crowded street in vain for Rat-face, her husband's spy. In a minute she recognized one of his associates, shabbily dressed, loitering across the street.

Promptly at nine, as the sun came from behind a cloud, Marthe walked out on to the street, a basket on her arm, and set off slowly in the direction of the Central Markets. She wore a bonnet that largely concealed her face, and her steps seemed painful. The spy followed her. Anne followed them at a safe distance.

As Marthe approached the market, the spy left her and went into a tavern. Anne paused for a few seconds, and then she quickly closed the distance to Marthe. To Anne's surprise, Marthe passed by several food stalls and went directly to the great merchant church of Saint-Eustache. Blinded by the bright light outside, Anne's eyes took a few moments to adjust to the dark interior. Marthe had gone to a side altar and was lighting a taper. She stiffly lowered herself to the floor on her knees and soon began to sob.

Anne approached and put a hand on the woman's shoulder. Marthe stopped sobbing, crossed herself, and tried to struggle to her feet. Anne lifted her up and offered her a handkerchief.

Only now did Marthe recognize her. A look of horror came over her battered face. 'Oh no! You mustn't come near me. If my husband were to find out, he'd beat me again, even worse than before. I'm not supposed to go to the puppet theatre or to ever see you again. He's convinced that you're a friend of the priests and are plotting against him.' She hesitated briefly. 'Fortunately, he doesn't know about Patrick, or he'd kill me.'

'I understand. Don't worry,' Anne insisted. 'I'll not keep you long. Let's move to another chapel that's less exposed.'

When they were alone, Anne asked, 'Do you recognize this man?' She showed Marthe one of Michou's sketches of The Red Rooster's barman.

Marthe held the sketch at arm's length, squinted, drew it close. 'I've seen him before. He spoke to my husband a few years ago while I still could hear and Jacques seemed interested in me. We were walking in the garden of the Palais-Royal. This man came up to us like an old acquaintance and said his name was Aristide Blanc. At first, Jacques seemed annoyed but he invited the man to our apartment. For an hour they were alone. I listened at the door but could only hear the rumble of their voices. When the man left, I must have looked curious. Jacques remarked, "He's an uncle from Chartres, needs money, and is looking for work." Later, I found out that he was unlucky in the gambling dens.'

Marthe's brow furrowed. 'Why do you ask about him? Has he done something wrong?'

'I can't say yet. He's now the barman at The Red Rooster and may be the last person to have seen Armand Flamme alive.'

Marthe became very still as she appeared to realize that her husband might be linked in yet another way to Flamme's death.

Anne continued. 'So it's all the more important to search your rooms for that gold watch you told me about yesterday. It appears to be a crucial piece of evidence. Does Boyer know that we're interested in it?'

'I don't think so. I said nothing.'

'Good. I need to know a time when both of you will be away from the apartment.'

'Boyer said, if I behave as he commands, he will treat me to an equestrian show at the Circus in the Palais-Royal. That would be three days from now. I should be more or less healed by then.'

'Perfect. For now, all I want you to do is to give me a plan of your rooms and show me how to get into them.' She paused. 'And, by the way, a spy working for Rat-face followed you to the market and is waiting in a tavern for your return.'

She smiled dryly. 'He takes Rat-face's place across the street from me. Tipples strong spirits. By nightfall, he's too drunk to stand. I'm sure he's not pretending.'

Hmm, Anne thought. The spy wouldn't notice Marthe if she were to slip out later at night to help Patrick. She shuddered at the thought of these two ill-starred persons clubbing Flamme to death. Unfortunately, the idea was at least plausible. She would have to work hard to prove it false.

Later that morning, Anne met Patrick at the institute for the deaf for a lesson in speech. He read words and phrases from cards, while she articulated them slowly and clearly. With frequent repetition he mastered them, though with a heavy 'deaf' accent. She could then say them at a conversational speed. The process was painfully slow and uncertain. Yet he persisted, usually with a smile. By nature he didn't seem to be a patient man. She wondered if some of his patience came from working with her.

Anne felt a sense of urgency in these exercises. His father's death had thrown the young deaf man on his own in an unfriendly, sometimes hostile environment. To survive he needed every skill in communication that she could impart. To do that well she had to know him better.

She began gently. 'What are your plans, Patrick, now that Father O'Fallon is gone?'

'I want to begin training in the printer's trade. He left me a small trust fund for that purpose.'

'Have you thought of starting a family?'

He nodded, a wry expression on his face. 'I've thought of it often. But to have a family I would need money.'

And a woman, Anne said to herself. In his eyes Anne detected a powerful pent-up feeling. He was thinking of Marthe. Nearly the same age, they were a good match and coping with the same disability. Both were religious. And, finally, they seemed to be in love. But of course there was a major obstacle: Marthe was married.

Unbeckoned, Anne shuddered. The temptation to remove that obstacle must be powerful. She tried to sound out Patrick's attitude towards Boyer.

'In the past you've said that you held both Flamme and Boyer responsible for your father's death and would like to kill both of them. Now that one of them is dead do you still feel that way about the other?'

'I do,' he replied. 'Though Boyer didn't throw the stone, his bitter words against priests encouraged Flamme.'

Anne pointed out that Boyer and Flamme disagreed about killing priests. Boyer argued that it should be done only at the conclusion of a legal process, similar to trying someone for acts of treason. Seen in that light Boyer perhaps wasn't responsible for Father O'Fallon's death.

Patrick shook his head. 'That sounds like a distinction without a difference. Armand Flamme and Jacques Boyer are two rogues cut from the same cloth. Both are atheists, enemies of God and of the friends of God, such as Father O'Fallon. In addition, Monsieur Boyer is cruel towards his wife, Marthe. For that reason alone, he deserves to be severely punished.'

'I'm sure he does. But must you be his executioner? That should be a magistrate's job.'

He scoffed at the idea. 'Unfortunately, the police and the magistrates of this new regime don't act fairly and impartially, however much they chatter about liberty and equality. They neglect the poor; they prevent workingmen from organizing unions. And, they render justice according to a person's political opinions and the club to which he belongs. Jacques Boyer must be punished for his crimes. If the law won't do it, I will.'

Anne felt her heart pounding with anxiety, but she held Patrick in a level gaze. 'It's true that the present regime is weak and often incompetent, and it fails in many of its responsibilities. But I can assure you that at least one magistrate, Pierre Roland, upholds the highest standards in the law. He and Colonel Saint-Martin, my husband, will bring Monsieur Boyer to justice. I urge you to cooperate with them.' She paused to focus his attention. 'Will you promise to avoid any rash act of revenge?'

Patrick averted his eyes, wrung his hands, and was grimly silent. Anne stared at him intently. Minutes passed. Finally, he sighed, then signed, 'I'll do as you say. My father told me that the colonel is an honourable man and a brave and skilful officer. I'll trust him.'

That evening at home, Anne related to Paul what she had learned from Marthe in Saint-Eustache and from Patrick. 'Can you imagine? Her husband promised to take her to the Circus if she behaved.'

Paul shook his head in disbelief.

Anne continued. 'Poor woman, married to a devil. One day he charms her; the next day he beats her. For her sake, if for no other reason, Patrick would surely want to kill him. But I think he'll keep his promise to me and leave Boyer to you.'

Anne showed him the plans of the Boyer rooms. 'In a few days, while they are at the Circus, we could search his study and hopefully find the gold watch.'

Paul reflected for a few moments. 'Georges and I shall visit Boyer tomorrow morning in advance of the search. Georges might have an opportunity to survey the study with an eye to where Boyer might hide his secrets. Meanwhile, I'll question him about Flamme and who might have killed him.'

SEVENTEEN
Failed Alibi

12 June

At mid morning the next day, a Sunday, Saint-Martin and his adjutant arrived at Boyer's door, equipped with authority from Mayor Bailly. He had ordered them to inquire into the death of Armand Flamme. Marthe showed them into a small entryway and went to fetch her husband. Saint-Martin began to feel a bit apprehensive. Boyer had a mercurial temperament and an acidic tongue. He also publicly condemned the monarchy. But he was capable of a disarming smile and a gracious manner. An official visitor like Saint-Martin didn't know what kind of reception to expect.

This morning, for whatever reason, Boyer chose to be a good host, perhaps to suggest that he had nothing to hide. He greeted the officers with proper courtesy and led them through the apartment to his study. It was a large room, a scholar's haunt. Books filled shelves from floor to ceiling, precarious piles of newspapers covered most of the floor. Ink had spattered Boyer's housecoat. His fingers were inky, and there were streaks of ink on his chin. Saint-Martin imagined him writing his pamphlets in a furious, inky haze.

'We are looking into the death of Armand Flamme,' began Saint-Martin, taking a chair across the writing table from Boyer. Georges sat off to one side. Boyer merely nodded with polite interest.

'We've been told,' Saint-Martin continued, 'that you knew him better than most. You and he were members of the same political club that meets at The Red Rooster. He also has been a visitor in this apartment and your ardent supporter in the city.'

Boyer's genial expression scarcely changed, only his eyes grew wary. 'Flamme and I shared certain political opinions. You might say that we were allies in the struggle for greater freedom and equality in this country.' He seemed about to launch into a speech.

'But,' interjected Saint-Martin. 'You were heard to quarrel at the club. He aggravated you to the point that you walked out of meetings. What were the issues?'

'He was inclined to rash or precipitous actions and ignored my counsels of prudence. I disapproved of his insult to Monsieur Guiscard and his assault on the priest O'Fallon in the garden of the Palais-Royal. He took the law into his own hands. In a truly democratic republic only the representatives of the people would have the authority to judge or punish those men.'

'Do you know who might have killed him?'

'I suppose it was someone whom he had unwisely offended. My list of suspects is probably similar to yours. Monsieur Guiscard, the master builder, and Patrick, the priest's servant, both had strong motives to harm him. There may be others unknown to me. For much of our lives Flamme and I moved in different circles. He was a rude, ignorant, and uncultivated man.'

'I must ask you, sir, as I have other acquaintances of the victim, where were you on the night of his murder?'

'I was at The Red Rooster for a meeting of the club. Afterwards I went to the Café Marcel on the Boulevard. The rest of the night I spent in Madame Lebrun's brothel in the Palais-Royal. Both institutions are well known.'

Saint-Martin glanced at his adjutant. Georges shook his head. He had no questions. 'We'll move on then. We may have more to ask later.'

Out on the street, the colonel asked, 'What do you think, Georges?'

He drew a handkerchief from his pocket and reflected for a moment. 'The café and the brothel might confirm his alibi. We must check. Our problem is to discover a sufficient motive.' The adjutant patted perspiration from his bald pate. 'I wonder, where does his money come from? His writing earns him nothing. And he isn't living off an inheritance – his father died a pauper. Yet, he owns a substantial library and buys many newspapers. His apartment consists of three large, well-furnished rooms and is located in a decent area north of the Palais-Royal. He frequents fashionable cafés, restaurants, and brothels.'

'He must have a hidden patron, possibly the Duc d'Orléans,' said Saint-Martin. 'What else, Georges?'

He tucked his handkerchief back into his pocket. 'We must find out where he hides his diaries, letters, and perhaps that gold watch. I'll have to check the usual places: in a cabinet behind a shelf of books, under a floorboard, behind a wall panel, in a hidden drawer in his writing table.'

'That's a task for another day,' Saint-Martin declared. 'Let's have lunch. Afterwards we'll check his alibi.'

Later that Sunday afternoon, Saint-Martin and Charpentier set out to trace Boyer's movements on the night that Flamme was murdered. They knew that Boyer left his political club at The Red Rooster early. At Café Marcel on the Boulevard a waiter confirmed that Boyer was there with friends until ten.

The two officers followed his tracks from Café Marcel to the Palais-Royal's Valois arcade. Madame Lebrun's brothel was above an elegant café. A cluster of painted women were soliciting customers outside the entrance. Though it was Sunday, business seemed brisk. Georges asked one of the older women if the mistress of the house was available.

Yes, was the reply. She was upstairs overseeing the preparation of food and drink for the evening's entertainment. The colonel asked the doorman to take them to her. The servant hesitated for a moment, anxiety gathering in his eyes. In full uniform, unsmiling, the two visitors presented an intimidating appearance. The servant studied them closely, realized he had no choice, and led them upstairs into an expensively furnished parlour.

In a few minutes Madame Lebrun arrived, painted and powdered for the evening, and gave them a warm welcome. A decade or more past her prime, she still had the grace and fine features of a successful courtesan. Her cooperation with Saint-Martin and his adjutant – and with police in general – was an important reason for her long and profitable career. They could count on her for credible information. In return, they refrained from harassing her or closing down her establishment.

She seated them and asked with an engaging smile, 'What may I do for you gentlemen?'

Saint-Martin spoke first. 'Monsieur Jacques Boyer has told us that he arrived here a little after ten on the 9th and stayed several hours. Would you please check your records?'

Madame Lebrun replied, 'That's unnecessary. I recall his arrival – it was earlier than usual. He also announced the time with fanfare so that I would take notice and surely remember. I realized that he was preparing an alibi for some nefarious reason. In the same manner, he announced his departure at dawn.' She smiled. 'Your questions lead me to believe that my impression was correct.'

Saint-Martin didn't doubt her word. She had proven trustworthy during previous investigations. He signalled to Georges to go ahead with questions.

'Could Monsieur Boyer have slipped out of the building for a couple of hours and sneaked back in?' he asked.

'I suppose he could have,' she replied. 'He's a frequent guest and probably knows the building well. He could have gone out the back way.' The madame shook her head. 'But he was in bed with one of my women all night. She would have noticed him leaving.'

'May we talk to her?' asked Georges.

'She's getting ready for the evening's guests,' replied Lebrun grudgingly. 'But I'll summon her.'

A few minutes later, a pale young woman entered the parlour in a dressing gown. Yes, she knew Boyer from previous visits. He was one of her more agreeable customers. Georges pressed her to contradict Boyer. But she insisted that she and he had slept together through that night.

'Did you have something to drink before going to bed?' Georges asked.

'Yes,' she replied. 'Monsieur Boyer had brought a bottle of red wine. When we got to the room, we drank it with a little bread and cheese. Then he served the two of us a few small glasses of cognac, and we went to bed.'

Georges tilted his head, as if curious. 'When you've been drinking in the evening, do you usually get up in the middle of the night to relieve yourself?'

'Yes, I'm sure. But this time with Monsieur Boyer I slept through the night like a log.' She paused uneasily and reflected. 'I suppose he drugged me. Why would he do that?'

'We think,' replied Saint-Martin, 'that he may have left you at about eleven and sneaked out into the street to kill a man, then returned to your bed.'

Her eyes grew large as saucers; her hand flew to her mouth in horror.

*　　*　　*

Once outside in the garden again, the two men sat on a remote, shaded bench. The colonel asked, 'What do you think, Monsieur Charpentier?'

'Boyer could have killed Flamme. That's all the more plausible since he's gone to such lengths to create an alibi.'

'Yes,' Saint-Martin agreed, 'though he hasn't given us an obvious motive, he's now high on our list of suspects.'

'So, where shall we look for a possible motive?'

'Not in the usual places,' the colonel conceded. 'Neither money nor women appear to be involved.'

Georges reflected for a moment. 'When he and the victim have quarrelled, it's been over politics. And it's been hot and personal.'

Saint-Martin fanned himself with his hat. 'Perhaps Flamme went too far with a malicious, insulting remark. It might have touched Boyer on a particularly sensitive spot and provoked a powerful desire for revenge. Our task now is to uncover that spot.'

That afternoon at home, Paul joined Anne for a cool fruit drink under a tree in the garden. He passed on to her the results of the investigation into Boyer's alibi. 'He could have killed Flamme, but we just don't know why. I don't expect to find evidence directly linking him to the crime until I can search his rooms.'

'Probably, the answer to his motivation lies hidden in his character,' Anne suggested. She showed Paul a placard. 'I found it in the garden of the Palais-Royal. Boyer is going to speak at a meeting of the Jacobin club early this evening. The public is allowed in the balcony. We could observe him.'

Paul agreed. 'He should have something to say about Flamme's murder. It's on everyone's lips. Georges will join us.'

EIGHTEEN
The Jacobins

12 June

Early in the evening, Paul, Anne and Georges went to the Jacobins' hall near their home and were fortunate to find good seats in the public balcony. In a few more minutes it was packed – and very warm. For comfort's sake, she wore a light muslin, high-waisted gown and carried a fan. Paul's suit was made of a thin silk fabric. Still, he was soon patting his brow. Georges was dressed as a provincial businessman in plain brown wool. His face was bright pink and perspiring.

With the aid of her opera glass, Anne searched the balcony for familiar faces and found Guiscard sitting at a distance. He was alone and appeared anxious and preoccupied, not at all his robust self. She handed the glass to Georges. He studied Guiscard intensely for a minute or two, then returned the glass.

'He's not the same,' Georges remarked. 'His porter reports to me that ever since Flamme's death, Guiscard has been unusually irritable and disorganized, often snaps at people. He's probably here tonight out of fear that Boyer might implicate him in Flamme's murder. That could damage Guiscard's good reputation among leaders of the new regime and force him into a costly and uncertain legal defence.'

Among members of the club on the benches below, Anne recognized Pierre Roland the magistrate, seated near the balcony. He and she made eye contact and discreetly waved. Paul leaned towards Anne and whispered. 'Mayor Bailly is also here today, the slender, dignified man dressed in black, seated in the centre. He's a member of the club but attends rarely.'

Anne studied Bailly with her glass. 'His face is gaunt and pale. He looks ill.'

Paul nodded. 'The pressures on the mayor have undermined his health. Still, as the city's chief magistrate, he apparently believes that he must listen to what Boyer has to say about

Flamme's murder and perhaps take certain precautions. Otherwise, this day could end in a riot among the lower classes. He also must glance over his shoulder at his political rivals.'

Paul pointed to a man making his way to a front bench. 'There's one of them, Monsieur Pétion. I've heard that he aspires to the mayor's office.'

After the meeting was called to order, the presiding officer asked the seated members and guests of the club if any of them wished to speak. Boyer rose and approached the speaker's podium. The president gave him a sceptical glance and asked for the issue that he wished to address.

Boyer said loudly that he would comment on the cruel murder of the patriot Armand Flamme. There was a stir of anticipation among the members.

The president remarked, 'We're aware that you knew him. Go ahead.'

With a polite bow, Boyer thanked him, then climbed up on to a raised speaker's platform. For a moment he silently surveyed the audience, gathering their attention. Then he briefly introduced himself. His voice was clear, powerful, and well trained in public speaking. When he came to speak of Flamme, he lowered his voice to a tone of awe and reverence. 'Armand Flamme,' he declared, 'was a great tribune of the people, akin to the brothers Gracchi in the ancient Roman republic. He fought tirelessly for our liberty, equality, and fraternity. Unfortunately, a cowardly conspiracy has struck him down from behind in the dead of night. His killers must be identified and punished.'

'Do you know who did it?' demanded a doubtful voice from the members' benches.

Another member shouted, 'Flamme was a vile demagogue. Good riddance!'

Other voices joined in a discordant mêlée of opinions concerning Flamme, mostly negative. Pétion and a few others futilely urged Boyer on.

The presiding officer hammered for order. The roar slowly subsided and Boyer was allowed to continue. He adopted at first a conciliatory tone. 'Armand Flamme was a zealous patriot, but was sometimes given to rash or intemperate remarks. I myself have felt the lash of his tongue. Still, our fraternal quarrels must not divert our attention away from the enemies who would enslave us. Their agents lurk in dark places, eager to strike down our leaders. Flamme was the first to fall. We should resolve that he be the last. I've gathered enough evidence to identify the chief suspect and shall report him to our National Guard. At this time, I'll not name him. I'll only say that he's the servant of a nonjuring priest. The police know him from earlier, violent attacks on patriots in the Palais-Royal.'

Boyer paused while the audience buzzed with speculation about the killer's identity.

Anne turned to Paul and whispered into his ear, 'He's accusing Patrick!'

Paul whispered back, 'That's a clever tactic to divert suspicion away from Boyer himself.'

Georges borrowed the opera glass. 'I'm focused on Guiscard. He's smiling now and looks relaxed, perhaps relieved that Boyer didn't accuse him. Still, I wonder what else is going through his mind?' He returned the glass. 'I'll leave now. I must speak to his porter again. You can tell me later what our speaker said.' Georges worked his way out of the balcony.

Now Boyer began to raise his voice. 'Citizen Flamme's killer is merely a tool of the forces arrayed against us: the king and his ministers, erstwhile aristocrats, nonjuring clergy, and many less obvious minions of despotism.

'Enemies from within will continue to threaten our liberty until the National Assembly tears up the new constitution it has written, that bastard compromise between liberty and tyranny. The Assembly must establish instead a truly democratic, secular republic.'

Pétion and a few radicals applauded. But many in the audience began to murmur. Disputes broke out in the hall.

Anne looked to Paul. 'Is the idea of a republic so unpopular here among the Jacobins?' She didn't follow politics closely.

'Most members of the club have committed themselves to the new constitution and the idea of a limited monarchy.' Paul pointed to a man, waving his arms and shouting, leading the protest against Boyer. 'That's Monsieur Barnave. With Lafayette and Bailly, he believes that the people need leaders endowed with sound judgement and experience in public affairs, wealthy propertied men like themselves. They've stripped the king of any real power. He's largely a ceremonial figure, a symbol of the nation's unity.'

Anne glanced down at Pierre Roland. He was rigidly still, as if in pain.

Paul followed her eyes. 'Boyer's perversion of justice seems to drive our poor Roland to distraction.'

By now Boyer was shouting over the noise. 'The king and his allies, the clergy, are traitors to the revolution and must be eliminated. Having killed Armand Flamme, they are devising schemes to further undermine our liberty. I intend to expose them.'

His remarks produced uproar. 'Give us proof,' cried the protesters in unison. For a moment Boyer ceased speaking. When the president had restored order, he told Boyer that he wouldn't be allowed to continue. 'You've said enough.'

He ignored the president and continued from where he left off.

The president ruled him out of order and commanded him to take a seat. He refused to leave the platform and launched into a tirade against the new constitution. The president ordered bailiffs to eject him. As they dragged him from the room, he threatened to expose the president and other leading club members. He shouted, 'You're in league with these traitors and guilty of crimes against the people.'

'I wonder,' Anne mused, as they left the hall, 'if there's any substance to Boyer's charge of a royal conspiracy against the people? Surely it's false as far as Patrick is concerned. If he killed Flamme, he did it solely for personal, not political, reasons. So what's left of Boyer's claim?'

'It has a basis in the facts,' Paul replied. 'Over the past two years, partisans of the king, like the Baron Breteuil, have tried at home and abroad to forcibly restore the old regime. Boyer may have discovered evidence of a plot and will try to expose it. I must find out what he means by the king's treachery.'

'I hate to think that Boyer could persuade the public that Patrick was involved.'

Paul shook his head. 'Paris has just become a more dangerous place for Patrick.'

NINETEEN
Treachery to be Exposed

12 June

Georges hurried from the Jacobins to The Nimble Heifer. He had another appointment with Guiscard's porter, Luc Thierry, at seven in the evening. Arriving a few minutes early, Georges entered the tavern by the back door and went directly to the room that Cécile Tremblay had reserved for him. This extra caution was due to the porter's growing fear that Guiscard's men might become suspicious of these meetings and report him to their master. Precisely at seven Thierry also came in through the back door and joined Georges. He seemed unusually agitated.

While they were settling down at the table, Madame Tremblay arrived with a jug of red wine and a pair of glasses. 'Behave,' she said with a wink and left them.

Georges poured. They raised the glasses, saluted each other, and nearly emptied the glasses before getting down to business. Thierry needed that first glass of wine to calm his nerves.

'I've news for you tonight, Georges. My agent – Guiscard's clerk – has found a key to the office and made a copy.'

'Perfect!' Georges exclaimed. 'Now we'll watch for an opportunity to search unobserved. In the meantime, I'll try to imagine where he might hide his secrets. Under the best of circumstances, we won't have time for a comprehensive search nor perfect conditions. I'd like to go directly to the hiding place. And I have an idea.'

When Georges first interrogated Guiscard in his office, he had focused on its centrepiece, the enormous writing table. Since then he had speculated on what the table could mean to Guiscard and how he might use it.

It was an obvious symbol of his wealth and importance that he delighted to show off. But it wasn't just about vanity. Guiscard also had a practical bent: the table should serve a useful purpose.

And what could seem more useful to such a man than to house the true record of his success in business.

The account book and other secret papers *had* to be hidden in the table.

It was growing dark as Boyer hurried from the Jacobins' hall to The Red Rooster tavern. Tonight was the Citizens club's first meeting following Flamme's death. He felt he had to regain the members' trust, reassert their republican principles, and revive their hopes for the revolution. Last but not least, he had to persuade them that a royalist agent had killed Flamme.

By the time he arrived, breathless and sweating, the club had already assembled in the back room, more sombre than usual, and was engaged in a desultory discussion of recent events. He took a few minutes to greet members personally, addressing individual concerns, and cultivating good will especially among the artisans who followed Flamme. The violent death of their leader seemed to have chastened them.

When drinks were served and everyone settled down, Boyer called the meeting to order. First, he addressed their questions about the death of Flamme. 'A suspect has been interrogated,' he reported, 'and the investigation continues.'

Several members asked almost in unison, 'Who is the suspect?'

'He's the servant of a certain deceased, traitorous priest, known to the National Guard for his violence towards patriots. A guard recalled having noticed him loitering on the square, stalking Flamme. The servant's motive is revenge for the death of the priest his master. But he is also suspected of being part of a wide-ranging plot to overthrow the revolution and restore the old despotic regime.'

The members gave Boyer closer attention and more respect than in the past. One of the artisans remarked to him, 'You don't need to give us the villain's name. We know him and will find a way to deal with him ourselves. We don't trust the courts to do the right thing.'

Boyer turned next to the issue of the royalist plot. Rumours of such plots were rife and intrigued the public. So his audience was disposed to hear him out. They were discontented with the slow, fitful pace of reforms that favoured the rich and brought few benefits to the common people.

'The king,' Boyer insisted, 'may seem patriotic but deep in his heart he's the sworn enemy of a truly democratic nation. His recent public protestations in support of the National Assembly are false and hypocritical. He and the queen have also tried to deceive the public with certain patriotic acts, such as attending Easter mass with clergy who had taken the oath to the constitution. But at heart he remains a dangerous tyrant, a false patriot.'

Suddenly, a powerful anger overcame Boyer. He clenched his fists until the knuckles turned white. 'I'm convinced,' he declared ominously, 'that a great treachery and betrayal of the nation is afoot. And I intend to stop it.'

His audience turned to each other, with sceptical glances. A man shouted, 'We all hear the same unfounded rumours. What do you know that we don't?'

'And what will you do about it?' asked another.

'You'll soon find out. Politics in France will never be the same.' He took a long draught, emptying his glass, and left them shaking their heads.

Outside the tavern Boyer breathed in the fresh night air. He had to clear his head. A strenuous task lay ahead. Weeks ago, he had picked up on rumours of the king planning to flee from Paris and organize a counter-revolution. He had begun in earnest an investigation among servants at the Tuileries. Some of them could surely be bribed to reveal the royal secrets.

He now set off in the direction of the palace, hoping to contact a maid, Paulette, the mistress of a National Guard officer. She seemed willing to share inside news from the royal court. As *porte-chaise des affaires* to Marie Antoinette, the servant in charge of the queen's personal privy, Paulette was well placed to keep a gimlet eye on the activity of the royal family.

When Boyer first met her, she claimed that she could confirm rumours about a royal attempt to escape from Paris. He was wary and suspicious. She called herself a patriot but she also wanted money for any information that she gave. He paid her but kept this contact to himself for the time being. If he worked alone, he reasoned, he might be able to extort money from persons who were implicated in the plot. He might also greatly enhance his own reputation as a patriot and not have to share it with rivals.

At subsequent meetings with Paulette, he tried to gain more precise details of the supposed royal plot. On a recent occasion the maid told him that the queen had suspiciously packed and shipped her cosmetics case, as if about to go away on a long trip. The maid had also reported that Count Fersen, the queen's Swedish lover, was frequently sneaking in and out of the palace in disguise, dressed in a long grey coat and a round hat. What was he up to? He didn't need a disguise in order to visit the queen. Finally, she noticed that Fersen seemed to place unusual trust in one of his servants, Jeanne Degere.

Boyer checked her out. She had worked for Fersen for years and earlier also for his father. Suspecting that the Swede might use her as a courier, Boyer followed her on several occasions from the palace to rooms rented on Place des Victoires by a rich Russian baroness, Madame de Korff, known as Fersen's friend. She was scheduled to leave Paris for Russia in June. Mademoiselle Degere also visited a coachmaker who was building an unusually large and sumptuous vehicle ostensibly for the baroness. Boyer asked himself, Why would Fersen be so interested in a Russian aristocrat's travel arrangements, unless as cover for a royal escape? Over the next few days, Boyer had devised a plan.

Tonight, Paulette was waiting for Boyer at a small, dark, private door to the palace. She whispered in his ear. 'Jeanne Degere has just spoken urgently with Count Fersen and is about to leave the palace through this door. From hiding, I saw him give her a message to deliver to an address on Place des Victoires. She'll hide it in her bodice. He told her that the message contains vital information in a matter of the utmost importance.'

'How shall I recognize her?'

'She's wearing a black woollen cape with a hood. You'll see her soon when she passes by. We must hide now.'

Boyer assumed that Jeanne would walk to Place des Victoires. He quickly reckoned that he might be able to intercept her en route.

He and Paulette hid behind a nearby hedge. Within a few minutes, the door opened. Holding aloft a lantern, the count stepped out, looked around, then beckoned Jeanne. She slipped out quickly. They exchanged a few brief words. Then she walked rapidly towards Rue Saint-Honoré. Boyer set his plan in motion.

The bells of Saint-Roch tolled midnight.

TWENTY
The Courier

13 June

Jeanne Degere patted the message sewn into her bodice, then set off at a brisk pace from the palace. The bells of Saint-Roch were ringing midnight. At Rue Saint-Honoré she turned right. She felt safe late at night in Paris only on well-lighted main streets. Even at midnight she wasn't alone on this one. Men and women in fashionable clothes were travelling to or from their pleasures in brightly painted carriages, equipped with oil lamps. A small part of her envied them. But there was scant place in her life for fashionable clothes or restaurants. Since childhood, she had worn only the plain woollen garb of a domestic maid.

For the most part, she was content. Count Fersen was a generous and considerate master. She had a pleasant room and good food in the house he rented on Rue Matignon. Above all, she enjoyed his trust – it gave her great satisfaction. And he sent her on missions that were challenging, sometimes even dangerous. She was also grateful to him for the company of her older brother Benoit Degere, a retired soldier from Fersen's regiment. The count had hired him as a servant last year. Apart from a damaged leg, he was still agile and strong, a reassuring companion on a dark night.

In this spring of 1791 Jeanne was serving as a secret courier between Fersen, the queen and certain others involved in planning an event that had to be secret. Early on, Jeanne determined not to pry open the messages as other couriers sometimes did. They would sell the contents. She'd rather not know any more than the count wanted her to know. Even under torture, she wouldn't reveal his secrets. She often carried messages between him and Madame de Korff. Recently, she became concerned that someone might be following her.

Today she had complained to her brother.

He had replied, 'We'll lay a trap and catch him tonight.'

As she passed Rue de Richelieu, she glanced to her left. From across the street, her brother signalled that she wasn't being followed. That eased her mind. She gave another reassuring pat to the message.

Benoit limped across the street and joined her. 'Does it hurt?' she asked, pointing to his damaged leg.

He nodded. 'Fersen had me running all day with messages. He has a big, complicated scheme on his mind.'

Together they continued on Rue Saint-Honoré a short distance, then turned left into Rue des Bons Enfants. This was the route that she usually followed on her missions to the de Korff rooms on Place des Victoires. Earlier in the evening the street would have been crowded with tipsy revellers from the Palais-Royal nearby, filling the air with their shouts and songs.

But at this time, late at night, the street was empty and sparsely lighted and felt strangely silent. She was happy to have her brother at her side. Though war had taken its toll, he was still a brave and powerful man. Her missions usually took place during the daylight hours. But this week was different. The count was running from place to place in Paris, arranging something really important. She knew better than to ask. He said he was sorry to send her out at night, but he had no choice. There would soon be an end to it, God willing.

These musings began to raise vague apprehensions in her mind. She shuddered but continued walking. Then she detected a movement in the darkened entrance to an abandoned building on her right. Suddenly alert, she lightly touched her brother on the shoulder and pointed.

TWENTY-ONE
A Missing Husband

13 June

Early in the morning, Georges joined Anne and Paul at breakfast and reported on last night's secret conversation with Luc Thierry. 'At their meeting on Rue Colbert, Guiscard and Boyer apparently struck a deal to shift suspicion for Flamme's murder entirely on to Patrick.'

Paul remarked, 'It sounds like a pact conceived in Hell. Those two rogues are trying to pervert the course of justice and hang a man who may be innocent.'

'Didn't Boyer's republican views trouble Guiscard?' asked Anne.

'Not at all,' replied Georges. 'Guiscard is a practical businessman, a schemer without a conscience. His greedy eyes are fixed on former church property, like a dog on his bone. Above all, Guiscard wants a secure title to what he has already bought. And he intends to buy a lot more. If the king were to prevail and bring back the old regime, he would return church property. Guiscard would lose everything. However, if the republicans come to power – anticlerical as they are – they would guarantee Guiscard's investment.'

'You're right,' said Paul. 'Every thinking person knows that the monarchy now rests on a weak foundation. Guiscard will hedge his bet and put money on Boyer.'

'So, Boyer can be bought,' Anne persisted. 'Doesn't he claim to stand on moral principles, such as honesty?'

'So he does,' Georges granted. 'Still, Thierry said Boyer looked very pleased as he left Guiscard's office with five thousand francs in his pocket.'

'Good work, Georges,' said Paul. 'But politics have made this an unusually difficult case. The Jacobins and other clubs are involved, not to speak of factions within the National Assembly. We'll need more evidence before Magistrate Roland would dare to put anyone on trial.'

Georges nodded. 'I'll continue to pursue Guiscard with the help of his porter and perhaps other spies. It's a labour of love.'

At mid morning Anne met Marthe Boyer in a side chapel at Saint-Eustache. Marthe had again pretended to shop in the Central Markets and had eluded one of Rat-face's spies. Anne described Boyer's speech at the Jacobins' meeting and the subsequent danger to Patrick.

The news brought tears to Marthe's eyes. Anne wondered if the two lovers continued to meet. That would now be even more difficult than before.

With Georges' revelation of a possible pact between Boyer and Guiscard in mind, Anne described the master builder to Marthe. 'Have you ever seen him?' Anne asked.

Marthe struggled with the question. 'I don't think so. But Monsieur Boyer once left a contract for use of a room at The Red Rooster on a table in the salon. He and Monsieur Guiscard had signed it.'

'So, they must have met,' Anne concluded. 'By the way, where is your husband?'

'I don't know. He hasn't returned home this morning. That's unusual. He didn't leave word that he would visit a friend or travel from the city.'

For a moment Anne thought of using this opportunity to search his study. She probably could pick the lock. But he might come home at any time, and must not find her there.

'We'll meet again tomorrow. If he's not home then, we'll go to the police.'

As Anne parted from Marthe in the church, she suddenly began to experience a powerful sense of dread. With every step she grew more convinced that Boyer was dead. On an impulse she hastened to the Boyer residence. Across the street loitered Rat-face. Anne strode directly up to him. 'We need to talk,' she said and gestured towards the tavern.

'If you wish,' he said, without a hint of surprise.

They sat in a quiet corner and Anne asked him point blank, 'When did you last see Monsieur Boyer?'

For a brief moment, he studied Anne, as if unsure of her intentions. Then he scratched his head and replied, 'Late last night. Near the Tuileries. He was perfectly sober. I lost track of him in the darkness.'

'Why were you following him?'

'He owed me for a week's work. I needed the money to pay my helpers. Without money they are useless.'

'Do you think Boyer is dead?'

'Yes,' he replied. 'I came here this morning, still hoping he would pay me. But I realize now that I'll never get my money.'

Suddenly Anne saw an opportunity. Rat-face's demeanour seemed strangely serene, suggesting a certain integrity of character. After a moment's hesitation, she asked, 'Would you work for me?'

Rat-face slightly raised an eyebrow in surprise.

Anne continued. 'Yesterday at the Jacobins, Boyer accused Patrick O'Fallon of killing Armand Flamme. Did you give him any evidence?'

'Madame, I'm a professional spy. If you want information, you must pay for it.'

'How much?'

'I spent a week on O'Fallon. Boyer should have paid me four francs per day, plus expenses. Shall we say thirty in all?' With a hint of teasing in his voice he added, 'And I'll pay for our wine.'

'Agreed.' She handed him the money.

Rat-face appeared to breath a sigh of relief. 'Before the meeting at the Jacobins, Boyer asked for a report on O'Fallon. I said that at the time of Flamme's murder, O'Fallon was alone in the Louvre.'

'Are you sure?' Anne was stunned. Two days ago, Marthe Boyer had tearfully confessed to spending the night with Patrick. He had denied it. 'I have reason to believe that he was with someone.'

'Boyer asked the same question and didn't like the answer either. He insisted that I testify before a magistrate that I'd followed O'Fallon to Place des Victoires. I refused.'

Anne felt a surge of disbelief. Who should she believe? Marthe, Patrick or Rat-face?

'Yes,' the spy continued, 'Odd as it may seem, I always tell the truth. My reputation depends on the accurate, factual reporting of what I see and hear. Lying would undermine my credibility with the police and other clients. If deceived, they would punish me.'

'Would you give this information under oath to Magistrate Roland?'

'First, I would weigh the risk. Powerful men have chosen to accept Boyer's idea of a royalist conspiracy as the cause of Flamme's death. I'm reluctant to contradict them. They would have me killed.'

Anne left the man staring into his glass.

She found Paul and Georges in Paul's office involved in a serious discussion. 'May I interrupt?' she asked.

'Of course,' Paul replied, raising an eyebrow.

'I have a strong feeling that Boyer's dead.'

The two men exchanged incredulous glances. A stunned silence gripped the room.

Then Paul asked, 'How can you be sure?'

'Marthe told me that he did not come home this morning. That's most unusual. Then I confronted his spy, Rat-face, and he shares my suspicion.' She related her conversation with the spy. 'He contradicts Marthe Boyer's story of being with Patrick at the time of Flamme's murder but still gives Patrick an alibi. Unfortunately, Rat-face fears retaliation and may refuse to testify before a magistrate.'

Georges stirred restlessly in his chair. 'There's no time to lose in Boyer's case. Evidence could be destroyed. Let's identify potential suspects and determine where they were last night.'

Paul turned to Georges. 'Could Guiscard have wanted to kill Boyer?'

'Possibly,' Georges replied. 'Boyer might have extorted that five thousand franc payment to deflect Guiscard's guilt in Flamme's death. Guiscard might have reasonably feared that Boyer would come back again and again for more. Boyer wouldn't be the first extortionist to be murdered.'

Anne spoke up. 'You seem to overlook another likely suspect, Antonio Diluna. We know that he stalked Boyer on Place des Victoires. Perhaps I might use my Italian to help Georges question him.' She gazed at Paul. 'Who do you suspect might have killed Boyer?'

'According to Rat-face, Boyer was last seen near the Tuileries late last night. I'll have a word with my former comrade in arms, Count Fersen. He's often at the palace, looking after the queen, so to speak. He just might have the key to this murky business.'

Paul addressed Anne. 'When you meet Patrick for lessons, find out where he was last night. Remember, Patrick threatened to kill Boyer as well as Flamme.'

Anne remarked, 'I hope to be assured that he was in his Louvre rooms and that Marthe was with him this time. I must warn him that if the public learns that Boyer has been murdered, it will turn on him with mindless fury.'

Early in the afternoon, Anne met Patrick at the Institute for the Deaf for a lesson in articulating simple words and phrases. They smiled and greeted each other as if the violence of the past few days had not occurred. Still, the suspicion that he might have killed Boyer gnawed at the back of her mind.

They sat facing each other at a small table, his eyes bright with anticipation. Following a method she had learned while working in Mr Thomas Braidwood's school in England, she positioned Patrick's tongue with a slender silver spoon, while he mimicked the movement of her lips. The process was tedious and his progress was slow and meagre. Still, his face beamed with pleasure at every simple word mastered, like *oui* and *non* and *merci*.

For the last word Anne deliberately chose *meurtre* or murder. He reacted with a thin, wry smile, but he received her instruction without protest and got the sounds nearly right.

At the end of the lesson, Anne explained that Boyer had publicly accused him at the Jacobins' meeting of Flamme's death.

Patrick frowned. 'Did he offer any evidence?' His signing hinted at suppressed anxiety.

'Nothing new or convincing,' Anne reassured him. 'It's widely known that you hated Flamme for good reason and that you stalked him at The Red Rooster. But Boyer's accusations are misleading and unfair. I'm sure that he could not convince an honest magistrate. I think he's trying to deflect suspicion from himself in the eyes of the public.'

Patrick appeared to relax.

Anne hastened to warn him. 'Take care. You are in great danger. Many in the audience were already turned against you and your father and believed Boyer's charges. They will be even more convinced when they learn this morning that he has disappeared. Frankly, he has most likely died.'

Patrick received the news thoughtfully. 'For Marthe's sake, I hope he's dead.' He smiled wryly. 'I suppose you wonder if I killed him as I said I would. He deserved to die. As a "free-thinker", he ridiculed true religion. He was also a loud-mouthed leader in the National Assembly's campaign to dismantle the church. But I didn't kill him. Again I was alone last night, so I have no alibi. And I don't want Marthe to invent one.'

'I believe you,' Anne signed, then raised a warning hand. 'If Boyer is found dead, especially if there's evidence of foul play, the gullible public will quickly accuse you and perhaps take revenge. A mob could form spontaneously and hang you from the nearest street lamp. It has happened to many innocent persons in the city during the past two years.'

'What should I do?' His anxiety had returned.

'Avoid the Palais-Royal. Before going out into the city, disguise yourself. Remember that Boyer's friends will try to keep track of you and Madame Boyer. So, be cautious, at least until we find out who really killed Armand Flamme and what has happened to Jacques Boyer.'

Patrick nodded. But his eyes were hooded. Anne wasn't at all sure that she had persuaded him.

During the afternoon, Georges devoted his mind to the need to search Guiscard's office. Its secret papers could expose the master builder's hidden connections to the murder of Armand Flamme and perhaps throw light on Boyer's dis-appearance.

When Georges first thought that Guiscard might keep secret papers, it seemed likely that his great writing table could have been built to store them. If so, its locks would be unusually strong and complicated, its construction very stout. Georges realized that he couldn't break into it. He had to find a quicker, more subtle way.

Georges' search led to the cabinet maker, Monsieur François Lacroix. Georges knew him from previous investigations and had also questioned him about special locks and secret drawers. Now elderly, he lived in comfortable retirement in rooms above his shop. Late in the afternoon, Georges paid him a visit.

'What brings you here, Monsieur Charpentier?' Lacroix

extended a bony hand in greeting and gestured Georges to a chair. A servant brought wine and sweetmeats and withdrew.

They toasted each other, then Georges began, 'I've come to talk about one of your masterpieces, the great writing table that you built for Monsieur Jean Guiscard.'

Lacroix frowned. 'That fraudster and cheat! He had made a modest down payment on the table and periodic small payments while I built it. When it was finished in the shop, he seemed pleased and promised to pay in full upon delivery. By this time, I had heard rumours that he wasn't to be trusted. Still, I took a chance and delivered the table. Thereupon, he declared it to be worth no more than the sum he had already paid and he refused to pay more.'

'Frankly,' said Georges, 'I'm not surprised.'

The old man grimaced at the painful memory. 'I chose to absorb the loss. To bring him to justice would have meant years in the courts and the loss of as much money as the table is worth.'

Georges shook his head in a sympathetic gesture.

A mischievous glint entered the old man's eye. 'I'm glad you came, Charpentier. In a curious way, justice might still be served.' He instructed a servant, who returned with a small box. The old man shook it – and produced the rattle of keys. 'At the time, I had a vague premonition of trouble and made copies of all the keys to the table. They should still fit. Open the drawers and see what he has hidden there. Good luck!'

TWENTY-TWO
A Delicate Matter

14 June

L ate in the morning the next day, Anne set out to visit Marthe Boyer. Across the street from her apartment a glum Rat-face loitered as usual. He shrugged as Anne met his eye. Apparently Jacques Boyer had not returned home, nor had he given any sign that he was alive. In the apartment Anne found his wife, pale and drawn, overcome with anxiety. 'What will become of me?' she wailed.

Anne calmed her. 'We'll take one step at a time.' They went to the police bureau and reported Boyer missing. Anne brought Marthe back to her apartment and hurried home.

The door to the office was open. Paul was at his writing table, speaking to Georges. Anne waited a second and coughed lightly. Both men turned towards her and smiled.

'Boyer is definitely missing,' she said. 'A few minutes ago, his wife and I reported it to the police.'

'I'm not surprised,' Paul remarked. 'I expect to hear shortly from the mayor. In the meantime, Georges has news. He has the keys to Guiscard's office and his desk. We're waiting for an opportunity to search for his hidden records.'

A clerk appeared at the open door. 'Sir, the mayor requests you to come to his office. Monsieur Boyer has been reported as missing for more than twenty-four hours.'

Paul turned to Anne. 'We'll go to his apartment as soon as I'm through with the mayor.'

An hour later, Saint-Martin was pacing the floor in the mayor's anteroom in the Hôtel de Police. A familiar feeling of anxiety crept into his spirit. On similar occasions in the past, Lieutenant General de Crosne of the old regime and his successor Mayor Bailly of the new one had called him to this office. Then he was asked to conduct unusually thorny investigations. Now he suspected that Mayor Bailly and Commandant Lafayette would ask him to investigate Boyer's disappearance.

Since politics seriously complicated this case, Saint-Martin was reluctant to be involved. He wished to stand apart from the country's factional quarrels and simply serve justice and the common good without fear or favour. To that end, he had given up his noble title and other privileges – as had his aunt Marie de Beaumont and her recent husband the former Count Savarin.

Mayor Bailly opened the door himself and invited Saint-Martin into the office. Lafayette stepped forward to shake his hand, then seated him at the writing table. Both men appeared more tense than usual.

'We recall your service two years ago,' the mayor began. 'You ably investigated the assassinations of the intendant of Paris, Berthier de Sauvigny, and his father-in-law Foulon. Their killers were apprehended without unduly upsetting the fragile political process.'

Lafayette leaned forward, a worried expression on his face. 'Today, we must deal with two more cases with strong political overtones, the murder of Armand Flamme and the suspicious disappearance of Jacques Boyer.'

Bailly added, 'We are especially concerned that Monsieur Jérôme Pétion, president of the National Assembly, has supported both men. Tomorrow, he will be elected President of the Criminal Tribunal of Paris. You can expect him to show keen interest in this investigation.'

'Thank you for the warning. Monsieur Pétion and I have differed in the past, but I will do my best to work with him. Still, I'll pursue the facts wherever they lead.'

Bailly went on, 'Because of the overheated political environment of the day, many citizens are already construing Boyer's disappearance as foul play. Some claim that the queen leads a conspiracy to assassinate republican leaders and enemies of the court. Others charge that the Jacobin club itself is responsible and has purged a troublesome member from its ranks.'

Lafayette sighed. 'The police have no obvious suspect and no dead body.'

'We want you to lead the investigation,' said the mayor. 'We trust you to use the utmost discretion.'

Saint-Martin objected, 'Boyer might simply have had too

much to drink and couldn't find his way home. Give him time to come to his senses.'

'He's never been lost before,' said the mayor. 'At least in this case, it's wise to seem concerned and react quickly. Otherwise Pétion and other radicals will accuse us of covering up a conspiracy of Boyer's enemies.'

Lafayette explained, 'We're telling the public that this investigation hopes to find Boyer alive. He may have stumbled into a pit and is unable to help himself or call for help. He could have suffered a mental collapse and can't remember his name or where he lives. Granted, these are thin stories, but they are the best we could concoct.'

Saint-Martin agreed reluctantly. 'Then, I'll try to find him. Frankly, I doubt that he's alive, but I'll pretend.' He wondered what hidden, dangerous traps lay ahead in the investigation: the public's moods were unpredictable, sometimes violent. Prominent persons might be involved. Among the suspects would be Fersen or his agents. Was Boyer's 'disappearance' premeditated? Had someone taken care to conceal the evidence?

Early in the afternoon, Saint-Martin returned home. Anne was waiting for him in the salon. He described his commission from the mayor. They agreed that the first step should be to visit Madame Boyer and search her apartment. She couldn't be expected to regret his disappearance. Still, her reaction to it could be revealing. Given the abuse she suffered at his hands, she had a strong motive to be rid of him.

A few hours later, Anne and Paul called on the putative widow. Georges accompanied them but remained in the background. Having assumed that her husband had died, she wore black. But that was her only obvious sign of grief. Instead, to judge from her pallor and bright, shining eyes, she was experiencing a mixture of shock and relief. It took a few minutes and many soothing words, but Anne managed to put her at ease.

At a signal from Paul, Anne began to question her. She claimed to have been at home alone during the night. That couldn't be substantiated. Her servant lived outside in the neighbourhood and came in to work during the day.

Finally, Anne asked her, 'Would you object if my husband and his adjutant were to search your rooms for clues that might throw light on Monsieur Boyer's fate?'

'I would be grateful if you would,' she replied, and then hesitated. 'But if he returned home while you're searching, he would be very angry. After you left, he would probably beat me again.'

'Frankly,' Anne signed, 'he's not likely to come back this afternoon.' Or ever, she added under her breath. 'In any case, we'll protect you.'

When the men left to search the study, Anne signed to Marthe, 'My husband and his adjutant will be busy for about an hour. I'll make tea for us, and you can help.'

After they had settled themselves at a tea table, Anne ventured a question. 'Has your husband ever failed to come home after twenty-four hours?'

Marthe shook her head. 'When he knows that he'll be away, he leaves written instructions. He hasn't done so this time. That's why the police are concerned.'

'Has he recently seemed anxious or afraid, as if he felt under threat of harm?'

'Yes,' she replied. 'He may have thought his life was in danger. A few days ago, he began to carry a pistol even in the daytime.'

Anne wondered what might have prompted Boyer's concern. Almost immediately, the angry face of Antonio Diluna came to mind. 'Have you by chance noticed a muscular, dark-complexioned young man loitering near this building?'

'Why yes, I've seen him a number of times. My husband warned me to avoid him.'

'Did he tell you why the man was dangerous?'

'No.'

'He's Antonio Diluna, the brother of Magdalena, your husband's *former* mistress. Antonio hates your husband. He pretended that he was a widower and then seduced the young woman. She's pregnant.'

Marthe flinched. 'I'm sorry for her. If her brother killed Jacques, I hope he escapes punishment.'

'Even if someone else is blamed?' Anne asked.

'This is too much,' Marthe signed. She buried her head in her hands and wept.

Meanwhile Paul and Georges searched in the study, the most likely room for Boyer's secrets. Georges had picked the lock. Madame Boyer couldn't offer any helpful suggestions because her husband usually shut the door while he worked.

It was a large, airy room. One wall was lined with book-shelves. Dark, varnished wainscot covered the lower third of the other walls. Richly framed obscene engravings hung on the white plaster walls. The finest piece of furniture in the room was the highly polished brown mahogany writing table that stood by the window. Its drawer was locked, but Georges opened it with ease. Inside was only an account book recording payments to printers for pamphlets and placards.

As Saint-Martin searched the bookshelves, he was reminded of Boyer's serious interest in religion and philosophy. Atheism was prominently represented from the ancient Roman Lucretius to the modern Baron d'Holbach. Among the books were also folders of pornographic sketches. But no hiding place was to be found.

The colonel and his adjutant stood in the middle of the room and looked around them. 'We must try to imagine him here,' Georges said. 'Where would he have kept his secret papers and treasures?'

'He was a writer,' Saint-Martin replied, 'and probably made daily entries in his journal. It needed to be close and acces-sible.' He reflected for a moment, then pointed to the wall beneath the window within reach of the writing table. 'That's where his journal has to be.'

Georges closely inspected the wainscot, tapped gently, and pushed. A section of the wall yielded to his pressure and unlatched. He pulled it open, revealing a cabinet. On shelves inside were journals and file boxes and a small velvet pouch.

'Here's the watch, sir,' Georges exclaimed. He laid the pouch on the table and removed a pocket watch in a plain gold case. With his magnifying glass he examined the watch.

'Breguet's name is on the main dial.'

'Tell me about it,' said Saint-Martin as Georges handed him the watch.

'It's one of a kind, sir. Abraham-Louis Breguet is the best watchmaker in France. Unless it's a counterfeit, he made it in his workshop on the Quai de l'Horloge. The movements of your body wind up the mechanism. At the touch of a button it sounds the hours, half-hours, and quarter hours, each with different tones.'

Saint-Martin laid the watch on the table and studied it closely. The main dial was silver with a subsidiary dial for seconds and an opening for days of the week. On the right side was an opening for the age and phases of the moon; on the left, a sector to indicate the state of winding.

'It's an amazing piece of work,' said Saint-Martin, as he returned the watch to its pouch. 'What do you suppose the owner paid for it?'

'About three thousand francs. It's hard to imagine that Boyer could afford it.'

'That's true,' Saint-Martin granted. 'But, it's even stranger that no one has reported having lost it and offered a reward for its return.'

'Perhaps it was taken from Breguet's workshop. He might not have missed it yet.'

Saint-Martin put the watch in his pocket. 'Anne and I shall pay him a visit. In the meantime we need to find out how this watch came into Boyer's hands.'

'The barman told us that Armand Flamme showed off his gold watch late on the night that he died.'

'But the barman saw it at a distance and can't tell us for sure that it's this one. We must go to Boyer's journals.'

Georges reached into the cabinet and pulled out the most recent one. The entries were written by a careful, meticulous hand but in code. Georges studied a page and sighed, 'This is too difficult for me.' He handed the journal to Saint-Martin.

He fanned the pages, stopping to study a few entries. 'I can't read it either. It's a task for Monsieur Savarin, our expert in code. The Foreign Office keeps him busy. Hopefully, he can find time to help us. Until then, we can't safely assume that Flamme stole the watch or that Boyer got it from Flamme, either freely or violently.'

Anne, Paul and Georges left Marthe Boyer and returned to Paul's office. Anne related her conversation with Marthe and added, 'I'm very concerned about her. She has money for only a few days and will soon become destitute. Unless her husband is legally declared dead, she can't touch her dowry or dispose of his things. In the meantime, she has no way to pay rent for the apartment and no family or friends in Paris to turn to.'

Paul remarked, 'It could be months or years before a court might declare Boyer to be dead.' He frowned. 'Her adulterous relationship with Patrick has tainted her reputation and will make it harder for her to find support. The public will soon believe that Patrick killed Boyer as well as Flamme. As Patrick's lover, Marthe has an obvious interest in her husband's death. Even a fair-minded magistrate like Pierre Roland would have to suspect her as well as Patrick.'

Georges waved a hand. 'Marthe was once a butcher. I know a widow, a kindly, sensible woman, who sells meat in the Central Markets. She could put Marthe to work until her situation improves.'

'Contact her,' said Paul. 'Perhaps she could use Patrick as well. He must soon leave his father's rooms in the Louvre. In the meantime, we must move ahead with our investigation. We'll begin with the Jacobin club this evening. They should be keenly concerned about the missing Boyer.'

That evening at the Jacobin club, Saint-Martin and Georges discovered how fast and far the news of Boyer's disappearance had travelled. An atmosphere of dread seemed to fill the hall. It was sparsely attended. No speech was scheduled. A few club members had huddled together in anxious conversation.

In his speech to the club Boyer had declared Flamme to be the first but not the last victim of a conspiracy of enemies of the revolution. It now appeared that Boyer himself was the second. The members assumed the worst from his disappearance. With hushed voices, they asked each other, who would be next? Boyer's warning of imminent royal treachery gained credence.

With Georges at his side, Saint-Martin interviewed the club's president and its leading members. They agreed that the missing man was a notorious libertine. 'He may have cuckolded one too many husbands,' suggested one man. Another offered that Boyer's strident, personal attacks on the royal family and the clergy had earned him many enemies.

A third conceded that his demand for a republic was unpopular in the club. Most members favoured a constitutional or limited monarchy.

'However,' asserted the president, 'none of the Jacobins would have harmed, let alone killed, Boyer. They had a certain grudging respect for his courage and audacity. He professed out loud the secular and democratic ideas that many members share but keep to themselves.'

During these conversations, Monsieur Pétion had stood apart. Saint-Martin made a point now of engaging him. 'I believe, sir, that congratulations will soon be in order. Tomorrow you will be elected President of Paris' Criminal Tribunal – a signal honour and a heavy responsibility.'

Pétion regarded Saint-Martin with cold, hostile eyes and said, 'Be warned, Colonel. I shall require the police to rigorously pursue the enemies of the people. My tribunal will judge them without pity and order the punishment their crimes deserve.'

'With due regard for a citizen's rights,' Saint-Martin added dryly, then asked, 'Who do the Jacobins think has caused Boyer to disappear?'

Pétion replied, 'Most of them suspect the old priest's servant, Patrick, and they want him arrested and prosecuted. But they correctly consider him merely the tool of a dangerous conspiracy located in the Tuileries. The royal court is attempting to silence its critics.'

Georges pointed out that Boyer had threatened to expose the club's leaders of receiving secret payments from the royal court. Could a club member have retaliated?

Pétion made a dismissive gesture. 'Boyer was irritated that many in the club rejected his political views, so he made that empty, silly threat.'

On the way back to the office, Georges asked Saint-Martin if they should investigate whether the court had secretly paid certain club members to silence Boyer? On that point the club and the court had a mutual interest.

'We'll leave that question to another day,' said Saint-Martin, who was reluctant to spend time on dubious rumours. 'Tomorrow Anne and I will visit Monsieur Breguet with the watch we discovered in Boyer's study. Meanwhile, you should try to determine who was the last person to have seen Boyer.'

'I'll start with Antonio Diluna. We know that he stalked Boyer.'

TWENTY-THREE
Frustrated Rage

15 June

Georges made his way to the tavern near Saint-Sulpice and met the waiter/spy Bernard Fontaine. As it was mid morning, and few patrons sat at the tables, Bernard was free to move to the back room and speak to Georges.

After they were seated, Bernard smiled mischievously. 'When I heard rumours that Jacques Boyer was missing, I said to myself that Monsieur Charpentier would soon pay me a visit. How can I help you, Georges?'

'Antonio Diluna has been observed stalking Boyer. Do you think that he intended to harm the man?'

'Diluna is not stupid. He hasn't announced to the world that he's planning to cut Boyer's throat. But there are disturbing signs. His mood has changed. He used to be a joyous, carefree man who laughed easily and would often break out in song. Since his confrontation with Boyer here two weeks ago, he broods, never smiles or sings, and looks preoccupied. You might conclude that he is calculating how to punish Boyer for deceiving and seducing Magdalena.'

'How frequently do you think he has stalked Boyer?'

'One of my associates, who tried to keep track of him, reported yesterday that Diluna frequently followed Boyer to different places and at different times of the day, as if looking for an opportunity to strike when his guard was down. Diluna appeared to realize that he had to be cautious since Boyer was armed and alert. He stopped stalking Boyer at about the same time that he disappeared.'

'When can I question Diluna?'

'Today, he is performing with his sister in the Théatre des Italiens on the Boulevard. Last night, he was here with his sister. I don't know when they might be back again. They haven't spoken to the barman about supper.'

'Should I come here anyway on the chance that I might meet them?'

Bernard hesitated. 'I prefer that you don't question them here. They would suspect that I directed you to lay in wait for them. In my profession I need to appear detached from the police. Try to meet them at the theatre. You should ask Madame Cartier to help with the Italian. She might also pry useful information out of Magdalena.'

'I'll ask Madame Cartier.' Georges rose to leave.

Bernard came with an afterthought. 'I think Diluna is making plans to leave Paris and probably will soon return to Naples, presumably to ease his sister's pregnancy. He doesn't talk about it, so he might try to keep his departure a secret. Keep that in your calculations.'

Georges pressed a small silver coin into Bernard's hand. 'You've been most helpful. I'm sure we'll do business again.'

At the Théatre des Italiens, Diluna and his sister Magdalena were engaged to perform on stage during the intermissions. Georges and Anne arrived on time to watch one of their acts. Dressed in brightly coloured, festive garb of Italian peasants, Antonio played a medley of fast fiddle tunes while his sister danced with incredible energy and grace on the slack rope. She'll soon have to give that up, thought Anne.

A helpful manager allowed Georges to use a small office upstairs. Harlequin masks covered its walls. After the Dilunas' last act at eight o'clock, the manager brought them up for the questioning. Georges sat behind the writing table in his gendarme's uniform; Anne sat off to one side in a plain, blue, high-waisted muslin gown. The brother and sister arrived still in their costumes, surprised and irritated.

Georges began gently, with Anne translating. 'We have a few questions for you. This seemed the most convenient place to ask them. Please be seated.' He motioned them to chairs facing him.

'We need to rest between acts,' complained Magdalena. 'I'm exhausted.'

'I'll be brief and try not to tire you.' He asked Antonio directly. 'Why were you stalking Boyer?'

The question seemed to catch Diluna by surprise. For a moment he searched desperately for an answer. Finally he blurted out. 'I wanted to frighten, not hurt him. I hoped I could force him to admit that he owed something to my sister.' He threw a glance in her direction. 'Boyer should support their child and compensate her for lost income. This is probably her last performance for many months. And that's unfair.'

Georges nodded sympathetically. 'When and where was the last time you saw Boyer?' In her translation Anne mimicked Georges' insinuation that he already knew the answer and that it would be pointless to try to deceive him.

Antonio hesitated again, shifting nervously in his seat. 'The last time was the night between the twelfth and the thirteenth of this month. I had followed him to the palace of the Tuileries. He met a woman there. I figured that he intended to bed her. That's how he typically ended the day. I couldn't foresee any further opportunity to scare him that night, so I left.'

Georges leaned forward and met the Italian's eye. 'And where did you go?'

Diluna again glanced at his sister, this time with a hint of shame. 'I went first to a gambling den, then to a brothel in the Palais-Royal.'

Anne asked Magdalena. 'Is that true?'

'He didn't come home. That's all I know.'

Georges got the name and address of the den and the brothel, then asked Antonio. 'Do you realize that Boyer has disappeared and that you are among the last persons to see him?'

'I've heard the rumours. But I didn't kill him, if that's what you're getting at. And I've no idea where he is.'

Magdalena muttered under her breath, 'I hope he's in Hell.'

Out on the Boulevard Anne and Georges sat on a bench across from the theatre and watched the crowds pass by.

Anne asked, 'Do you think Antonio killed Boyer and hid his body?'

For a moment Georges seemed to struggle with his thoughts. He replied carefully, 'I don't think so. He wanted to do it, he looked for opportunities, but he was unwilling to risk failure or arrest.'

'His love for his sister restrained him, didn't it?'

'That's right. He's a decent man.'

Anne added, 'But unfortunately we may have lost a promising suspect.'

'Still, we've gained a significant piece of information about Boyer's movements shortly before he disappeared. He was seen with a woman close to midnight near the Tuileries.'

TWENTY-FOUR
The Tuileries

16 June

The next morning Saint-Martin walked the short distance from his office to the Tuileries. At breakfast Anne told him that Jacques Boyer had been last seen with a woman near the palace late in the night of his disappearance. Could the Court's partisans have killed him and concealed his body? But why would they have bothered? Boyer's anticlerical republican rants were no more dangerous to the Crown than hundreds of others whom the Crown simply ignored. Still, Saint-Martin had to find out what Boyer was doing at the palace that fateful night.

He would begin with his well-connected acquaintance, Count Axel von Fersen. Since Baron Breteuil, Saint-Martin's patron, had gone into exile in Switzerland, Fersen was virtually the only man left in the royal family's inner circle with whom Saint-Martin could speak confidentially.

Fersen's maid Jeanne Degere showed Saint-Martin into the antechamber of the room that Fersen kept in the palace's second floor of the south wing. 'Count Fersen will see you in a few minutes,' she said in her direct, rustic manner. She was utterly loyal to the count and carefully guarded his secrets. Saint-Martin knew better than to try to pry any sensitive information from her.

Fersen himself soon invited Saint-Martin into his room. They sat at a window overlooking the garden of the Tuileries. Jeanne served hot chocolate and started to withdraw. With a silent movement of his lips Fersen gave her a command; she nodded in return and left, closing the door behind her.

Meanwhile, Saint-Martin surveyed the room – it was small and sparsely furnished. Near a window stood a writing table with pen and ink and a few sheets of paper. The floor was bare; empty bookshelves lined a wall. There was also a sleeping alcove. The count apparently did most of his work elsewhere. Aware of the count's intimate relationship with the queen, Saint-Martin felt certain that a secret passage connected this room to hers, but he couldn't detect it.

For a few minutes, the two men carried on a rather strained, polite conversation. Finally, when the chocolate was finished, Fersen said, 'I suppose you've come here on business. How can I help you?'

Saint-Martin gave him a hopeful smile. 'I'm looking into the possibility that partisans of the royal court might be involved in Boyer's disappearance or supposed death. He had publicly declared at the Jacobins that he was investigating a royal conspiracy against leaders of the revolution. Moreover, he was last seen with a woman near the palace. Could you point out any potential suspects for interrogation?'

Fersen replied with a firm, dismissive shake of his head. 'You are looking in the wrong direction, Paul. I can't think of anyone at the Court who would harm him. Assassinating demagogues like Boyer is as pointless as swatting flies or cutting off the heads of Hydra. The Jacobin club, even its radical members, has found him embarrassing. They may have done away with him and then blamed the royal court.'

Saint-Martin nodded. 'I'll look into that possibility – my investigation has only just begun. But I think that a few hot-headed fanatics, unknown to you, could have taken it upon themselves to avenge the victim's insults to the royal family. You must recall that on 28 February a large band of young nobles attempted to invade the Tuileries in order to protect the king.'

Fersen shrugged. 'I'm aware of that incident. Many were bruised, but no one was killed. I don't know of anyone who would resort to murder.'

Sensing that this line of interrogation seemed to make Fersen anxious, Saint-Martin continued. 'I grant that it may be difficult, but I'll proceed nonetheless with the interrogation of palace servants.' He noticed an expression of alarm growing on Fersen's face. 'And I must include servants of the royal family and . . . your personal servants. My adjutant, Georges Charpentier, is already at work in the palace.'

Fersen's expression darkened. Through thin, tight lips he remarked, 'His Majesty will be affronted.'

Saint-Martin acknowledged the royal displeasure with a slight nod. As he left the room, he understood that Fersen would hinder rather then help the investigation. There must be a reason and it might explain the mystery of Boyer's disappearance. Stony-faced, Jeanne Degere opened the door for him and met his eye as he passed her. He felt certain that she had listened to the conversation.

Meanwhile, Georges Charpentier moved through the palace, talking to National Guards, trying to gather information relevant to Boyer. Several hundred guardsmen were stationed there to protect the royal household. But everyone knew that they were also supposed to prevent the king and queen from running away. Georges approached several guards who had served in the police of Paris. They shied away from him.

One of the former policemen looked nervously over his shoulder, then took Georges aside into a ground floor storeroom and offered to help. Georges explained that he was investigating the disappearance of Jacques Boyer.

'I've heard tell of him,' said the guard. 'He comes here often. Pesters the maids. Tries to dig up dirt on the royal family. I didn't know he had disappeared.'

'I first heard of it three days ago,' Georges said. 'Mayor Bailly and Commandant Lafayette put Colonel Saint-Martin and me on the case. It could be thorny to handle. Boyer seemed to enjoy provoking powerful people. Could anyone from the palace have done him in?'

'I wouldn't know,' replied the guardsman. 'But there's a maid who might help you. She works on the first floor in the south end of the palace. Our commander placed her there to spy on the royal household – it's a poorly kept secret. Her name's Paulette and she's a patriot. Promise her a few coins and she'll probably help you.'

Georges found her cleaning an antechamber in the royal apartment. Suspicious at first, she opened up when Georges showed his commission from Lafayette. For a few copper coins, she agreed to meet him a half-hour later when she went off duty.

They went to a nearby tavern on Rue des Orties and sat in a quiet corner. Georges ordered wine for both of them. She was a short, sturdy woman, perhaps thirty years old, plain featured but spirited. Her eyes had a shrewd look.

'The officers here don't pay attention to what I report,' she complained. 'It's not specific enough, they say. I've told them that the royal family is about to leave on a long trip. I can tell from the way they are secretly packing. A few days ago, the queen sent a large box of her cosmetics to Brussels. That's specific enough to my mind.'

'Did you also tell this to Monsieur Jacques Boyer?'

Her eyes narrowed with suspicion. 'Why do you want to know?'

'He has disappeared. I'm trying to find out why.'

'So it's true,' she remarked. 'This morning I heard the rumour. I'm not surprised or sorry. He's a conceited ass. Yes, I told him about the cosmetics. Why not? He paid. As I spoke, his eyes lit up, and he said, "Then I'm on the right track." He asked me to keep him informed. I said I would.'

'He might have come to a bad end. Do you know anyone here who would have harmed him?'

She took a draught of her wine. Her brow creased with reflection. 'His rants against the royal family have made many enemies here, but I haven't heard anyone say that they wanted to kill him.'

'Did you see him the night of 12–13 June?'

She nodded. 'Yes, near midnight. Count Fersen had come, disguised, earlier in the evening and seemed tense. Usually, he seems so calm. Later, when I saw his servants, I thought they were tense too. Something was going on. So, I decided to watch them closely, and I sent a message to Boyer. About eleven, he arrived. On previous nights, he had been following Jeanne Degere, as she delivered messages to someone on Place des Victoires. I told him I thought a major event would happen tonight. He paid me, and I promised to help him get started.

'Soon, he and I watched from hiding as Count Fersen sent the servant, Jeanne, out into the city, almost certainly with a message. Boyer said he would follow her. That was the last time I saw him. A few hours later Jeanne came back with her brother.'

'Do you have any idea where they went?'

'I don't know. But they must have done more than just deliver a message. She dragged her feet and leaned on him. He was bent and limping. They looked exhausted.'

Georges thanked Paulette, gave her the copper coins, and left her in the tavern to finish her drink. In the palace garden, he met Colonel Saint-Martin and they walked to a quiet, shaded bench overlooking the Quai des Tuileries and the Seine. It was a warm day; the sun was high in a clear blue sky.

'What did you discover, Georges?' the colonel asked, fanning himself with his hat.

'My investigation in the palace led me into Count Fersen's own household. The woman whom Boyer met outside the palace was Count Fersen's servant, Jeanne Degere. Boyer had been following her for some time. The night of his disappearance Paulette, the patriot maid, told him that Jeanne would be carrying a message of critical importance. The count himself sent her off. That excited Boyer, and he followed Jeanne. The patriot maid never saw him again.'

Saint-Martin reflected for a moment, stroking his chin. 'It won't surprise you, Georges, that Count Fersen denied that he or his household or the Court could be involved in Boyer's disappearance, or in any conspiracy against leaders of the revolution. The king, he claimed, is reconciled to the limited role he'll have to play under the new constitution.'

Georges frowned. 'That sounds like a bold-faced attempt to deceive us. Perhaps Fersen is engineering a major grasp for power on behalf of the Crown, and Boyer got wind of it. Fersen then panicked and ordered Jeanne Degere and her brother to assassinate Boyer.' Georges paused to search his commander's countenance. 'Sir, you know Fersen as well as anyone. Do you think he's capable of such a drastic measure?'

For a moment Saint-Martin struggled with the question. He liked the Swede and enjoyed his company. But beneath his suave, charming exterior was a subtle, calculating, even ruthless mind.

In reply to his adjutant's question, the colonel carefully measured his words. 'Fersen's ultimate loyalty is to the queen, not to any abstract idea of justice or the nation. If the circumstances of the royal family were to become dire, he would use any and every means to save them. By all reports, Jeanne and her brother would do whatever Fersen asked of them. Why not murder?'

Georges scratched his head. 'But the royal family's circumstances today hardly call for such a drastic solution. No doubt
they are unhappy with the turn of events over the past two
years. Their freedom of movement is restricted, but they live
comfortably. No one threatens their lives. The king, if not the
queen, still enjoys the people's respect, and he recently professed
publicly to be satisfied with his reduced role in public affairs.'

'That's true, Georges. But could Fersen's servants have acted
on their own?'

'Possibly. Boyer has been dogging Jeanne's steps. If he were
to attempt to violently extract information from her, he would
surely incur her brother's wrath.'

'Still,' mused Saint-Martin, 'it seems highly unlikely to me
that either he or his sister would freely do anything – murder,
for instance – that would embarrass or discredit their master.'
He sighed. 'For the time being, Fersen's intentions are
inscrutable.'

TWENTY-FIVE
The Watch

17 June

Anne and Paul set out early on Friday morning for Monsieur Breguet's workshop on the Quai d'Horloges. Their challenge was to determine who stole the Breguet watch and how it ended up in Boyer's secret cabinet. That might lead to discovering why Boyer disappeared.

They had sent ahead a messenger to ensure that they could meet the watchmaker. He was a busy, highly productive man. To win his attention Paul mentioned that he had questions concerning the authenticity of a Breguet watch. On their arrival a clerk led them into a show room and sent an errand boy upstairs to the family apartment to fetch Breguet.

While they waited, the clerk showed them several pocket watches under glass, their simple elegant gold cases opened to expose the dials. From one watch the dial had been removed to reveal the complex inner mechanism, including a self-winding system similar to that of a pedometer.

Ten minutes later, Monsieur Breguet arrived. His expression was welcoming though not servile. He seemed a bit on his guard, perhaps uncertain why a police colonel would come to the shop with his wife to discuss a watch.

'Shall we speak in my office?' he suggested, and showed them into a simple but tastefully appointed room with fine furniture upholstered in silk. He had made a fortune selling watches to the royalty and aristocracy of Europe. Some of the transactions probably took place in this room. Breguet and his visitors sat around a green velvet covered table. As he gazed expectantly at them, Anne retrieved the watch from her bag and placed it on the table.

'Does this piece come from your workshop?' Paul asked. 'It carries your name, but so do some counterfeits.'

Breguet grimaced. 'The truth lies inside.' He opened the dial, studied the mechanism, and breathed a sigh of relief. 'Yes, this is one of mine. No counterfeit can match the quality of this workmanship. It also has a serial number etched inside. I finished it about a month ago for a distinguished client.' His expression slowly grew troubled. He asked hesitantly, 'Is there a problem? The watch seems to function perfectly.'

'We found the watch under unusual circumstances,' Paul replied. 'Could you tell me for whom you made it?' Paul's tone was insistent.

Breguet gently shook his head. 'My client demanded that the watch must be kept a secret, and I promised.'

'Then I must reveal that it's a crucial piece of evidence in a criminal investigation.' Paul showed the watchmaker his authority from the mayor.

Breguet sighed deeply, pulled a bill of sale from a file, and handed it to Paul.

He read it and said to Anne, 'A month ago, Lady Elizabeth, Countess of Sutherland, wife of the British ambassador Earl Gower, purchased this watch for 4,000 *livres*.'

Paul turned to Breguet. 'Why do you suppose she insisted on secrecy?'

The watchmaker shrugged. 'She said only that the watch would pleasantly surprise a certain gentleman. At the time I assumed – and still do today – that she was referring to her husband, the ambassador. The countess is a beautiful, gracious woman with a mind of her own. Still – *o tempora o mores* – one really doesn't know what to think. I trust that both of you will be discreet.'

Anne understood that Breguet was gravely concerned to maintain the good will of his aristocratic clientele, far and away his best customers. Who else could or would pay the equivalent of 167 pounds sterling, a sum sufficient to support a family of the middling sort for ten years?

Out on the street Paul asked Anne, 'Granted that the countess is one of the richest women in Britain, why wouldn't she report the loss of this watch? We're not dealing with a trifling matter.'

She replied, 'We need to know the circumstances surrounding her purchase of the watch. Is she involved with a gentleman other than the ambassador?'

Paul reflected for a moment. 'If she were in a scandalous relationship, then why was Boyer holding the watch? Could he have planned to extort money from the countess before returning it? I see no way to answer these questions other than to confront her. We must ask with due deference for an appointment.'

Anne agreed. 'Deference, to be sure. I realize that the Countess of Sutherland is no ordinary mortal.'

Early that afternoon, and with growing anticipation, Anne and Paul approached the grand town house of Earl Gower and his wife, Countess Elizabeth, on Rue Saint-Dominique, near Les Invalides. Paul had made an appointment with the countess through her personal secretary. Fortunately, the countess happened to be free this day – usually she had a full schedule of events.

Anne was surprised that he had received the appointment. The countess was discriminating with requests for her time and her money. Paul's message was brief and vague as to the visit's purpose. He wrote only that he would like to speak about a matter of serious concern to her. Anne wondered if Paul's reputation as a police colonel and his status as a former aristocrat might have intrigued the countess.

Their coach passed through a monumental portal, drove down an allée of plane trees into a vast forecourt, bordered by gardens to the left and right. The house was a two-storey, elongated, and perfectly symmetrical building, monumental in its dimensions but neither ponderous nor pretentious. Pierced by tall windows and decorated by columns, its facade had a sober elegance. The sight reminded Anne of a miniature palace of Versailles.

'Tell me about this place,' Anne asked Paul.

He smiled. 'Most of what I know comes from Georges. Almost a year ago, Gower, the British ambassador to France, leased the property, known as the Grand Hôtel de Monaco. It had been the Parisian residence of Marie de Brignoles, the estranged wife of Honoré de Grimaldi, Prince of Monaco. She had built the town house fourteen years earlier in the recent revival of the classical Grecian style. In the early, chaotic days of the revolution, she feared for her life and emigrated to England. The building was left sumptuously furnished and unoccupied.

'It now serves as a symbol of Britain's power and significance in the world. Spacious and centrally located, it's also a suitable working space for the embassy. Next door is a much smaller building for servants and other members of the household staff. Behind the house is a large formal garden that echoes the building's palatial aspect.'

A handsome young liveried servant met Anne and Paul at the door, led them through an oval vestibule into a library and left to announce their arrival. An older liveried servant stood by a tea table set for three. Several accomplished watercolour paintings hung on one wall. A mountain landscape caught Anne's eye. Its palette was dark and brooding, devoid of people. She asked the servant about it.

'The countess painted it, Madame. It's a scene from Sutherland, her county in the highlands of Scotland.' Anne wondered what the scene might reveal of the artist. According to the countess' critics, the poor crofters who lived there were beneath her notice.

On another wall was the portrait of a young woman. 'An attractive, spirited person,' said Anne to her husband. 'She appears remarkably self-confident.'

'Proud, perhaps wilful, as well,' he added softly.

The servant took a step towards the portrait and said evenly, 'That's the countess herself at seventeen. Mr George Romney was the painter.'

Promptly at the appointed hour the countess entered. Self-assured, a woman accustomed to managing things, she studied her guests with a quick, searching glance, then smiled politely and gestured for them to be seated. Her expression indicated that Anne and Paul should feel honoured. They were apparently worthy of her time and attention.

While the tea was being poured and candied fruits served, Anne reflected on the countess's reputed charm among men. She had begun to show it towards Paul, meeting his eyes with a level gaze, seeking his views and commenting sagely on all sorts of things. She rather ignored Anne. But that was not surprising. The countess was said to regard most women, even of her own class, as witless and servile. But she didn't know Anne.

The countess was undoubtedly attractive, if not precisely beautiful. Though she was slender, stood barely five feet tall, and was only twenty-five years old, she had acquired a commanding presence. Her hair and eyebrows were light chestnut, her eyes dark chestnut. She had a small mouth, inclined to an ironic rather than a good-natured smile. Her chin was round and determined; her forehead, low and stubborn. On this warm morning she was wearing a becoming light pink, high-waisted muslin gown and a pink ribbon in her hair.

At a gesture from the countess, the tea ended, the table was cleared and the servant withdrew. The countess's expression grew serious. 'I'm curious, Colonel, as to the purpose of this visit.' She leaned back and observed him sharply.

'I've deliberately avoided giving the appearance of an official police investigation, out of respect to the ambassador, his home and his sovereign. Still, a man of public significance has been murdered in the city and another has mysteriously disappeared. Certain evidence pertaining to them has led me here.'

The countess frowned, her brow creased. 'Colonel, what can you mean?'

'Have you lost a watch recently, Countess?' asked Paul abruptly.

'No, Colonel,' she replied. Her tone grew more irritated. 'Since the streets of Paris are thick with thieves, I'm always on guard when I go out. Thus far I've not lost a sou, much less a watch.'

Paul nodded to Anne. She retrieved the gold pocket watch from her bag and laid it on the tea table. Paul asked the countess, 'Do you recognize it?'

She picked it up gingerly and studied it. 'I surely do. It must be a duplicate of mine. For all I know, Monsieur Breguet might have made several that look alike.'

'That's possible, Countess. But could we compare your watch with this one?'

'Mine is hidden away and meant to be a surprise gift to someone, but I'll fetch it. Can we keep the secret?'

Paul looked towards Anne and nodded. 'We'll be discreet.'

Anne expected the countess to ring for a servant. Instead she excused herself, returned the watch to the tea table and left the room. A few minutes later, she returned with a small red leather-covered box, tied shut with a black silk ribbon. 'You may open it, Colonel,' she said, sounding both pleased and annoyed.

Paul could feel the weight of something inside. Nonetheless he untied the ribbon, opened the box and gave it to the countess.

She looked inside, then gasped. 'Good God! What's this?'

She held a small, round flat stone in her hand and stared at Paul. 'You seem to have known that my watch has gone.'

Paul shook his head. 'I could only guess that this was your watch and that you were unaware of its loss.'

'Well, I thank you for recovering the watch.' Her eyes darkened with anger. 'It must have been stolen. I may have a traitor in my household.'

'That would be an especially serious problem in the embassy of his Britannic Majesty,' said Paul. 'We may be able to help you, Countess. Have you seen either of these men?'

Anne placed Michou's sketches of Armand Flamme and Jacques Boyer on the table.

The countess shook her head. 'I don't recognize them. They appear to be of the common sort of men. My servants are more likely than I to have known them. In any case,' she added, 'as strangers, they wouldn't realize that I had hidden the watch, nor could they imagine where to look.'

'Who might have known?'

The countess hesitated. 'My personal maid. She has served me for years. I can hardly bring myself to suspect her. But she's the sole person to whom I've shown the watch. She even suggested the hiding place. She must have given the watch to the thief, or at least told him where it was and unlatched a window for him to enter the room.'

Paul raised a cautionary hand. 'She might have casually mentioned the watch and its location to another servant who was less trustworthy. May we go to the watch's hiding place and speak to the maid there?'

'Follow me,' said the countess. Her expression was grim and unforgiving.

She led them into an adjacent, spacious, and richly decorated bedroom on the garden side of the house and went directly to a roll top writing desk. The roll top was unlocked. 'It's usually locked if I leave the house,' she said while opening it. 'I put the watch in its box at the back of this drawer behind other empty boxes.' She grimaced with irritation. 'As I said, that's where my maid told me to put it. I'm now more sure than ever that she stole it.'

Paul shook his head slightly, urging patience. 'May I question her?'

The countess rang a bell and a stout, middle-aged woman appeared. She looked alert and ready for service. Paul could detect no guile.

'Colonel Saint-Martin would like to speak to you,' said the countess with frost in her voice. Disconcerted, the maid nearly stumbled into the room.

Paul gave her a reassuring smile and gestured to a tea table. They sat facing each other, Anne and the countess off to the side. 'Do you recognize these men?' he asked handing her Michou's sketches.

'I believe I've seen this one more than once. He was in the street, peering at the house.' She was pointing to Flamme.

Paul asked a few more questions about her background, work, current interests, friends and acquaintances. From her remarks he deduced the portrait of a simple honest woman, no thief. Serving the countess was her passion.

'That will be all, Madame. I may have a few questions for you later.' She left the room looking bewildered.

'Colonel!' said the countess, exasperated. 'Why didn't you confront her with the watch?'

'She didn't take it,' he replied gently. 'You are fortunate to have her, possibly the only reliable servant in the house. Have any of your servants been discharged or quit since you hid the watch?'

'Well, I can't speak for the entire staff. The steward would know them. I can recall one young woman who cleaned these rooms occasionally. She left a few weeks ago. But how could she have known about the hidden watch? I'll call the steward. You may wait here. I'll only be a moment.'

As soon as she left, Anne said to Paul, 'If Georges Charpentier were with us, he would point out that this building was empty for more than a month between the departure of the Princess of Monaco and the arrival of Earl Gower and his family. Could someone – even the French government – have installed means of spying in these rooms?'

Paul considered the question for a few moments while he surveyed the room. Then he replied, 'It's a plausible idea. Let's test it.' Their suspicion focused on small openings in the rich antique ornamentation above the pilasters decorating the walls. Several leering satyrs in high relief looked down at them. Their eyes could serve as peepholes.

Anne tapped on a wall. 'It could be thin in strategic places to allow a concealed spy to overhear private conversations.'

A few minutes later, the countess returned with the steward, a handsome man with the supple bearing of a courtier. He explained that the young maid who cleaned the rooms had previously worked in this building for the Princess of Monaco.

'Describe the maid,' said Anne.

'A small, agile woman, and clever as well,' said the steward, 'quite excitable, I recall.'

Anne had a sinking feeling that she knew the person who fit that description. Doctor Pinel had placed Renée Gros in this household and she had recently disappeared. But how could she have carried out this theft?

'I have a suspect,' Anne said to the countess. 'She might be willing to tell us that she stole the watch. She could also name the man who engaged her to do it.'

'Remarkable!' exclaimed the countess. 'Please get to the bottom of this affair.'

Paul added, 'I'd also like to call in my adjutant, Georges Charpentier. He's familiar with this building and could help us discover who was behind the theft of the gold watch that we found in Jacques Boyer's study.'

Late in the afternoon, Anne and Paul went to Doctor Pinel's institute. Paul had sent a messenger ahead. The doctor was occupied, but he had instructed his assistant, Berthe Dupont, to help them. Anne knew her from three years ago. A tall, sturdy woman with natural authority in her voice and manner, she had great influence over Renée. She would help Anne try to persuade the young woman to return to the Hôtel de Monaco and explain what she had done there.

Thanks to Anne's suggestion, the magistrate Pierre Roland had moved Renée from a Châtelet prison cell back to Pinel's clinic. She had a small, pleasant room for herself and Princess, a charming feline, mostly a short-haired tiger with a white spot on the tip of her tail and bits of calico in her fur.

When Anne entered the room, Princess was leaping upon shadows on the floor and batting a ball across the room. Renée was playing dominoes with another patient. Berthe announced Anne and Paul, the game was put aside and the visitor quietly left.

Anne took the lead. 'We've been to the British ambassador's house, talked to Elizabeth the Countess of Sutherland, and found a way to improve your relations with the police and keep you out of prison.'

Renée signalled the cat and it leaped into her lap. 'Tell me more,' she said in a soft ironic voice.

'Would you accompany us to the Hôtel de Monaco and show us how you managed to snatch the countess' watch? We would also like to know who was your accomplice.'

The young woman grimaced. 'I didn't exactly steal the watch, but I'm willing to show you how it all happened. I want my friend and guard, Berthe Dupont, to come along and look after me. Doctor Pinel says I'm improving but I'm not yet fully responsible for what I do. I think that means I'm still a little crazy. Since that keeps me out of prison, I don't quarrel with him.'

The countess, her steward and Georges were waiting in the vestibule when the others arrived. Georges' face brightened when he saw Berthe. They were good friends.

Saint-Martin quickly brought his adjutant up to date on the theft of the Breguet watch. 'You know this building, Georges. Could you explain how the theft was possible?'

Georges pointed to the ceiling. 'The original architect allowed about two feet between the floors, crawl space for a thief, so to speak. The architect could then raise the building's height by as many feet and increase its monumental appearance on the outside. Lower ceilings also created more pleasing proportions in the interior architecture.'

As they walked through a salon, Georges remarked, 'Someone has opened small peepholes into many of the rooms.' He pointed up to a decorative face mask beneath the moulding. 'I suspect that a spy could remove the eyes and look down into the room.'

Paul offered an explanation. 'Behind this trick was perhaps the desire to spy on the Princess Marie of Monaco. It may have been her ex-husband, Prince Honoré, who lived in a nearby town house. Or perhaps even the French government.'

'It was none of them,' interrupted Renée. 'Armand made the peepholes when the house was vacant.'

Anne asked Renée. 'Then tell us how you and Armand schemed to steal from the countess.'

While the young woman composed her thoughts, the others

gathered around her. She began to speak quite lucidly and without a trace of embarrassment. 'Armand knew the building very well. He had helped build it years ago. When he heard that it was empty and that a very rich British ambassador and his family would soon move in, he figured out how to spy on them and earn some money. He laid boards across the ceiling supports in the crawl space so I could easily and quietly move about and spy through peepholes into the rooms. The ceilings are very thin. If people spoke normally, I could understand them.

'Armand got the idea to earn money by spying for the royal government. For a month, I listened to Earl Gower and his visitors and told Armand what I'd heard. He sorted out what I'd probably got wrong and added things from his own imagination. At the end of the month he approached a man in the government's department of foreign affairs and asked if he'd hire us to spy on the British ambassador. Armand showed him our information, but didn't say how we got it. The government man glanced at it, laughed at Armand, and said, 'You're trying to sell me a pile of *merde*. It's worthless.'

'We then looked for opportunities to take things the family really didn't need, but could earn money for us. Watching them through the peepholes, I learned their hiding places and told Armand. He sneaked in and grabbed some coins and tableware and substituted paste for real diamonds.'

'Weren't you afraid that the steward would catch you?' Anne asked.

'No, he didn't seem to notice things missing. He and the maids pilfered too. Sooner or later the countess would find out but I would be gone by then.'

'That's a lie,' exclaimed the steward. He turned to the countess for support. 'I haven't taken a penny. Why would anyone believe the tales of a confessed thief?'

She stared at him coolly for a second, then curtly motioned to Renée to go on.

Renée continued apparently unperturbed. 'I honestly think Armand and the steward had an understanding. They met sometimes in the city and talked as if they had something to hide.'

The countess said to the steward. 'You and I shall have a conversation after this.'

The man nodded, crest fallen and tongue-tied.

Paul took the lead. 'We'll move now to the countess's room.'
When they had reassembled, he asked Renée, 'How did you
manage to steal the watch?'

Renée smiled with a hint of pride. 'One day, the countess
came home with a small box, holding it in her hand as if it
were precious. Otherwise she always had a maid carry her
things. So I crawled into the space above us.' She pointed to
the leering face of a faun in high relief directly above the
countess' roll-top desk.

'As I was watching through the faun's eyes, she opened the
box and took out a pocket watch in a gold case. She and her
maid admired it. They said it even wound itself and told the
days of the week and the phases of the moon. When they hid
it in the desk, I was sure that it was valuable.

'A few weeks ago, the family left the city on an outing. Only
a few servants remained in the building. In the evening, while
they were eating and drinking, I unlatched the garden window
for Armand. He picked the desk's lock, replaced the watch with
a stone, and put the watch in his pocket. I latched the window
behind him.'

She paused and glanced slyly at Anne. 'So you see, Armand
snatched the watch, not I.'

'Why did you quit your job here?' Anne asked.

'Armand thought that Countess Elizabeth would soon miss
such a valuable item and would call the police. They would
discover all the thieving that was going on in the house, and I
might be suspected. But nothing actually happened until now.'

Up to this point the countess had been mainly an observer,
albeit a keen one. Her expression had grown increasingly tense.
Her brow was furrowed, her eyes had narrowed to mere slits;
their chestnut colour had turned nearly black. Renée's tale of
deception and crime in her household had clearly both humiliated and angered her. Anne feared an explosion was coming.

Renée darted numerous glances towards the countess.
Apparently sensing her changing mood, the young woman grew
nervous. She still spoke freely but more rapidly, slurring words.
Her eyes opened wide and grew bright, her cheeks flushed.
Anne gave Paul a warning glance, then said to Renée, 'We've
heard enough. You've been very helpful. Now we shouldn't tire
you.'

The countess erupted. In an unnaturally high voice she

shouted at Anne, 'Are you about to take that little thief back to Pinel's clinic? I should think not. She must go to jail. I'll have my husband press charges. She and her accomplice have affronted the honour due to His Britannic Majesty.'

At the mention of jail, a look of alarm crossed Renée's face. Her lips began to quiver; her breathing came in gasps; her body trembled. Berthe put an arm around her shoulder to steady her.

Saint-Martin addressed the countess as her equal with authority in his voice. 'I understand your feelings, Countess. You and your husband have been wronged. But the noise of it is still confined within these walls. The chief villain, Armand Flamme, has been murdered and thus silenced. The damage he caused you has been repaired. We have returned the stolen watch and have recovered the other stolen items from Flamme's apartment. They will be sent to you.'

'Will *no one* be punished, Colonel?' She glanced again at Renée.

'Would it be wise, Countess, to bring this affair to the public's attention? Much of the thievery came from your own staff. Moreover, to press charges against Mademoiselle Gros, mentally ill and merely the villain's tool, would seem vindictive and unworthy of an enlightened noble lady.'

The countess's anger seemed to abate. By character and upbringing, she was averse to histrionics and rather inclined to practical solutions. When Saint-Martin finished, she said, 'I'll leave Mademoiselle Gros to you, Colonel, and deal with my own staff.' She drew the pocket watch from her bag. 'I thank you for recovering this watch. My husband will receive it on our wedding anniversary.'

Anne gave Berthe a signal.

She said softly, 'It's time to go, Renée,' and took the young woman under the arm. She staggered towards the door, eyes unfocused, head lolling. Before she could fall, Berthe scooped her up, carried her to the coach and drove off.

'I wonder if she'll ever be fit to live on her own,' Anne said to Paul as they returned home.

'At least, Doctor Pinel is committed to caring for her,' Paul remarked. 'To the police, if they ask, we can make the case that Flamme directed her.'

Georges added, 'We've also learned that he had the Breguet watch. He either gave it to Boyer or Boyer took it from his dead body. That should make him our prime suspect in Flamme's murder and free Marthe Boyer, Patrick O'Fallon, and Monsieur Guiscard from suspicion.'

Saint-Martin shook his head. 'A magistrate would remind you, Georges, that we have only a strong presumption of Boyer's guilt, rather than solid proof that he actually killed Flamme. For all we know, Flamme's killer could have given or sold the watch to Boyer.'

'That's unlikely but possible,' Georges admitted. 'Monsieur Guiscard could have done it. He and Boyer appeared to have reached an accord.'

TWENTY-SIX
Secrets Revealed

18 June

The following day, business for the gendarmerie kept Colonel Saint-Martin at his desk, but the Breguet watch continued to occupy his mind. At a pause in his work he glanced at a detailed drawing of the watch that Michou had prepared. It was hard to keep his mind from wandering back to Boyer's study. How did the watch get there? His mind resisted the most likely conclusion that Boyer had taken it off Flamme's dead body.

Saint-Martin regretted that he had no one with whom to discuss the case today. Anne had resumed her tutoring of Patrick O'Fallon and other special students at the institute for the deaf. Georges was at the Ministry of Finance, investigating Guiscard's devious purchases of church property.

Georges returned early in the evening, just as a messenger arrived with a cryptic, unsigned message from Aunt Marie's town house on Rue Traversine: 'Puzzle solved.' Saint-Martin guessed that it concerned Boyer's watch and his secret papers and came from Monsieur Savarin, a cautious man who covered his tracks.

Saint-Martin and Georges hurried to the house. A servant showed them to Savarin's study, a modest, pleasant room, designed for his leisure hours. His cello leaned into a corner with a music stand nearby. Small oil paintings of pastoral scenes hung on a wall. The books on his shelves were mostly *belles lettres* that he read for entertainment. The Foreign Office housed his professional library and his files on members of the French aristocracy.

Three comfortable chairs were arranged around a tea table by the hearth. On this cool evening in June a low fire was burning. A carafe of sherry stood on the tea table together with three glasses. Savarin was waiting for them at his writing table near a window, a rare, triumphant smile on his face. He rose and extended his hand not only to Saint-Martin but also to Georges, whose intelligence he had learned to respect.

With a simple, gracious gesture he seated them at the tea table. A servant poured the sherry and withdrew. Savarin raised his glass in a toast: 'To the occasional victory of justice and truth.' His two guests joined in the toast. Then he handed Saint-Martin two pages of closely written text.

'Jacques Boyer has given you a nearly full confession. You could hardly ask for more. I've translated the last two weeks of entries in his journal and all his loose papers. The code, though amateur, is quite challenging and the journal entries are very revealing. The last is dated the morning of 12 June.'

Saint-Martin read the text with mounting interest. Boyer had written a detailed account of his quarrel with Flamme over his thieving habits and in particular the gold watch. Boyer demanded that his followers aim at a higher moral level in their lives. How could they otherwise criticize the vices of the clergy and aristocracy? Stealing the watch was only the latest and most egregious of Flamme's missteps.

Saint-Martin could understand how the ruffian would resent Boyer's criticism and, even more, the patronizing tone in which he delivered it.

Boyer demanded the watch – he would ensure that it got back to its owner. Flamme refused to give it up, insisted he had found it and didn't know the owner. Boyer called him a liar. He grew angry and slapped Boyer with such force that he fell to the floor.

Saint-Martin read aloud from Boyer's journal: 'That vile blow was the last straw. I swore by God to punish his insolence.'

Savarin smiled. 'It tickled me to see a professed atheist swearing by God.'

'There's more,' said Saint-Martin. 'As we suspected, Boyer paid the barman at The Red Rooster to set Flamme up. The journal goes on to describe in detail Boyer following Flamme into a dark street, beating him to death, and retrieving the gold watch. It gave Boyer immense satisfaction.'

Georges asked Saint-Martin. 'Would a magistrate agree, sir, that we've sufficient evidence here to convict Boyer of Flamme's murder?'

'I believe that our magistrate Pierre Roland would agree. We'll speak first with Mayor Bailly, then with Roland.'

Georges asked Savarin, 'Did you find out where Boyer got his money?'

Savarin shrugged. 'In the diary, he refers to a source but not by name. In recent letters a member of the National Assembly gives him information and advice and perhaps money. My colleagues at the Foreign Office believe he's Monsieur Jérôme Pétion, who uses Boyer to promote the republican cause among the citizens of Paris.'

'Pétion, my nemesis!' exclaimed Saint-Martin. He sighed, then studied the secret letters. 'They discuss Flamme's thefts. Boyer asks, "What should I do?" The source replies, "Do whatever it takes to stop him." Boyer could understand that to mean, kill Flamme if you must.' Saint-Martin glanced at his companions for a reaction.

They nodded gravely. 'We must confirm the name of that source,' said Georges and looked to Savarin.

He sipped thoughtfully from his glass. 'I'll find a way to pry into Monsieur Pétion's files. An ambitious man, he has made enemies who might help me.'

'According to these letters,' Saint-Martin went on, 'Boyer is convinced that Fersen is arranging for the royal family to secretly flee from Paris. Fersen's servants, he thinks, know the date and the destination. For weeks, he has been following them about the city. "Finally," he writes, "I must force the truth out of them." He underlines the sentence, then confides, "At the same time, I must beware of the angry Italian, Antonio Diluna, who dogs my heels. He would slit my throat."'

Georges sighed. 'Unfortunately, we don't know if Boyer ever confronted them, or if Diluna got to Boyer first.'

TWENTY-SEVEN
A Quandary

19–20 June

Early in the morning, Saint-Martin hastened to Mayor Bailly's Louvre apartment – he had sent a messenger ahead. The mayor sat waiting at his writing table, as usual dressed plainly in black, calm and collected but with a wistful look in his eyes, as if hoping against hope that his visitor would bring him good news. His greeting was polite but lacked warmth and enthusiasm. He would be happy to retire to his home in Chaillot.

The colonel took a seat by the table. 'Sir, you will be pleased that we have recently discovered evidence in the Armand Flamme case that proves beyond doubt Monsieur Boyer's guilt. The evidence also suggests that Monsieur Pétion might be complicit.'

The mayor raised an eyebrow in a gesture of interest. 'Really? Pétion? That would be extraordinary. Please continue.'

Saint-Martin went on to relate the story of the stolen watch found in Boyer's study. 'In his diary and other secret papers he describes killing Flamme, then devises a scheme to blame Patrick O'Fallon for the crime. According to Boyer's notes, Monsieur Pétion approved the scheme.'

The mayor's expression turned sceptical. 'I'd be surprised if Pétion had in fact approved. But your evidence against Boyer seems convincing,' the mayor granted. 'If you were to present it to the magistrate Pierre Roland, he would probably issue a warrant for the man's arrest.'

'What would be its political consequences, sir?' The mayor's lack of enthusiasm was beginning to intrigue Saint-Martin.

'A conscientious, dispassionate magistrate, like Pierre Roland, and other reasonable men could easily acknowledge Boyer's guilt. But men – Pétion foremost among them – who believe that royal agents have caused Boyer's disappearance and threaten other revolutionary leaders are sure to protest vigorously.'

'I'm sure they would, sir. They allow themselves to be governed by political passions. But we should nonetheless follow the evidence.'

The mayor leaned forward and met Saint-Martin's eye. 'Colonel, your stubborn pursuit of wrongdoing among our reformers, as well as your connection to the Baron de Breteuil, has led some of my acquaintances in the political clubs to wonder where your loyalty lies. They would go so far as to claim that you've put the gold watch as well as a falsified diary and similar secret papers into Boyer's study in order to incriminate him. They might also argue that it would be wrong to arrest a man who cannot presently defend himself.'

'Sir, my record of eight years as a police officer speaks for itself. In the old regime as well as the new, I have pursued criminals regardless of their social class or political persuasion. My critics wilfully ignore the facts of this case. Shouldn't we go ahead with the judicial process, in spite of protests? If we prove that Boyer was a murderous devil, we might disarm most of our critics and isolate the rest.'

Bailly lifted a warning finger. 'Need I remind you, Colonel, that Monsieur Pétion is now President of the Criminal Tribunal of Paris. If Monsieur Roland were to convict Boyer, Pétion would reject it.'

'He wouldn't dare,' objected Saint-Martin.

The mayor shook his head. 'I believe we should suspend the process at least until Boyer is found, dead or alive.'

'If or when that happens, sir, do you think there will be less protest?'

'Who knows, Colonel. I'm concerned about today's problems, not tomorrow's. To prosecute the missing Boyer would arouse controversy and distract us from completing the chief business at hand, the new constitution. We should let sleeping dogs lie.'

With that cliché ringing in his ear, Saint-Martin left the mayor's apartment, a frustrated man. He faced a quandary. Should he pursue Boyer's arrest without the mayor's backing and risk the wrath of Boyer's supporters? Or should he compromise his principles and simply go along with the mayor? It took less than a minute for him to decide. He set off towards the office of the magistrate Pierre Roland.

He arrived near noon. 'What do you have for me?' asked Roland gazing expectantly at Saint-Martin. Almost immediately, the magistrate seemed to sense that his visitor was carrying a burden. 'What's the matter, Colonel?'

'It's the Flamme case, sir. We've solved it. Boyer is the culprit, and here is the evidence.' Saint-Martin handed over the diary and the other secret papers, together with a full report on the investigation.

Roland scanned the materials, asking questions and commenting as he went along. 'You say that Flamme approached someone in our Foreign Office with a plan to spy on the British ambassador. Is that important to the case against Boyer?'

'The spying was brief and fruitless and only marginally related to the case,' Saint-Martin admitted. 'It could be omitted.'

The magistrate nodded and read on. 'I'll accept Monsieur Savarin's reading of the diary's code. The evidence against Boyer looks convincing. He has clearly confessed to killing Flamme. Impressive work, Colonel. You've exceeded my expectations.' He paused, gazing at Saint-Martin quizzically. 'What was Boyer's chief motive? He and Flamme held similar views on religion and political reform. Both wanted a secular republic.'

'Nonetheless, sir, they hated each other and had long-standing disagreements over revolutionary tactics. But it was Flamme's personal insult that finally moved Boyer to murder.'

'What insult?'

Saint-Martin returned to the diary and pointed to the passage. 'In the course of a hot argument over the watch and other issues, Boyer called Flamme a liar. Flamme was enraged and slapped Boyer. The affront of that blow, as much as the blow itself, touched Boyer's most sensitive nerve. Among aristocrats such an insult would taint a man's honour and could lead to a lethal duel with swords or pistols. Boyer felt as much aggrieved as any aristocrat, but as a commoner he didn't have the option of a duel. Instead he followed the base instincts of his class, took his enemy by surprise from behind and clubbed him to death in a dark alley.'

Roland engaged Saint-Martin's eyes. 'Though you've solved the case, Colonel, you aren't satisfied. Something is amiss.'

'That's true. Mayor Bailly objected that it would be polit-
ically inopportune to put Boyer on trial, especially *in absentia*,
when he couldn't defend himself. His sympathizers would
violently object that I was a partisan of the Crown and had
fabricated evidence and concocted false charges against him.
The magistrates in the case would have to defend their decision in the district tribunal, where Pétion's influence is strong,
and in the court of public opinion. That sort of controversy
could distract the country from the work remaining to be done
on the new constitution, and put the magistrates themselves
at risk.'

Roland lowered his eyes and gazed for a long moment at
the uncluttered, shiny surface of his writing table. 'So, in view
of the mayor's objection, why should we bring the case to trial
now? Couldn't it wait?'

'To begin with the most practical reason, we must coun-
teract, as soon as possible, Boyer's false accusations against
Patrick O'Fallon at the Jacobin Club and elsewhere. To deflect
attention from himself and Monsieur Guiscard, Boyer has insinuated that O'Fallon killed Flamme as part of a royalist
conspiracy to assassinate leaders of the revolution. I was present
at that meeting of the club and can tell you that many members
seemed inclined to believe Boyer.'

Roland frowned. 'His accusation is pernicious. I've heard
men repeating it in the cafés of the Palais-Royal. No doubt, it
would now be difficult for the deaf man to receive a fair trial
in the city.'

'I agree,' said Saint-Martin. 'And there's an even more
pressing concern. I think Boyer intended to go around our judicial system. His accusation was a call for mob justice and a
"trial" for Patrick, like the baker's two years ago, where the
unfortunate man was falsely accused of profiteering, then hung
from a street lamp outside his shop. To prevent a similar injustice we must expose Boyer for the fraudster and charlatan that
he was, or perhaps still is. An honest, well-publicized trial is
the right, the only way, to do it.'

The magistrate rested his hands on the table and slowly tapped
with his fingers. 'I need to think about this problem for a day
or two and consult a few trustworthy magistrates at the district
court. They have the authority to reverse my decisions on appeal
particularly in capital offences. I'll keep you informed.' Roland

paused. 'By the way, isn't the deaf man also suspected in Boyer's disappearance? I've heard rumours that he was having an affair with Boyer's wife.'

'Unfortunately, the rumours contain a grain of truth. I believe there are mitigating circumstances in that affair – Boyer severely abused his wife who is deaf. She found understanding and solace with the deaf O'Fallon. But, in the public's eye, their relationship can only hurt his cause.'

The magistrate gazed at Saint-Martin for a moment, then smiled gently. 'A part of me has always admired the Chevalier de Bayard, a knight *sans peur et sans reproche*. You have a great deal of his spirit, Colonel.'

'Thank you, sir. I look to Bayard as a model.' Saint-Martin left the magistrate's office, believing he had done all that he could to bring the absent Boyer to trial. Now he must find a way to safeguard Patrick from mob violence.

In the meantime, Anne and Georges hastened to the tavern near Saint-Sulpice in response to a brief message from the waiter/spy Bernard. 'Something is brewing here. Come disguised,' he had written. Anne assumed it had to do with Antonio Diluna and his sister Magdalena. Georges put on a plain brown woollen suit and a wig; Anne wore the plain woollen clothes of a kitchen maid.

When they arrived near noon, the waiter nodded their eyes towards a large table where several men were in a lively discussion. Their leader's fleshy, animated face looked familiar to Anne, most likely a politician, but she couldn't put a name on him. Georges whispered in her ear, 'Monsieur Danton.'

Voices occasionally rose but not sufficiently for Anne or Georges to make sense of what was being discussed. For the most part, the men seemed conspiratorial and malicious. Gradually, Anne recognized three or four other members of the group. Her heart skipped a beat. She whispered to Georges, 'Some of those men are from Armand Flamme's gang that assaulted Father O'Fallon in the Palais-Royal.'

Then Georges made eye contact with Bernard who was serving the men. He mouthed the word, 'Wait.'

After about ten minutes the group broke up, but a few lingered over their drinks. Bernard again caught Georges' eye and mouthed, 'Be at the church in ten minutes.'

They met near the church's entrance, but didn't acknowledge each other. Once inside, Bernard led the way into a small supply room, and latched the door. As they sat down at a table, he remarked, 'In my line of work I must keep a discreet distance from the police even in disguise. Otherwise, I would lose the trust of the rogues I investigate. The leader Danton and half the group you saw at the large table are Cordeliers, the most radical of the city's political clubs. They frequently visit our tavern. I pretend to sympathize with them, and so they allow me to serve them. The others at the table are hired cut-throats.'

'What were they talking about?'

'Patrick O'Fallon. They were planning how to kill him. Danton and the other Cordeliers in the group sympathized with Boyer and shared his fear of a royal plot to overthrow the present revolutionary regime. In the several days that have passed since he disappeared, they have grown convinced that Patrick O'Fallon, the priest's servant and an agent of the royal family, has killed Boyer and hidden his body. These villains believe that the police do not wish to find the body and will not arrest his killer. So they are going to take matters into their own hands. You saw them at the table making arrangements with the cut-throats to seize O'Fallon when he emerges from the Louvre. They have engaged Boyer's spy, Rat-face, to inform them of O'Fallon's movements. Once they catch him, they will hold a mock trial, convict him of murder and adultery and quickly hang him from a street lamp.'

'When will they set their plan in motion?' asked Anne, her heart beginning to pound.

'Soon, as early as today. Maybe tomorrow. Rat-face will determine the time and place. Apparently, Patrick frequently goes out disguised to meet his lover, Marthe Boyer, most often in the Central Markets or in Saint-Eustache. Sometimes she comes to his rooms in the Louvre. Fortunately, he's aware of danger. His movements aren't predictable, but if he's careless, the cut-throats will be ready to pounce.'

'Thank you, Bernard,' said Georges, 'we'll immediately take measures to thwart them.'

He hesitated for a moment. 'I know you can keep a secret. We have convincing evidence that Jacques Boyer killed Armand Flamme. We don't know yet if or when the case will go to trial. Politics may get in the way.'

As they rose to leave, Anne said, 'I meant to inquire about Antonio Diluna and his sister.'

'They have vanished,' Bernard replied. 'Three days ago, as they left Paris, they told the barman that they would perform in Versailles. But this morning, when they hadn't returned, he checked their room and it was empty. They had paid rent in advance.'

'They are probably travelling south to Italy,' Anne remarked. 'I think Antonio fears being accused of Boyer's disappearance.'

'I'll alert the gendarmerie,' said Georges with little enthusiasm. 'We aren't likely to find them. Still, Antonio remains a suspect.'

By mid afternoon, Saint-Martin was back in his office. Suddenly Anne and Georges rushed in. 'Patrick is in danger,' they exclaimed. 'A mob is forming to hang him.' Taking turns, they reported their conversation with Bernard.

Saint-Martin frowned. 'For the time being, Patrick won't be safe living on his own anywhere in Paris. We'll have to move him into my aunt's town house on Rue Traversine and put it under police surveillance.'

Anne added, 'Marthe Boyer can't afford to remain in her apartment.'

'I've suggested,' said Georges, 'that she could work in the widow's meat shop for room and board.'

'Or,' asked Anne, 'could we also find a place for her at the town house?'

'Possibly,' Saint-Martin replied. 'I must speak to Aunt Marie about these arrangements. In the meantime, Patrick has to be found. If he's out in the city, he's vulnerable to the conspirators' attack. He must stay in his rooms at the Louvre for the time being. Georges, can you see to that?'

'I'll try. Will Madame Cartier accompany me? I'll need her help communicating with Patrick.'

Anne glanced towards Paul with the question in her eye.

He rose from the table, opened a cabinet and handed her two small pistols. 'They are primed. Use them if you must.'

He turned to Georges. 'The two National Guards who patrol Rue Saint-Honoré are stout and trustworthy. Call on them for support.'

*   *   *

Accompanied by the guards, Anne and Georges hurried to Patrick's rooms at the Louvre. She wore simple street clothes. He was now in a gendarme's red and blue uniform, and armed with a cutlass and a pistol. The rooms were empty. The watchman at the north portal said Patrick had left an hour ago. 'He pretends to be an old man, bent and shuffling. But he doesn't fool me.'

'Nor Rat-face either,' Anne muttered to Georges. 'Was he carrying a shopping basket?' Anne asked desperately.

'Yes, he was,' replied the watchman.

'Then let's try the most direct route to the Central Markets,' said Georges to Anne. They set off on Rue Saint-Honoré to Rue de la Tonnellerie and turned left into the market district. The street was clogged with bustling late afternoon traffic. The bedlam grew worse as they wormed their way deeper into the markets and faced a torrent of carts and wagons loaded with produce and people headed out into the city. Anne wondered how they could ever hope to see Patrick. Then off to the right on the corner of Rue de la Cordonnerie she noticed a commotion. Some people were pushing towards the scene, trying to see what was going on, while others were trying to flee from it.

'This is it,' said Georges. 'Follow me.' He plunged into the churning crowd, Anne close behind him. Stern-faced, the National Guards followed her.

In front of a boot maker's shop a half-dozen men surrounded Patrick. His arms and legs were tightly bound. Two of the men were fixing a noose around his neck. Another man threw the loose end of the rope over a nearby street lamp. Two others tended to a companion, sitting barely conscious against the wall of the shop, holding a bloody rag to his nose. Patrick had gone down fighting.

Meanwhile, the leader of the group, a short, heavy-set man with a florid complexion and a big, booming voice, harangued the crowd. 'He's the man who killed Armand Flamme and Jacques Boyer. He must be stopped before he kills another patriot. The police do nothing. We'll give him the punishment he deserves.'

Georges moved quickly up to the speaker and confronted him, face to face. Taken by surprise, he stopped in mid-sentence and glared at Georges.

Georges announced in a loud voice, 'I've come to take citizen Patrick O'Fallon to the Châtelet for questioning. Tell the crowd to disperse. Untie the prisoner.'

'Go back to your barracks,' muttered the speaker. 'The people are in charge here.'

Georges's voice went to a deeper, menacing level. 'I know my duty, sir. I serve the people. Do as I say.'

Confused and fascinated, the crowd grew silent and gaped at the two men. The speaker's face turned purple with rage. Screaming obscenities, he lunged at Georges who nimbly stepped aside and tripped him as he passed by. He fell heavily face down on to the filthy pavement.

As he struggled to rise, some in the crowd began to snicker. Fresh dung dripped from his face and splattered his coat and breeches. He yelled to his men for help.

Meanwhile Anne had rushed up to Patrick and signed encouragement to him. The rogues who were about to hang him momentarily stood still, mouths agape. She yanked the rope down from the street lamp.

When their leader called out, they started to move towards him. Anne drew her pistols and ordered them to stop. They hesitated, glanced at each other, then at Anne. At the same time, Georges drew his pistol and told the guards to help the speaker struggle to his feet.

Georges raised his pistol to the speaker's temple. 'Order your men to release the prisoner and tell the crowd to disperse.' Georges half cocked the pistol.

The speaker was now wobbling on his feet, the guards gripping him tightly. He was short of breath and panting. He croaked to the crowd to leave, then turned to his men. 'Do as he says.'

For a moment, time seemed to stop, leaving everyone frozen in place. The rogues muttered to each other and snarled at Anne and the police, obviously tempted to attack them. But the dwindling crowd gave them no support. Their humiliated leader offered them no further direction. Finally, most of them bolted and disappeared into the crowd, leaving behind their injured comrade on the ground.

Cowed by Anne's pistols, one rogue remained by the street lamp. At her command he untied Patrick. The guardsmen then shackled the rogue, the speaker and the injured man and led them away to prison, to be charged with stirring up a riot.

At that moment, Marthe Boyer emerged, trembling, from the bootmaker's shop where she had hid. At the sight of Patrick she nearly fainted into Anne's arms. His face was bruised. He stood unsteady on his feet. But he managed to smile at her and reached out a hand.

She clasped it and wailed, 'What shall become of us?'

'I must go to the Châtelet,' he said dolefully.

'I think not,' said Georges. 'I misled the rogues in case they might attack again. We'll go to the colonel's office instead. He may have made arrangements for you.'

Saint-Martin had reached his Aunt Marie. She was willing to offer room and board. Marthe could assist the cook; Patrick could work in the stable. By nightfall Anne had installed them in the town house's attic.

Their situation was much improved. They were now decently lodged and employed. Above all, they were safe from mob violence. However, the arrangement was temporary. Marthe was still Boyer's wife until his death could be certified. His property was beyond her reach. How much, if anything, she might inherit was unknown. She received little support from society where her relationship with Patrick was regarded as adulterous. Patrick had scarcely any means of support and lived under a thick cloud of suspicion, widely believed to have killed Boyer and hidden his body. Their situation added urgency to the investigation.

TWENTY-EIGHT
Fraud Exposed

19–20 June

Meanwhile, Georges had received a note from Luc Thierry. 'Come immediately to The Nimble Heifer. An opportunity has arrived.' Georges had been prepared for days. He packed his tools and a small pistol, disguised himself to resemble one of Guiscard's servants, and set out. Though he had done missions like this many times, he still felt a strong surge of energy.

Luc was waiting anxiously in Cécile Tremblay's back room, wringing his hands. 'This evening,' he began, 'Guiscard plans to watch his mistress perform at the Théatre des Italiens and then spend the night in her apartment. What do you say?'

'You and I should search the office tonight. I have an idea where his true account book and secret papers are hidden. Your wife should watch at the front gate; your agent the clerk should keep an eye on the back of the property and the rear gate. This is the best opportunity we could hope for, but it's risky. Guiscard's mistress might send him home, or his workmen might stumble upon us. That would expose your agent – and your ties to Madame Guiscard. Her scheme would be ruined. Still, if we find her husband's secret accounts, she would prevail in court and you would surely receive a handsome reward.'

Georges met Luc's eye. 'Shall we proceed?'

The porter's face had turned livid. For a moment, he stammered bits of nonsense. Finally, he croaked, 'Go ahead.'

Georges stood in the middle of the office, Luc at his side. At eight o'clock, a dim light came from outside. Drapes only partially covered the windows facing the courtyard and the porter's house. Luc's wife could give them signals. But, like two blind men, they must search without lanterns. Otherwise,

Guiscard's workers might notice them. And, of course, he might return unexpectedly.

So, with a certain measure of anxiety, Georges patted Lacroix's keys in his pocket and walked directly up to the table. The first key turned smoothly, Georges breathed a sigh of relief and pulled out the drawer. There they were: Guiscard's secret papers lay in neat bundles together with the account book. He and Luc carried them into the clerk's office and pulled the drapes over the window. Luc began reading the account book, Georges the loose papers.

While browsing in copies of messages, Georges came upon the name Jacques Boyer. Under the date, 12 June, Guiscard had paid him five thousand francs with the note, 'As per our agreement concerning Flamme.' Georges scratched his head and asked Luc, 'What can Guiscard possibly mean?'

'Boyer must have received that money in person. A week ago, early in the morning, he arrived on foot at the front gate on Rue Colbert. I directed him to Guiscard's office.'

For a long moment Georges stared at the copy and tried to tease out its meaning. For a start, Guiscard and Boyer had little in common, except contempt for religion and a hostile relationship with Armand Flamme. Both men, together with Patrick, were suspected of having killed him. During that visit a week ago, Georges concluded, Guiscard and Boyer must have agreed to channel the public's suspicion towards Patrick and convict him in the public's eye. Guiscard paid Boyer five thousand francs to speak for both of them. That same day in the evening at the Jacobins, Guiscard at first seemed anxious. He probably didn't fully trust Boyer to fulfil his part of the bargain. Later he must have been pleased and relieved by Boyer's indictment of Patrick.

'This is evidence of a felony,' Georges said to the porter and put the message in his pocket. 'In normal times, written proof like this would put both Boyer and Guiscard in prison. But considering the public's present, excited mood, I'll search for still more evidence to strengthen the case against them.'

For about an hour the two men took notes on Guiscard's secret records. Finally, Georges stretched. 'Luc, we've seen enough. It's time to put everything back as it was, except for the most incriminating messages and the secret account book.'

'What happens next?' asked Luc, a hint of anxiety in his voice.

'Tonight, I'll report our findings to Colonel Saint-Martin and give him the evidence. He has been arranging the next step. It should be swift. You will witness a dramatic scene tomorrow.'

At dawn the next day, Colonel Saint-Martin and Georges hastened to the Ministry of Finance. It was not yet open for business, but a trusted finance officer and a magistrate were waiting for them just inside the gate. Behind them in the court-yard was a coach with finance inspectors inside. Several National Guards stood by their mounts.

'What have you concluded from your study of Guiscard's secret records?' Saint-Martin asked the finance officer. He had received them late last night.

'I gladly gave up several hours of sleep,' he replied. 'We've strongly suspected him of fraud; now we have solid evidence. We can prosecute him, despite his powerful political connections. We're ready to go to Rue Colbert.' He gave a command and they set off.

Wide-eyed, Luc opened the gate and the cavalcade passed through. Guiscard's clerk unlocked the office and the destruction of the master builder's criminal business began. The inspectors emptied the hidden contents of the great writing table into boxes and took the files from the shelves as well. The National Guards hauled all the confiscated material outside and loaded it into the coach.

When the operation was nearly completed, the magistrate said to Saint-Martin, 'We'll leave now. It's time to meet Monsieur Guiscard. He is said to lie in the arms of his mistress.'

Georges led the way. At the door a maid opened for them, then promptly fainted. A National Guard moved her to a couch. The sound of heavy riding boots on the tile floors soon stirred up several bewildered servants. One of them dropped a large silver breakfast tray and its contents on the stairs to the first floor.

At the door to Mademoiselle Barcome's boudoir, Georges neglected to knock and marched right in.

'What in God's name is going on?' shouted a naked Guiscard climbing out of bed. His partner, the pretty Yvonne, slid under the covers.

The magistrate arrested Guiscard on suspicion of fraud and

Mademoiselle Barcome as a witness or accomplice. They were allowed to dress and then taken to prison. One inspector immediately began an inventory of the apartment's furnishings. The other assembled the servants for questioning.

As they left the apartment, a worried-looking Luc asked Georges, 'What will happen next?'

'Unfortunately, the Ministry of Finance, like other parts of the government, is in disarray. Three ministers have come and gone in less than two years. Many of its experienced staff have retired or emigrated. It will take months to audit Guiscard's accounts, figure out his crimes and determine his accomplices, then put him on trial. In the meantime, a finance officer will oversee Guiscard's properties and his business. You will continue as porter at the house on Rue Colbert. Guiscard's clerk will look after the office and the workshop. In the end, both of you should receive a substantial reward.'

Luc's brow creased with concern. 'And my employer, Guiscard's estranged wife?'

'She will get her dowry back. But, the Ministry of Finance is desperate for money. They will confiscate her husband's ill-gotten gains and heavily fine him, then send him off to prison. Little will be left over for his wife.'

TWENTY-NINE
A Problem of Conscience

20 June

In the afternoon, Saint-Martin and Georges were back at the Tuileries palace, continuing their investigation into Boyer's mysterious disappearance. From his diary, as well as from the patriotic maid's observations, it was clear that Boyer believed Jeanne Degere and her brother to be agents of a royal conspiracy to reverse the revolution. He might have been killed in the course of following them. So Saint-Martin and Georges had arranged to question Jeanne and afterwards a reluctant Fersen.

They met her in the anteroom to Fersen's apartment. Saint-Martin assigned the questioning to Georges while he sat to one side and observed. Jeanne sat up straight, hands folded in her lap. Her gaze was straight and steady.

'Mademoiselle,' Georges began, 'you were seen leaving the palace at midnight between the twelfth and the thirteenth of June. Where did you go and what was your mission?'

'I delivered a message to a person on the Place des Victoires whom I recognized only from his or her clothing and gestures. I have no idea what the message was about.'

'Count Fersen chooses his messengers wisely,' Georges said with a slight bow to Jeanne. 'Monsieur Boyer's diary states that he frequently followed you in the belief that you carried important messages concerning the royal court. Were you aware of him? And did you encounter him that night on the way to or from your destination?'

'On previous occasions I was aware of being followed, but I couldn't recognize the person. During the night in question, my brother Benoit observed me from a hiding place on Rue Saint-Honoré. He later joined me and said that no one was following me.'

'Describe your route to and from Place des Victoires that night.'

'We took Rue Saint-Honoré to Rue des Bons Enfants.'

'Was that your usual route?'

'It varied.'

Georges had noticed that Jeanne had evaded his initial question, so he repeated it. 'Did you encounter Monsieur Boyer?'

'No,' she replied without blinking.

'When did you return to the palace?'

'Early in the morning before dawn. I don't recall the exact time.'

Georges glanced towards the colonel. 'Any questions?' he asked.

Saint-Martin shook his head.

Then Georges gave Jeanne a friendly smile and said, 'That will be all for now.'

The colonel and his adjutant left the palace and strolled in the Tuileries garden at a safe distance from spies.

'What do you think, Georges?'

'Jeanne has been well coached and is giving us less than the whole truth. Her brother would give us the same story. Her mysterious contact person is probably one of Madame de Korff's servants. De Korff has rooms on the Place des Victoires.'

Saint-Martin reflected for a moment. 'The message could have to do with a delicate assignation. Fersen's appetite for romantic adventures is notorious. At one time, he and Madame de Korff were lovers.'

Georges merely nodded. His mind had moved to a different problem. 'We should search Rue des Bons Enfants for evidence of a violent confrontation. Jeanne's denial seemed a little too emphatic.'

Saint-Martin shrugged his consent, then added, 'Suppose Boyer in fact didn't follow her. He might have changed his plans after leaving the Tuileries.'

'What did he do instead?' Georges persisted.

'We have no idea, only another complication.'

'Perhaps Count Fersen will shed light on our problem. Still, he might baulk when he realizes that Jeanne and her brother are prime suspects in Boyer's death.'

At the appointed time, Saint-Martin and Georges arrived at Fersen's door. Jeanne opened for them, then disappeared. The handsome count was at his writing table in shirtsleeves and breeches. His military coat, sword and pistol hung on pegs, his boots stood just inside the door. Saint-Martin sensed that this man was ready for a quick departure. He looked up at his visitors and pushed aside a low pile of papers. His dark bluish grey eyes were evasive and unwelcoming.

For this interrogation, Saint-Martin took the lead and sat in a chair facing Fersen. Georges stood off to one side, arms folded over his chest. His sceptical posture was meant to rattle the urbane Swede.

Saint-Martin omitted the conventional pleasantries and asked directly, 'On the night of Boyer's disappearance, you sent your servant Mademoiselle Degere with a message to the Place des Victoires. What was the message she carried?'

'I won't tell you,' Fersen replied through thin, pressed lips. 'The message is secret. I may add that it doesn't concern the royal family.'

'Do you know what happened to Jacques Boyer?'

'No I don't.'

'We've found his diary. Are you aware that he was attempting to discover why your friend, the Russian baroness, Madame de Korff, has bought a large, luxurious coach? On several occasions, her servants were seen late at night on the Place des Victoires, ready – it would seem – to receive messages delivered by Jeanne Degere. He had also learned that the queen has shipped a large chest of cosmetics to Brussels in the Austrian Netherlands. He deduced that you were preparing for someone in the royal family to secretly leave Paris. It could be the king's brother, the Comte de Provence. But the cosmetics shipment indicates that it would more likely be the king and queen.'

Fersen glared at Saint-Martin. 'Monsieur Boyer's deductions are the product of an overheated brain. You couldn't possibly be insinuating that I killed Boyer, or had him killed, to put an end to his investigation.'

'That idea isn't as absurd as you wish me to believe. The stakes are high enough for murder. Even the most casual observer of our country's present precarious situation would agree that the flight of the king from Paris would have enormous and unpredictable consequences. If persistent rumours are true, the king is nonetheless planning to secretly flee to a distant safe-place. Should the attempt fail, the king would find himself in an untenable position, especially if, as is likely, the public were to interpret his flight as a repudiation of the revolution and all its works. How could he rule in a constitutional regime that he condemned and abandoned? And what had he planned to do once he was safely out of France?'

Fersen replied, 'I'm not privy to His Majesty's secret intentions. Perhaps he'd breathe a sigh of relief.'

'Yes,' rejoined Saint-Martin, 'then return with an army of German mercenaries and end the reforms achieved thus far? That could lead to civil war. Why would he take such a risk?'

'Because his present situation seems hopeless and unbearable,' Fersen replied. 'He's deeply troubled by the Assembly's drastic measures depriving the church of its property, suppressing the religious orders, denying it self-government, repudiating the spiritual authority of the Bishop of Rome, and so on.' He paused. 'The oath required of the clergy to support these measures was the last straw, intolerable to the king's conscience.'

'Then where do you stand on this issue?'

'I agree with you concerning the consequences,' granted Fersen, 'and have discussed them with His Majesty. Fortunately, like any reasonable man he rejects the idea of flight. Therefore he has had no reason to fear Boyer's investigation. While the reforms of the church and many other aspects of the forthcoming constitution greatly distress him, the nation's peace and tranquillity are first and foremost in his mind. During the past two years, he has publicly professed his patriotic sentiments and has accepted his role in the new regime. The royal family even receives Holy Communion from a priest who accepts the civil constitution of the clergy, which the king privately regards as abhorrent.'

Saint-Martin said evenly, 'I'm grateful for your informed opinion of our king's intentions. Nonetheless, the disappearance of Jacques Boyer remains a mystery that I must solve.'

Saint-Martin and his adjutant walked out of the palace in silence. When they came to a secluded part of the garden, the colonel could no long restrain his irritation. 'Fersen is too clever by far, trying to pass the king off as a true patriot. In fact, he's a decent dullard who should apprentice himself to Breguet and be content making watches. By temperament the queen is more

suited than he to govern the country.' Saint-Martin struggled
to master his feelings. 'In fact, neither of them is up to the
task. I fear the country will lose patience with them. If that
happens, they are doomed.'

Georges grimaced. 'It's a fate of their own making. In public
they pretend that they are reconciled to the new constitution.
But they really are false patriots who deceive the people. As a
competent military officer, Fersen may have honestly explained
to the king and the queen the possible consequences of a failed
escape as well as the slim chances of a victorious march on
Paris. But the king and especially the queen probably insist on
going forward with their scheme. They may have thought that
Jacques Boyer stood in their way and asked Fersen to do something about it.'

Saint-Martin nodded gravely. 'If they asked, no doubt he
would order Jeanne Degere and her brother to remove Boyer
as neatly and quietly as possible.'

THIRTY
Flight to Varennes

21–25 June

Early the next morning, Paul was at breakfast in the garden, enjoying peace and fresh air before the day's noise and stench spread over the city. Dew glistened on his roses as they awoke and spread their petals. He picked three of the yellow ones for Anne. As he began to trim off their thorns, Georges burst in.

'The cat is out of the bag, sir. The royal family is gone!' He paused to catch his breath. 'They escaped from the Tuileries late last night and are now well on their way to wherever they're going. Paulette the patriotic maid just told me. She got the news only a few minutes ago.'

Saint-Martin felt shocked and angered. 'What brazen deception Fersen practised on us yesterday! Imagine! Louis, a reasonable man who preferred the peace of his people to his own troubled conscience. A patriotic king indeed!'

Georges pulled up a chair. 'Yes, this must have been Fersen's work, an incredibly clever, well-executed trick. No one else could have herded a dozen such witless swine beneath the eyes of a thousand spies and guards. How did he do it?'

At this moment the clever Swede no longer mattered. Saint-Martin scarcely heard the question. His mind had switched to the principal suspects in the Boyer disappearance.

'We must find Jeanne and Benoit Degere. I'm assuming Fersen's gone with the royal family. They will sorely need his tactical skills. Find out if the servants are with him or have left on their own. They may still be somewhere in Paris. Take a couple of trustworthy gendarmes with you and report back to me as soon as possible.'

At mid morning Georges returned. Saint-Martin was waiting anxiously in his office. During the morning, he had conferred

with Mayor Bailly and Commandant Lafayette. They were especially chagrined, since they had visited the king late last night,
while the rest of the royal family was probably sneaking out a
side door of the palace. The king had seemed quite calm.

'He's a better actor than we give him credit for,' said Georges.

'That's true,' granted Saint-Martin. 'Neither Bailly nor
Lafayette had a clue to where the royal family was. Bailly
guessed that they could have gone to the royal château at Saint-
Cloud. It's the queen's favourite palace and it's nearby. Lafayette
thought they might have travelled to Rouen in Normandy. The
people there are said to be more sympathetic to the royal family
than in Paris.'

Georges sniffed. 'The two fools were busy making excuses
for their bumbling failure to prevent the escape.'

'What did you learn this morning, Georges?'

'Madame de Korff pleaded total ignorance and acted aston-
ished. But a groom in her stable told me that her new, huge,
fancy yellow coach has vanished, I presume with the royal
family inside.'

'That's hardly a subtle way to travel incognito. Certainly the
queen, not Fersen, made that choice.'

'Fersen's clearly gone,' Georges continued, 'But I don't know
about brother and sister Degere. They just might be hiding in
Paris, spying for their master.'

'At this point we'll assume they are with Fersen. If not, we
can look for them later. Prepare to leave. As soon as we discover
the route, we'll be going after the royal coach. Our suspects
may be riding on top.'

Two hours passed. Rumours abounded. But no one really knew
the royal family's whereabouts. Then a gendarme arrived at
Saint-Martin's office and reported the royal coach was on the
road to Chalons-sur-Marne.

This news came shortly before noon. The colonel instantly
called Georges. 'We'll leave immediately and follow the coach's
tracks. With luck we may reach the fugitives before the frontier. Lafayette will surely send a detachment of National Guards
to catch them, but he moves slowly. I'd like to get there first.'

Georges added, 'And we could interrogate them while they
were still stunned, or confused, or frightened and haven't yet
concocted tales to tell the world.'

'Be prepared, Georges. Anything could happen. Local fanatics might stop the coach and massacre the royal party, Fersen and the Degeres included.'

The chase ended in Varennes, a small town, a few miles west of the Austrian Netherlands. The colonel and his adjutant, together with a small party of gendarmes, reached the town early in the morning of the twenty-second. It had been an exhausting thirteen-hour ride.

A local postmaster had identified the king. The local authorities had stopped the coach, detained its occupants in the village inn, The Golden Arm, and awaited instructions from the government in Paris. The townspeople were thoroughly aroused and milling about; the local National Guard was armed and excited. Would the king's German mercenary cavalry charge into the town and rescue him?

Saint-Martin explained to the local authorities that he and his men had come simply in pursuit of two fugitive suspects in a murder case. Lightly armed and non-threatening, the gendarmes were well-received. They fanned out in two groups, the colonel leading one, his adjutant the other.

Over the course of a few hours, they were disappointed to learn that Count Fersen and his servants were not in the royal party after all. Saint-Martin himself spoke briefly with the king, who seemed even more lethargic than usual. Another attempt to escape was out of the question. But he didn't seem unduly distressed. It was as if he wouldn't or couldn't face the consequences of his reckless act.

The queen was another matter. The shock of this failure had visibly aged her. Pale, mouth quivering with rage and despair, she said, 'This is the beginning of the end. It's all over for us.'

'What went wrong?' asked Saint-Martin softly.

She hesitated for a moment, as if uncertain whether to confide in him. But they had spoken before. She knew Saint-Martin to be an aristocrat and an honourable man. Besides, he was probably the only reasonable person in the vicinity she could talk to. Her own companions were in shock. So, she told him, 'After Count Fersen got us out of Paris he offered to lead us across the country to the frontier where loyal military forces were waiting. His Majesty politely declined the count's offer and said he could manage by himself. The result you see before you.' She gave Saint-Martin a knowing look and said no more.

Shortly afterwards, the gendarmes gathered in a room of the inn for a meal. At the table Saint-Martin learned that Count Fersen had left the country by a more northerly route and was presumably safe now in Brussels. His two servants had travelled with him and were also beyond reach.

The royal journey from the outskirts of Paris to Varennes had been more like a leisurely summer voyage in the country than a desperate escape from prison. The splendour of the coach itself attracted attention. The king had insisted on frequent stops and hearty meals along the way. The fugitives were often recognized. The king talked to people, even teased them to guess who he was. Consequently, much delayed, the coach missed its rendezvous with the loyal troops near Varennes. The royal family would be taken back to Paris to face ridicule and scorn, if not worse, from the betrayed citizens of the city.

After the meal while the gendarmes were resting, a messenger arrived from the National Assembly with orders that the royal family should set out on their return trip early that same morning. They would be met on the way by three commissioners from the National Assembly, led by Monsieur Pétion who would escort them into Paris.

Saint-Martin and his gendarmes caught a few hours of sleep, then left Varennes for Paris ahead of the royal coach. About halfway home on the road near Epernay, they met a detachment of National Guardsmen and the commissioners' coach.

Saint-Martin rode up to the coach's window, greeted the commissioners, then added, 'The royal family appears to be well.'

Pétion leaned out the window, frowning. 'What are you doing here, Colonel? This is *our* business!' His voice reeked of suspicion and distrust. 'Are you trying to aid the escape of the royal fugitives or to hinder their return?'

Saint-Martin tensed but managed to control his temper. 'I have authority from Mayor Bailly to pursue two suspects in the Boyer case. I had reason to believe that they escaped with the royal family. I've since learned that they travelled by a different route and are probably now beyond our reach in Brussels. *My* business is finished here. I'm returning to Paris.'

'Bailly should stay out of this matter. It concerns the National Assembly. Fortunately, he will soon no longer be mayor.' Pétion glared at Saint-Martin. His cold fishy eyes spoke his mind. 'Then you and I shall have a reckoning.' He pulled back into the coach and it drove off in a cloud of dust.

On 25 June, aided by an opera glass and a military telescope, Anne and Paul witnessed the royal family's entry into the city. The fugitives appeared hollow-eyed and haggard from the tedious, exhausting four-day return journey. As the coach drove down the Champs-Elysées, the crowds were immense – and mostly silent. Men covered their heads in a sign of disrespect. Likewise, National Guards lining the route held their muskets upside down.

At the entrance to the Tuileries garden, Anne aimed her opera glass at Pétion leaning out of a window of the royal coach. The man looked triumphant, basking in the ripple of applause that greeted him.

'This is probably the high point of his life,' remarked Paul. 'He has humbled the monarchy that he has hated for so many years.'

In the garden of the Tuileries a mob attacked the coach and might have massacred the royal family. But National Guardsmen intervened and escorted them safely into the palace.

The king was the last to enter, bent and shuffling. An officer gave him a push as the doors were closing. A shiver ran through Anne's body. 'The French king has lost every last shred of authority,' she murmured to Paul. 'Does anyone care?'

At home that evening over a bottle of white wine, Anne asked Paul, 'Since Jeanne and Benoit Degere have escaped to Brussels, how will you continue to investigate Boyer's disappearance?'

'I'll wait.' He stretched out his legs, leaned back in his chair, and sipped thoughtfully from his glass. 'I'm stalemated until I can interrogate them again. In normal times, the French government could state our case to the Habsburg authorities in Brussels and expect that the fugitives would be extradited. But since war is likely soon, Brussels is in no mood to cooperate with us and would surely refuse our request. We have no way to force Fersen or his servants to return, short of kidnapping them. I have no stomach for that.'

'Might he return of his own accord and bring the Degeres along?'

'I doubt that he would dare to come in the near future. There's a warrant for his arrest, though none for the Degeres.'

'And wouldn't the mob tear him to pieces?'

Paul waved a dismissive hand. 'Soon, the high price of bread, lack of work in the city, and a poor harvest this summer will distract the "mob". And, with time, other radical agitators, like Monsieur Jean-Paul Marat, will take on Boyer's role as "tribune of the people". The public demand to find him will fade.'

Anne gazed into her glass and recalled from memory Count Fersen and the queen walking side by side in the palace garden at Versailles, exchanging fond glances as if there was no royal distance between them. She sipped some wine and mused aloud, 'As the danger subsides, Fersen will long to visit the queen again. I feel that he will return, together with the Degeres.'

'You're right, Anne. He's willing to risk a great deal for her. I'll be ready.'

She hesitated a moment before asking, 'Suppose you catch him, what would you do?'

'I'm sure he knows what happened to Boyer. I'll force him to tell me. Then I'll let justice take its course.'

THIRTY-ONE
Fugitives Return

February 1792

Months passed without a trace of the missing Jacques Boyer. Meanwhile, a worsening political situation complicated the investigation. In the city government radical republicans, such as Jérôme Pétion, replaced Saint-Martin's two chief enlightened allies, Mayor Bailly and Commandant Lafayette. Elected Mayor of Paris in November, Pétion criticized Saint-Martin's failure to charge Patrick O'Fallon for Flamme's murder. Pétion also attempted to memorialize Boyer as a hero and martyr of the revolution.

Saint-Martin tried in vain to warn him off, suggesting that Boyer was more likely a murderer than a martyr. In the meantime, Saint-Martin consulted Monsieur Savarin.

'Patience, Paul,' he usually advised. 'Our spies in the government are like moles. They work slowly and silently in the dark towards their goal. I'm sure they will find what you need to force Pétion to do the right thing. Our politicians are incredibly corrupt – and sometimes careless with their papers.'

In early December, Pétion threatened to take Saint-Martin off the case and replace him with a more pliable investigator who would arrest Patrick O'Fallon. But magistrate Roland demurred and held back Boyer's diary and secret papers, insisting that first the body should be found and homicide determined. The politics of governing the city soon overwhelmed the new mayor and he dropped the issue.

Madame Boyer and Patrick remained prime suspects, their reputation in the public's mind severely compromised. Due to lack of evidence, Saint-Martin couldn't build a convincing case against them nor could he clear them. They lived in a legal limbo, confined to the town house on Rue Traversine under police surveillance. Madame Boyer had little money, since the

government withheld her missing husband's assets. Patrick
O'Fallon couldn't find meaningful outside employment.

The other suspects, Jeanne Degere and her brother,
continued to serve their master, Count Fersen, in exile. The
count himself was engaged in desperate negotiations with the
great powers of Europe, attempting to organize a grand coalition to intervene in France and restore the old regime. The
major powers, Austria, Prussia, and Russia, showed little
interest, for they were preoccupied with plans to carve up
Poland and digest the pieces. It began to look as if Fersen
would never return to Paris.

Nonetheless, Saint-Martin kept watch on Fersen's friends
and acquaintances in Paris who might shelter him. Anne
continued to tutor Marthe Boyer and Patrick O'Fallon in
signing and the reading of lips. Marthe took over the town
house's kitchen when the elderly cook retired. Patrick thrived
in the stables, lending his great physical strength to an ailing
groom.

Then, on 14 February, Anne invited Monsieur Savarin and Marie
de Beaumont to dinner. At table over roast veal and a white
wine from the Loire, Anne complained that Boyer's disappearance had prevented his wife from probating his will or settling
his financial affairs. Nor could she marry Patrick. Both of them
remained under a cloud of suspicion and in danger of mob
justice.

'What can be done?' Anne asked her guests.

'Ask Count Fersen,' Savarin replied with a sly look. 'The
handsome Swede and his adjutant Anders Fredrik Reutersvärd
have come to Paris with counterfeit passports and diplomatic
papers. Fersen is disguised as a Captain Granfelt on his way
to the Portuguese court on Swedish state business. Last night,
he stayed with the queen in the Tuileries – I don't know what
if anything transpired. This morning he met the king and made
a futile attempt to persuade him to escape from Paris once
more. The idea was so absurd that I wonder if Fersen used it
merely as an excuse to return to Paris.'

'Where is he now?' Paul asked, instantly alert.

'He has pretended to travel on to Orléans and Tours. In fact,
he is presently at 54 Rue de Clichy, the residence of his old
friend, Monsieur Quintin Craufurd, the rich Scottish banker.'

Paul was elated. 'I must tip my hat. You've been very diligent – and clever as well.'

'I confess that Fersen's code almost defeated me. He wrote several letters to the queen, as well as to Madame Eleanore Sullivan and others about this trip, none of which I could understand at the time. Though I've known Fersen for years and have read many of his letters for the Foreign Office, the key to this code eluded me. It differed with each message. Finally I discovered that he indicated to each correspondent the page in a book, *Plutarch's Lives*, where the key words could be found. Each correspondent had to have a copy of the book. There's also a copy in my library. With the keys in hand, I deciphered the letters and passed the information on to our agents. They've followed him to Craufurd's residence.'

'I'm grateful that you've shared this with me. Now I must pay Fersen a visit.'

'Wait. There's more you should know.' Savarin sipped his wine, patted his lips, and glanced mischievously at the others at the table. 'Craufurd doesn't know that his mistress, Madame Sullivan, is hiding Fersen in the attic.'

'Incredible!' Anne shook a finger at Savarin. 'You're teasing us.'

'My dear Anne, the truth can sometimes be stranger than fiction.' Savarin ate a piece of the veal, then continued, 'Craufurd's servants, Josephine and Frantz, are loyal to Fersen and bring him food from their master's table.'

'How can Fersen possibly manage this deception?' Anne asked. 'Is Craufurd blind and deaf?'

'Yes,' Marie replied, 'But only with regard to Eleanore and Fersen. Otherwise, Craufurd is a skilful connoisseur of fine art and spends most of his waking hours studying and collecting paintings and sculpture in the city. With the closing of the monastic houses, their treasures have become more accessible to him. For relaxation he also has recourse to a second mistress in the city – in reserve, so to speak.'

Savarin nodded. 'That leaves Fersen free to enjoy the house and Eleanore. She's a talented and beautiful Italian woman, née Franchi.'

'You can better understand Fersen's deception,' added Marie, 'when you realize that Eleanore was also once his mistress and remains a good friend.'

'What happens when Craufurd is at home?' Paul asked.

'My agents don't know. I'd guess that Fersen passes the time in the attic reading novels.'

Savarin lowered his voice to a confidential whisper. 'The Foreign Office doesn't wish to act upon this information and will not inform other offices of the government. Fersen's trip poses no threat to our country's interests. We believe that it's merely a romantic caprice. The royal family will not attempt another escape. We are also trying to avoid unnecessary provocations of the Swedish king, Gustaf III. He and Fersen seem close.' Savarin paused again and addressed Paul. 'Seriously, I know that you and Anne have dearly wanted to question him about last year's suspicious disappearance of the agitator Boyer. This is your best opportunity. I trust your good sense. Just don't cause a diplomatic incident, and please don't mention me.'

Now, with Fersen in Paris, Saint-Martin saw an opportunity to force him to explain what, if anything, he or his servants had to do with Jacques Boyer's disappearance early in the morning of 13 June. He should also tell where Boyer's body was hidden. If he were to refuse to cooperate, Saint-Martin could threaten him with an arrest warrant for his part in the royal family's failed attempt to flee Paris. That might stir up the public's wrath against him. In reserve was also the threat to tell Craufurd of his friend's amorous deception. That would deal a humiliating, perhaps a lethal blow to his keen sense of honour.

On the next day, 15 February, Saint-Martin and Georges set out for Craufurd's mansion on Rue de Clichy. They wore plain civilian clothes to avoid attracting unhealthy curiosity in the neighbourhood. Since Craufurd would likely get in the way of any serious interrogation, Saint-Martin and Georges waited until he left the house for a day in conversation with art dealers. At the door Saint-Martin gave his card and announced that he would like to speak to the visiting Swedish gentleman. For a moment the servant seemed nonplussed. 'I'll speak to my mistress.' He showed Saint-Martin and Georges into an anteroom.

A few minutes later, Eleanore Sullivan appeared, still a beautiful brunette with an ample figure. Her eyes dazzled with the colour of onyx. She had delicate features and a perfect rosy complexion. Saint-Martin had met her off and on in the city. She smiled politely and said, 'Colonel Saint-Martin, what a pleasure to see you. Why would you think that I'm entertaining a Swedish gentleman?'

'Reliable sources have informed me, Madame. The gentleman and I are well acquainted. Please tell him that we have unfinished business to discuss.'

Madame Sullivan's smile vanished. She studied Saint-Martin. Her eyes flicked nervously. She must have detected his strong resolve. 'I'll tell him that you've come with your adjutant. Please follow me.'

She led the two men into Craufurd's study, a collector's den. Paintings covered nearly every inch of the walls from floor to ceiling. On fine cabinets and tables stood small bronze statues and Sèvres porcelain. Saint-Martin was examining a Boucher portrait of Madame de Pompadour as a young woman when Fersen entered the room.

'Paul, what a pleasant surprise to see you.' Fersen's manner was gracious but his dark blue grey eyes were cold and un-fathomable. His voice hinted at hidden anxiety. He glanced at Georges. 'And you've brought your adjutant along. But then you did say that you've come on business.' He gestured Paul to the writing table and let Georges fend for himself. He sat off to one side, his face an enigmatic mask.

Saint-Martin began. 'I've waited months for this opportunity to find out what happened to Jacques Boyer.'

'Unfortunately, neither I nor my servants can enlighten you.'

'Then I'll begin with your servants. They came with you and are hiding in the neighbourhood. I have reason to believe that they know the truth about Boyer's disappearance and can clear a cloud of suspicion from other suspects. With your assistance I also intend to recover Boyer's body and certify his death, mainly for the sake of his widow.'

Fersen frowned. 'Is it wise to disturb sleeping dogs?'

'True, they may bite,' granted Saint-Martin. 'But in Boyer's case, it's safer now to reveal what happened than it was at the time. In the months following the royal family's return from Varennes, public interest in Boyer has declined. Jean-Paul Marat and other radicals now carry the republican banner. The magistrates are also better disposed to give your servants a fair hearing, if one proves necessary. Please call them and instruct them to give honest answers to my questions. You may wait outside.'

Throughout these remarks Fersen stared at Saint-Martin, his disbelief barely concealed behind his glacial nonchalance. 'If I didn't know you, Colonel, I'd think you were mad. Why should I allow myself or my servants to become embroiled in your investigation? It's bound to be a disagreeable waste of time and effort. You've just said that Boyer doesn't matter any more. So why are you chasing after his alleged killer while France descends into anarchy? You had better take care. Zealous partisans of our monarch could make life difficult, even dangerous for you and your wife.'

Saint-Martin waved a dismissive hand. 'You know me better than to think that I might yield to a threat. I'll see justice done, whatever it takes.'

Fersen nodded ruefully. 'Your practice of the Chevalier de Bayard's virtues is proving inconvenient for me.' He paused for a long moment, his eyes troubled.

Saint-Martin could easily imagine Fersen's calculations: An enemy of the revolution, he was in France on a false passport. Saint-Martin could arrest him. The Paris mob could hang him from a street lamp. Even worse for his honour, his friend Quintin Craufurd could discover his ignoble deception and resent it. From the Swede's perspective, this was a bad situation.

Finally, Fersen sighed. 'I'll send for Jeanne Degere and her brother and instruct them to cooperate.' Head high, he left the room.

While waiting for the servants to arrive, Saint-Martin turned to his adjutant. 'What do you think, Georges? Can we expect the truth from Fersen and his servants?'

'In my humble opinion, sir, the count is a clever, two-faced bastard. He lies to his friend Craufurd. He would lie to us if he thought he could get away with it. But he can't. We've got him by the throat. Coming to Paris like this was idiotic.'

'I agree, Georges. Apparently his passion for the queen got the better of his judgement. It's difficult to imagine any other reason.'

Saint-Martin now turned his mind to the forthcoming inter-rogation. 'Refresh my mind, Georges. What do we know about Boyer's disappearance?'

'The patriotic maid, Paulette, told us that Boyer was spying on Fersen and his two servants on the night of his disappearance. She had seen Fersen send Jeanne Degere out from the palace late on 12 June. Boyer had followed her. Early the next morning, the maid had also seen Jeanne and her brother return to the palace. They had seemed agitated. When we searched the area between Rue Saint-Honoré and Place des Victoires we found recent blood stains on the wooden floor of an empty building on Rue des Bons Enfants.'

'With that much already laid before them, they might as well tell the truth,' said Saint-Martin. 'They should at least claim that they killed Boyer in self-defence.'

'But why would they confess?' Georges asked, playing the devil's advocate. 'How is it in their interest? They depend on Fersen. They won't confess unless he agrees. Why should he agree? Their confession would implicate him, as well as themselves, in what could be a serious crime.'

Saint-Martin countered, 'But, like Fersen, they are now in a dangerous and illegal situation. If they refuse to cooperate with me, I could turn them over to the police and a highly uncertain fate.'

The two servants arrived, confused and anxious. Saint-Martin gestured them to chairs at the writing table facing him. He studied them silently for a few minutes. Then he said, 'I know both of you to be brave and honest. You cooperated with my wife and me three years ago to prevent a young deaf maid from being executed for a crime that she hadn't committed. Today, Marthe Boyer and a young deaf man are likewise wrongly suspected of killing Jacques Boyer early in the morning of 13 June. I want to get to the truth. So, tell me what happened on your way to the Baroness de Korff's rooms on Place des Victoires. The consequences of trying to mislead me will be very serious for the count as well as for you.'

Jeanne and her brother glanced at each other, uncertainty written large on their faces. Finally, Jeanne spoke for both of them. 'Late at night, a week before the royal family's flight from Paris, Count Fersen sealed a message and entrusted it to me. "Take this to Baroness de Korff," he said. "It is of the utmost importance. Under no circumstances should you allow it to fall into enemy hands."'

'Did you know what was in the message?' Saint-Martin asked.

'I didn't have any idea. In the past I had carried many
messages for him, several of them to the baroness's rooms at
Place des Victoires, and never knew what was in them. I didn't
want to know.' She paused apparently recalling the scene with
Fersen. 'I don't remember the count ever before so concerned
as with this message. While handing it over, he stared at me.
The blue in his eyes became incredibly intense. I recall shiv-
ering. I later learned that the message warned the baroness that
the royal family's departure was being put off one day. The big
coach was to go to a different place at a different time to pick
them up.'

'What happened next?'

'I had asked Benoit to go with me. On previous nights I had
sensed that someone was following me. It was a dark figure –
man or woman, I couldn't tell. I hadn't felt threatened or in
danger. But this night I couldn't take any chances. Benoit
agreed.

'I left the Tuileries by a side door. As I passed the church
of Saint-Roch, its bells were still ringing midnight. Near Rue
de Richelieu Benoit was watching me from across the street.
I wasn't being followed so he joined me. We continued on Rue
Saint-Honoré east to Rue des Bons Enfants. We checked again
to see if we were being followed. But there was no sign of the
dark figure. So we relaxed a little, turned left and started up
the street as I had done several times before.'

Her eyes widened as the scene grew more vivid in her
memory. 'Then, suddenly, halfway to Place des Victoires, off
to the right, I saw something move. A masked figure leaped
out of an entryway, levelled a double-barrelled pistol at us, and
ordered us into the building. It was empty and being rebuilt.
Scaffolding covered the front. He took us to a room deep inside,
lighted by a lantern. So we realized that he was expecting us.'

'Someone in the palace must have betrayed you,' Saint-
Martin suggested.

Jeanne nodded, a grim expression on her face. 'We call her
the patriotic maid. She spies on the queen.'

'Then what happened?'

'From his voice I could tell that he was a man. He ordered
me to tie Benoit's arms behind his back, checked that I had
done it, then tied my arms the same way and sat me on a stool.
Benoit had to sit on the floor. The masked man pointed the

pistol at my head and demanded to know Count Fersen's plans for the escape of the royal family from Paris.

'I know nothing,' I replied. 'I merely carry messages. I'm not told what they contain and I never read them.'

'"Then tell me where you've hidden the message." He cocked one of the barrels and brought it to my temple. "I warn you."'

I refused to tell him. He slapped me in the face. Hard.

'"Tell me, or I'll find it myself."'

'I still refused. So he put the pistol on a nearby table and untied my bodice. He soon found the message and laid it next to the pistol. But, he had become aroused. He threw a wary glance at my brother, then stripped me to the waist and fondled my breasts. Behind him Benoit slowly, quietly rose to his feet, a knife in his hand.'

'I had hidden it in my sleeve,' Benoit added. 'I was able to retrieve it and cut through the rope binding my arms.'

Jeanne continued, 'The masked man must have noticed my eyes shifting. He left me and grabbed his pistol. Before he could fire, Benoit leaped upon him and cut his throat. For a minute or more, we stared speechless at each other and at the dead man lying in a pool of blood.'

Benoit said, 'Finally, I pulled off the mask and studied his face. I recognized him, Jacques Boyer, an enemy of the church and of the king.'

'We didn't know what to do,' Jeanne went on. 'Boyer was an important public figure. We couldn't go to the police. The count's secrets in the message might come out.'

'We decided to tell Count Fersen,' Benoit said. 'Jeanne went on to the Place des Victoires and delivered the count's message. I returned to the palace, roused Count Fersen from his bed, and told him our story. He turned grey in the face and I thought he would be sick. But he recovered immediately, threw on his street clothes and left the room. In a few minutes he came back with a couple of stout men detached from his regiment. They were dressed like workmen but I recognized them. The count said, "Lead us to the body. My men will dispose of it. You and your sister must forget that this ever happened."'

Jeanne searched Saint-Martin's face, her lips quivering. Then in a voice barely above a whisper, she asked, 'Colonel, how could we ever forget?'

*   *   *

'What should we make of their story?' the colonel asked when the two servants left the room.

'On the face of it,' Georges replied, 'the killing of Boyer would usually be considered self-defence. However, there were no witnesses. We have only the word of Jeanne and her brother. By hiding Boyer's body, his mask and his pistol, Fersen left the Degeres with nothing to support a plea of self-defence.'

Saint-Martin was concerned that the servants be treated fairly. The days immediately following the flight to Varennes had not been normal. The public had turned vehemently against the king and queen and their partisans. Under such circumstances, the Degeres didn't dare reveal what had happened. The public would have considered Boyer's confrontation as a patriotic act, an attempt to halt the royal family's flight. Had he survived, he would have been a hero. Had he not, his death would have been seen as a kind of martyrdom. An angry mob would have hung the Degeres from a street lamp.

Saint-Martin thought that public attitudes had now changed and the two servants might receive a more open-minded hearing. Or, so it seemed at least on the surface. The public was also distracted by controversy over going to war against the Austrians and might be paying less attention to the Boyer case. Fersen's testimony would be crucial.

The count was called into the study. His demeanour was calm and collected. But a mixture of cold fury and unease filled his eyes. Saint-Martin said to himself, 'I've earned an enemy, but one who has capitulated at least for today.'

The count made himself comfortable in the chair and addressed Saint-Martin. 'It's my turn now,' he began. 'So I'll make a clean breast of it. What I say shouldn't compromise anyone else. I'll admit that I suppressed evidence and deceived the police investigators. Boyer's death took me by surprise. I knew he was following Jeanne Degere but I didn't expect him to provoke a violent confrontation. She was intended as a decoy to keep Boyer occupied and distracted. She thought the message was important, still does, I believe, but it contained only misleading information. My friend Madame Sullivan carried the authentic message.'

For a moment, Saint-Martin found himself admiring Fersen's tactical skill. How flawlessly, and without scruple, he used friends and others in this scheme. That was probably the main reason why it worked as well as it did.

'Once Boyer was killed,' the count continued, 'I had to hide his body until the royal family's flight had taken place. Preparations were nearly complete. The departure was to take place very soon. I hoped his disappearance wouldn't be noticed for at least a day or two. If his body were discovered and my servants arrested, the police investigation would almost certainly have unravelled our project. The royal family would have found itself in a worse situation than before.'

'What was so important about the true message in contrast to the one Jeanne Degere carried?' Saint-Martin asked.

'It gave Madame de Korff the correct date and time of the royal family's departure.'

Saint-Martin pointed out to him that the escape failed anyway, due largely to the king's ineptitude in carrying out Fersen's plan. The loyal military commanders failed as well. 'In brief,' Saint-Martin concluded, 'the plan was clever but utterly imprac-tical since it required an improbable level of human perfection and more good luck than any serious person should count on. As a consequence, the king is hopelessly compromised. Leaderless, the country drifts into anarchy.'

'True,' admitted Fersen. 'The future looks bleak.'

Saint-Martin challenged Fersen. 'Wouldn't both king and country have been better off, if Boyer had succeeded in exposing the plan and preventing the king's escape?'

Fersen glanced at his nails and shrugged a shoulder. 'God only knows. The people are hungry, angry and fickle. Their leaders are ambitious, witless and distracted. And the new constitution is a blighted, palsied creature about to die.' He looked up and met Paul's eye. 'If the king had returned to Paris, free and powerful, he might have saved France. War is coming in any case, is it not?'

For a moment the room turned quiet. Saint-Martin replied, 'Perhaps. But we digress. You've told us why you acted. We need to know exactly what you did.'

Fersen reflected briefly, then began his story, 'Benoit led me to the scene of the killing on Rue des Bons Enfants and showed me Boyer's body. His blood had spread over the floor and had soaked into the wood. We tried to clean it up, but I'm sure we left many traces.'

Saint-Martin nodded. 'We noted them but were reluctant to draw conclusions. Blood sometimes flows at a construction site.'

Fersen went on. 'It was about two in the morning. The city was quiet; the street was still empty. We had just a few hours before merchants and workers would fill the streets on their way to the arcades of the Palais-Royal and the Halle aux Bleds, the municipal grain market.

'A few years ago, I had studied the city sewers in the area of the Tuileries as a way to pass secretly in and out of the palace. At the time, the idea proved to be impractical. But a sewer could serve as Boyer's grave, appropriately, considering the man's character. So Benoit and I wrapped his body in a canvas and put it in a cart. My men dragged it to a drain near the Louvre. We lowered it into a work area in the sewer and stuffed it into a large barrel. I tossed in his pistol and his mask. It should all still be there.'

Saint-Martin said, 'We'll look for it.' He turned to Georges. 'Get Benoit and a couple of gendarmes. We'll leave immediately for the Louvre.' He said to Fersen. 'I expect to see you tomorrow.' As he left the house, he instructed a pair of hidden gendarmes to prevent the Swedish visitor from leaving the property.

Benoit and Georges came out of the sewer, grey-faced and gagging. Georges managed to say, 'We found the gun, the mask, and the body. I saw the face. It was Boyer and he wasn't pretty.' They brought the body to the morgue and officially identified it. A magistrate certified Boyer's death a homicide.

The next morning, after Craufurd had again left for the city galleries, Saint-Martin and Georges returned to the house on Rue de Clichy. Jeanne and her brother gave written depositions and promised to explain to a magistrate that they had returned to Paris to clear their names. Benoit would be given credit for bringing the body to light.

Saint-Martin sat down to tea with Fersen while Georges waited outside. After assuring the count that his servants would soon be cleared of any suspicions in Boyer's death, Saint-Martin added, 'I need a statement of your role in this affair. I won't use it unless to prevent an injustice. In the meantime, you may continue to enjoy Craufurd's unintended hospitality. I have no reason to become involved.'

Fersen wrote out a statement and handed it to Saint-Martin with a thin smile. 'This trip to Paris is probably my last in the foreseeable future. We'll soon be at war. My official mission to persuade the royal family to try once more to escape was unsuccessful. They intend to remain here to meet an uncertain fate. Frankly, I don't expect to see them again.' His gaze momentarily drifted, and his handsome face took on a deeply melancholy cast.

He sighed softly and glanced at Saint-Martin. 'But, the trip wasn't a total loss. At least I've helped clear up the Boyer affair and enjoyed the company of Madame Sullivan. I'll leave in a few days.' He hesitated for a moment, then said, 'Please remember me as a comrade in America in better days. Adieu, Paul.'

They shook hands and parted.

THIRTY-TWO
Case Resolved

Paris, 17–18 February 1792

At his writing table on the following day, Saint-Martin plotted his course of action. It would be difficult. Even as he promised Fersen a just outcome for his servants, he had felt uneasy. Pétion had to be seriously reckoned with. He had become one of the most powerful men in French politics. A popular mayor of Paris with great influence in the district criminal court, he was also well connected to leaders of the new Legislative Assembly. Finally, his distrust of Saint-Martin was visceral and seemed unbending.

Saint-Martin sent a note to Savarin at the Foreign Office. 'Any news?'

A note came back. 'Come to my study this evening. I may have something. Bring Magistrate Roland along.'

That evening Saint-Martin and Roland watched open-mouthed at the writing table as Savarin laid two packets of letters before them. 'Our spies recently found Pétion's correspondence with Boyer, together with a few other juicy titbits. I've just finished authenticating it.'

Savarin pointed to the packet tied in pink ribbons. 'These are copies of letters exchanged between Boyer and Pétion. The mayor agrees with Boyer that the deaf man, Patrick O'Fallon, is most likely an agent of the Crown and Flamme's assassin. O'Fallon tried to mask the killing as a robbery.' Savarin met Saint-Martin's eye. 'The fact that you have failed thus far to arrest anyone confirms Pétion in his opinion. He's convinced that you sympathized with Father O'Fallon and shared his views. Therefore, you must have a strong bias in favour of his son and are trying to shield him.'

'I'm not offended,' Saint-Martin remarked. 'The mayor is a poor judge of character, if I may say so.' For a few minutes, he browsed in the packet, then remarked, 'And he's gullible as well. He accepts Boyer's version of Flamme's death without seeing a shred of evidence. His enemies are free to insinuate that he was complicit in the murder of a troublesome radical comrade.'

Magistrate Roland concurred. 'I've heard that he's careless with details. In this case, he jeopardizes his lofty standing with colleagues and the public.'

Savarin handed over the packet tied with a blue ribbon. 'These letters reveal Pétion's financial transactions. Bribes from Guiscard passed through Pétion to certain officials in the Finance Ministry for government contracts and former ecclesiastical property. Some of it ended in Boyer's pocket. Pétion's personal benefit was small, and he probably was unaware that the money was tainted. Still it could be embarrassing to a politician who claims to be so high-minded.'

After a few more hours with the documents, Saint-Martin asked Roland, 'Do you think we have enough evidence of malfeasance to force Pétion's hand?'

Roland stared at the documents for a moment. 'They wouldn't convict him of a crime. However, they could threaten his reputation. That might persuade him to allow us to bring the Boyer case to a just and speedy resolution.'

'Then I'll arrange a meeting with him. Will you come?'

'Certainly.'

The next day, 18 February, the three men gathered in Pétion's office in the Hôtel de Police, off Place Vendôme. The room was a large, elegantly furnished symbol of the mayor's authority as the city's chief magistrate. Saint-Martin knew it well from many conferences with Bailly, as well as with the last Lieutenant General of Police, Thiroux de Crosne, now in exile.

As in previous encounters with Pétion, Saint-Martin felt a chill in the air. This would be an exercise in political manoeuvring rather than a meeting of fair, inquiring minds. Pétion had a politician's preoccupation with enhancing his power and a personal obsession with his reputation for civic virtue.

He settled into his chair and tilted his head at a sceptical angle. 'So, Colonel, are you finally ready to bring the deaf assassin Patrick O'Fallon to trial?'

Saint-Martin replied evenly, 'Sir, we are prepared to prove that Monsieur Boyer, not O'Fallon, killed Flamme. An accomplice, the barman at The Red Rooster, has testified against Boyer. Over the past several months we've also gathered strong documentary evidence to support our case.'

The mayor tried in vain to conceal his uncomfortable surprise. 'You should have given me this information in advance of our meeting. I might need to reflect on it.'

'That might have caused unnecessary complications. You will soon realize, sir, that this private, discreet approach is to your advantage. The facts are simple. To cover up his murder of Flamme, Monsieur Boyer led you to believe that the deaf man Patrick O'Fallon was a royalist assassin and committed the crime.'

Saint-Martin drew documents from his portfolio and laid them before the mayor, one after the other.

'The first is an authenticated transcript of Boyer's journal in which he describes his scheme. The second is the barman's confession of his part, and the third comes from Monsieur Guiscard who admits to paying Boyer five thousand francs to hire an assassin.'

Pétion glanced casually at the transcript, then read with increasing discomfort. 'The villain!' he finally exclaimed. 'Rather than pay someone else, he kept Guiscard's money and killed Flamme himself.'

Roland asked the mayor gently, 'It's clear, isn't it sir, that Boyer duped you?'

For a long moment Pétion seemed to ignore the question. His expression was impossible to read. Then he said, 'Boyer deceived me, as he deceived many others at the Jacobin club and elsewhere. We are all embarrassed.' He turned to Roland. 'You will put the record straight and that will be the end of it.'

'Not quite the end, sir,' said Saint-Martin. 'There's the matter of Boyer's disappearance.' He laid the Degeres' statements before the mayor and described the violent confrontation early in the morning of 13 June on Rue des Bons Enfants. He concluded, 'Benoit Degere killed Jacques Boyer in self-defence under severe provocation. Fearing retribution from the victim's followers, Degere hid the body and fled the country with his sister. He now believes he can receive a fair trial and has returned to cooperate with the investigation and to clear his name.'

Pétion scowled and shoved the statements aside. 'These are Fersen's servants, involved in the flight of the king. In this instance, Boyer acted like a patriot and was right to attack them. They are insolent traitors as well as murderers.'

Saint-Martin dismissed Pétion's contention with a wave of his hand. 'Boyer, a patriot? The same Boyer, sir, who murdered a radical comrade, implicated you in his crime, and shifted the blame on to an innocent deaf man? In the eyes of the law, the Degeres are neither traitors nor murderers. The National Assembly didn't include them among those guilty of aiding the royal family's attempt to escape from Paris.'

'Granted, Colonel, that Boyer was a bad subject. But had he succeeded in preventing the king's flight, this country would have been spared its present crisis of authority. We now have as head of state, Louis XVI, a proven renegade, whom no one can trust. The Degeres bear a heavy responsibility for that.'

'Sir, your conjecture about the nation's crisis is irrelevant. An armed, masked man attacked these two servants on a dark, empty street. What should they have done?'

The mayor glared at Saint-Martin. 'Colonel, you take too narrow a view of justice. The needs of the nation take precedence over those of individual citizens.'

'That sounds to me like the first step on the road to tyranny, an echo of the authority that our kings used to claim.'

Pétion shrugged. 'Furthermore, we have only the servants' word that they acted in self-defence. I shall urge a vigorous prosecution. Now, what else do you have to show me?'

Saint-Martin glanced at Roland, who nodded that it was time to apply pressure to the mayor. Saint-Martin put a packet tied with blue ribbons on the table. 'These documents record your financial arrangements with Jean Guiscard and prove significant bribery and fraud in the sale of nationalized church property. They come from his files as well as yours and they match. Granted, you didn't profit personally. But you showed poor judgement and culpable lack of attention, when you countersigned the cleverly hidden bribes that Guiscard offered to officials in the Ministry of Finance. You also imprudently forwarded Guiscard's secret payments to Boyer and other radicals.'

Pétion glanced with disdain at several of the documents. But as he read on, his hands began to tremble. 'This looks like extortion. What do you hope to gain? These letters are all clever forgeries. I'll deny everything. My reputation is as clean as the driven snow. It will defend me.'

'The documents have already passed a rigorous handwriting analysis that will stand up in court. While we speak, Guiscard is submitting a written confession of fraud to my adjutant and a couple of witnesses. And if I were to put these documents in the hands of Monsieur Robespierre, your former colleague in the National Assembly and soon your rival, what would he, "The Incorruptible", have to say?'

Pétion didn't respond. For what seemed like an eternity of minutes, Pétion remained silent. Then his muscles in his neck began to tighten. His eyes grew anxious and signalled his capitulation. Finally, he asked, 'What am I to do?'

'Monsieur Roland and I don't feel called upon to purge the new regime of its corruption. We merely want you to do your duty. Put politics aside and step out of our way so that we can conclude the Boyer case, quickly, fairly and strictly according to the rule of law. If you refuse to cooperate, we could severely damage your reputation. We prefer to leave that task to others who will eventually do it for us.'

Pétion grimaced. 'And what does my duty entail?'

'As mayor, you shall give Monsieur Roland written authority to proceed to trial at the earliest possible date. You shall advise your friends in the district criminal court to expeditiously review Monsieur Roland's decision. You shall allow the Degeres to leave the country exonerated and shall free Patrick O'Fallon and Marthe Boyer from police surveillance. Meanwhile, we'll keep this damaging material away from the public eye and return it to you when justice has been done.'

'How can I trust you?'

'I may be the only person in Paris you can trust. That's my burden. I can't save France, but I intend to save a few of its citizens from injustice.' Saint-Martin met Pétion's eye. 'Are we in agreement?'

For a long moment, the mayor sat rigid, tapping on the table, eyes averted. Finally, he looked Saint-Martin straight in the face and replied, 'Yes.'

EPILOGUE

In the following month, Roland's court declared that Jeanne and Benoit Degere had killed Jacques Boyer in self-defence and dismissed charges against them. They joined Count Fersen abroad. Marthe Boyer and Patrick O'Fallon were cleared of any involvement in the deaths of Flamme and Boyer. Police surveillance of them was lifted, Boyer's estate was probated and his property sold. With that money, Marthe and Patrick found a room in the city and planned to get married.

Guiscard was indicted of fraud, stripped of his ill-gotten wealth, and heavily fined. His wife received a legal separation and recovered her dowry but little else. Thanks to his political agility, Pétion's career continued to flourish for another year.

AUTHOR'S NOTES

Patriotism, or devotion to one's country, is an ancient concept, exemplified in Pericles of Athens. It evolved in late eighteenth-century France to become the pre-eminent moral standard in public discourse. A lofty, powerful idea, its devotees envisaged ennobling the entire nation. But the idea was elastic as well. Self-styled patriots of various stripes claimed to act on behalf of and for the 'people'. At the beginning of the revolution, they denounced the class-bound or self-centred attitude of aristo-crats and clergy, and the greed of speculators and profiteers. As the revolution progressed, 'patriotic' factions, such as the Jacobins, claimed the moral high ground for themselves alone and invoked patriotism to justify the destruction of their rivals. For an in-depth study of the concept, see Jay M. Smith, *Nobility Reimagined: The Patriotic Nation in Eighteenth-Century France* (Ithaca, 2005).

For the clergy's conflict with the new constitution, consult Timothy Tackett, *Religion, Revolution and Regional Culture in Eighteenth-Century France* (Princeton, 1985). See also his dramatic narrative of Louis XVI's attempt to flee from Paris, *When the King Took Flight* (Cambridge, 2003). John McManners, *The French Revolution and the Church* (New York, 1970) is a helpful overview of the National Assembly's attempts to reform the church.

Information on the stolen pocket watch in the story comes from George Daniels, *The Art of Breguet* (London, 1975). For a brief account of Lady Elizabeth Sutherland (1765–1839), see *Dictionary of National Biography*, vol. 23, pp. 99–100.

Arnold Barton's *Count Hans Axel von Fersen* (Boston, 1975) offers a judicious account of the Swedish nobleman's rela-tionship with the French queen. Fersen's secret visit to Paris in February 1792 is described in Émile Dard, *Un Rival de Fersen: Quintin Craufurd* (Paris, 1947).

Concerning marriage and divorce, see James F. Traer, *Marriage and the Family in Eighteenth-Century France* (Ithaca, 1980).

For a classic treatment of the Jacobins in 1791, see Crane Brinton, *The Jacobins: An Essay in the New History* (New York, [1930] 1961). Patrick Higonnet, *Goodness Beyond Virtue: Jacobins during the French Revolution* (Cambridge, Mass. 1998) offers a more detailed, modern analysis of the movement. Michael L. Kennedy, *The Jacobin Clubs in the French Revolution: The First Years* (Princeton, 1985), deals mainly with the provincial clubs and their connections to the mother club in Paris.

In April 1792, France declared war on Austria, launching twenty-three years of conflict that engulfed most of Europe. At the beginning, the French army was poorly prepared and suffered humiliating defeats. In the country's ensuing crisis Pétion and the radical Jacobins came to power, established a revolutionary republic, and executed the king (21 January 1793) and queen (16 October 1793). In 1793, Jacobin factions fell into fighting each other. On the losing side and a fugitive, Pétion took his own life near Saint-Émilion in 1794.

Saint-Martin's hero, Pierre Terrail LeVieux, Chevalier de Bayard (1473–1524), 'the knight without fear and beyond reproach', distinguished himself as a commander of French forces in the early sixteenth-century campaigns in Italy. Since then he has served as an exemplar of the chivalrous, incorruptible, and courageous soldier, esteemed also for his kindness and joyous spirit.

For the background to Anne Cartier's career as a tutor of deaf children, including the Abbé de l'Épée, the Abbé Sicard, and Mr Thomas Braidwood, see Harlan Lane, *When the Mind Hears: A History of the Deaf* (New York, 1984).